Cub

praise for Jeff Mann's *Cub*

"A warmly and poignantly written coming-of-age tale of two bear cubs in West Virginia."

—DAN STONE, author of *The Rest of Our Lives*

"It's a book for those boys out there who have discovered that they are different from many of their friends, but who also feel the division within the subculture they thought they could identify with. Their aloneness does not cease once they've figured out their sexual proclivities, but knowing who they are brings even more compartmentalization. *Cub* lets them feel there's room at the table for them. And I can think of no one better to write this story than Jeff Mann, whose table is as broad and wide as his heart. If this doesn't become a classic, there's no justice."

—JERRY L. WHEELER for *Out in Print*

"In *Cub*, you won't find the typical gay kid desperate to escape the farm for the bright lights of the city. Instead, you meet Travis: someone not at odds with his rural upbringing, a poet and a passionate young man who isn't like any youth I've read in gay young adult. ...Lyrical and possessing a raw honesty, *Cub* is Mann in fine form. Better, with Travis, Mann has given a voice to the youth who haven't found themselves in the gay young adult books that have come before."

—'NATHAN BURGOINE, author of *Light*

"An honest, engaging coming of age story about young gay love. Travis Ferrell's journey to self-acceptance will remain with you long after you have finished reading."

—HANK EDWARDS, author of the Charlie Heggensford stories

"Jeff Mann is so talented that he can write anything and do so successfully. But young adult, you ask? Yes, he can write that too. In this case he does so with the authority of someone who has experience on the subject. *Cub* fills an empty space within LGBT young adult reading materials by thoroughly connecting with the outsider, identifying and soothing the fears and opening up a whole new world to young cubs. Highly recommended."

—*Impressions of a Reader*

"Mann conveys the experience that most rural gays go through as they attempt to negotiate their homosexuality in a place that often discriminates against them.... This novel explores rural Appalachia in another context—and makes a significant contribution to the disciplines of Appalachian Studies and Queer Studies."

—Travis A. Rountree for *Appalachian Journal*

"Finally, a young-adult romance that features Bears and their friends. Travis has, with the aid of his now-off-to-college friends, come out. Living on the West Virginia farm that is a part of him, he dreams of finding his one true love. But wait! Travis is no ordinary country boy. He is a Wiccan leather bear who is going to be true to himself, no matter what. Travis meets Mike; they fall for each other and then have to learn one of life's meanest lessons together. *Cub* is another great read by Jeff Mann..."

—*OutSmart Magazine*

CUB

Jeff Mann

Cub

First published in 2014 by BEAR BONES BOOKS.
This edition published in 2018 by LETHE PRESS, INC.
6 University Drive • Suite 206 / PMB #223 • Amherst, MA 01002 USA
www.lethepressbooks.com • lethepress@aol.com
ISBN: 978-1-59021-339-1 / 1-59021-339-4
e-ISBN: 978-1-59021-257-8 / 1-59021-257-6

Set in Hoefler Text and Century Schoolbook.
Sugar-maple wallpaper: Brett Lamb.
Cover and interior design: Alex Jeffers.
Cover artwork: Ben Baldwin.

LIBRARY OF CONGRESS CATALOGING-IN-PUBLICATION DATA
Mann, Jeff.
  Cub / Jeff Mann.
     pages cm
  ISBN 978-1-59021-339-1 (pbk. : alk. paper)
  1. Gay culture--Fiction. 2. Gay teenagers--Fiction. 3. Popular culture--Fiction. I. Title.
  PS3563.A53614C83 2014
  813'.54--dc23
                              2013046138

For Steve Berman.
Thanks for suggesting that I write this novel and for many helpful
editorial suggestions.

For Ron Suresha.
Thanks for Bear Bones Books.

For Tiffany Trent.
Thanks for good advice and Chinese cooking.

For my high school buddies—Brenda, Bill, Laurie, Billy Jock, and Mike.
Thanks for helping me survive.

Thanks to Jamie Rand for information about the military.

Thanks to Alex Jeffers for designing this book.

In memory of Jo Davison, my high school biology teacher,
whose kindness and consideration made coming out an adventure,
not a nightmare.

CHAPTER ONE

"A<i>mo, amas, amat,</i>" murmured Travis Ferrell. Practicing his first Latin lesson, he made his way through dense rows of corn. He loved to stride through the satiny leaves, to listen to their rustle in September's afternoon breeze. It was like being sheltered inside a grove of emerald, a place where he was safe. He loved the high tassels of the plants, like frozen fireworks, and their scattered pollen, and the swathed ears themselves. Four of them he picked for dinner: nubbled and plump, with kernels so sweet that adding butter would be nigh unto superfluous. He shucked the ears over the compost, enjoying the ribbed-paper sensation of the husks, the gloss of the silk.

Tomatoes next. He plucked pungent suckers from a few staked plants, diverting their efforts from producing more leaves to supplying more fruits. He picked the ripest of the red-orange globes—descended from heirloom seeds passed down in his family—and placed them in the aluminum bucket beside the corn. Goddess-gifts, his Wiccan books would call them, though his Methodist grandmother would attribute them to Christ's bounty. "Habondia," he whispered, "goddess of abundance. Queen of the harvest." When he thought of freshly sliced tomatoes atop mayonnaise-slathered buttermilk biscuits, his belly rumbled.

Then the potatoes. "*America est patria mea. America est patria tua. America est patria nostra,*" he rehearsed, as he plucked off striped potato beetles and their ravenous larvae, crushing them beneath his boot. The bright orange eggs hanging like minuscule hives beneath the leaves he simply smeared up between his fingers, as his father had taught him. Travis hated to kill things, but he'd make an exception for garden pests and such like. When he washed his hands in a barrel of rainwater, colors oozed off in concentric circles: orange of the crushed eggs, chartreuse of the tomato suckers' juice.

Finished, Travis sat on the grass beside the bolted rhubarb patch and green featherings of asparagus. He wiped sweat from his brow and beard, fumbled loose his ponytail, and looked out over his family's Forest Hill farm. The late-summer garden was coming in fast: along with corn and tomatoes, there were cucumbers, squash, half-runners, okra, and eggplants to keep track of, and frowsy ranks of weeds to yank out when time permitted. The porch trellis was blue with twining morning glories; the two-story clapboard farmhouse, painted a pale yellow, was shaded by a great white oak. In the pasture up the hill, a few cattle grazed. To the east, waves of forest-covered blue-green mountains marched all the way to Virginia.

Hefting himself up, Travis grabbed the loaded bucket and headed for the porch. He found his grandmother there in the shade of the flowering trellis. She was a tiny woman, with a lined face and short wavy hair kept perpetually auburn by weekly visits to Mizz McNeer down in town. Stringing half-runners with her gnarled hands, she broke them into bite-sized sections and dropped them into a big zinc bowl. By her elbow, a cigarette smoldered.

"Here you go, Nanny," Travis said, displaying the bucket's garden-haul. "What else can I do? Besides put out your cigarette?"

Nanny sighed, giving Travis a tired smile. She was accustomed to his objections to her tobacco habit. "Honey, if they haven't killed me by now, they aren't going to. Why don't you take you a shower and get some homework done? Dinner won't be till seven or so. I should have gotten these beans on hours ago. We want them good and tender."

"With fatback?" Travis grinned, rubbing his belly.

"Lord, honey. Of course. Who wants to eat half-runners without some bacon grease or side-meat or fatback?"

"City folks? Vegetarians? Or those folks into Nouvelle Cuisine?" Travis's eyes filled with satiric amusement. "Remember that prettily arranged array of weeds they called a salad in that highfalutin restaurant in Lewisburg?"

"Didn't taste bad. But it did remind me of the purslane we used to feed the hogs. Get on now. And if you're hungry, there's some chips and dip in the kitchen."

Travis wasted no time in savoring that quick snack, followed by a big glass of sweet iced tea he flavored with squeezed lemon. He peeked into the big pot simmering on the stove, delighted to find a fragrant pot roast with vegetables. Even better, on the counter he found not one but two home-baked pies: coconut cream and cherry, his favorites.

Sighing with thoughts of the culinary comforts to come, he headed into the bathroom. There, he kicked off his work boots, peeled off his raggedy denim shorts and boxers, and tugged off his baggy T-shirt. Blue with golden letters proclaiming his allegiance to the West Virginia University Mountaineers, it was a gift from Bill and Brenda.

Turning on the shower and climbing into the warm stream, wistfully he thought of his friends: Bill, Brenda, and Jean, the pals that, during his junior year, had helped him come to terms with his feelings for men. How much he'd missed them since they graduated from Hinton High School that previous June. Bill, the butch woman with the short blonde hair, square jaw, and tough demeanor, toughness Travis aspired to but could never hope to match. And her girlfriend Brenda—soft-spoken, pretty, scholarly, sharp-tongued—who tossed Pepsi on Brent Vass when he called her a dyke.

And Jean, beefy-built lover of all things football. She and Travis used to cruise in her Jeep down the rough road to Brooks Falls, where they'd sip sneaked beers, watch white water rush over rock, and compare notes on their hopeless crushes. Travis's passion was for athletic classmates like swarthy Robbie Bowles and bearded Mike Woodson, or TV stars like Tom Selleck. Jean was ardent over Robbie's sister Sherry with her brandy-colored eyes and curvy figure, and Kate Jackson in reruns of *Charlie's Angels*.

Travis sighed, soaping up his furry armpits, then his beard, then his belly hair. Jean, Bill, and Brenda all left for college weeks ago. Over three hours' drive away, at the other end of the state, in Morgantown, they were studying at West Virginia University. It had been so much better to have them around, to have other gay folks to talk to. As much as he loved Nanny's farm, he was lonely with his secrets in

Summers County, where most people he met would think he was a sinner if they knew the truth about him. *One more year of high school to get through,* Travis thought, *and, if I keep getting good grades, I can follow my friends to WVU. Living in a city won't be so scary with my Sapphos to show me around. There, maybe I'll meet some wonderful man and fall in love. Then we can move back here, buy a farm, and spend our lives together.*

"So how was the first day of school?" Nanny asked, laying a slice of pot roast on Travis's plate, followed by a big spoonful of potatoes and carrots. "Did you see any of your friends?"

"They all left for college, Nanny. Remember?" Travis helped himself to the bowl of green beans and the plate of biscuits. "They moved up to Morgantown the middle of last month."

"Oh, that's right. Those big ole girls, Bill and Jean. Not very lady-like, if you ask me. Downright mannish. Now that Brenda, she's a different matter. So pretty in those sundresses of hers. I never did understand why you and she didn't date."

"We're just friends, Nanny."

"Yes, but...Lord, I remember my brothers courting and sparking girls when they were your age. And your daddy too, like his daddy before him." Nanny sighed, pushing her plate back. "And your cousin Johnny, getting that little girl pregnant. The Ferrell men are always chasing women."

"Are you saying they were all horndogs?" said Travis, applying mayonnaise to the biscuit halves.

"Vulgar! I don't know that word, but I bet I know what it means. Yes, I guess that's what I'm saying. I'm surprised you're not dating yet. Girls have always liked you. They can't help but admire your handsome face and good manners."

"I'm just trying not to be like Cousin Johnny." Travis winked and chewed at the same time.

"Thank God we got them married in time." Nanny wiped imaginary perspiration from her brow. "I'm just saying that you're a good-looking boy, Travis. There ought to be lots of girls at school who'd love for you to ask them out."

"Good-looking?" Travis rolled his eyes. "No one at school thinks that. They think I'm fat." Gingerly he patted his love handles.

"You're not fat. You're pleasingly plump. You're built like your daddy was at that age. And one of these days you're going to fill out like he did. You're going to grow up into a big strong man any day now. With those hairy legs and that manly new beard of yours, you already look like an adult."

"That's why I grew it." *That, and 'cause I think guys with beards are sexy, and maybe if I wear a beard, some other guy will think I'm sexy.* "I'm tired of folks treating me like a kid." Rubbing his chin, Travis smiled with pride. "You like it? It's pretty full for my age, isn't it?"

"Yes indeed. Your daddy tried to grow one in college, but it came in patchy, so he's been clean-shaven ever since."

"Most of the other guys at school couldn't grow one if they tried." Travis snickered. "Franklin Grimmett has this wispy stuff on his lip and cheeks that looks like someone glued pigeon feathers to his face. Downright pathetic."

"I'm sure you're right, honey. Those Grimmetts always were a sorry bunch. His daddy Givens is as homely as a mud-fence, bless his heart."

"Ugly as homemade sin." Travis snickered again, feeling pleasantly superior.

"True, son. True. But you got me off the topic. Beard or not, you should be dating at this age. I hate for you to spend so much time alone. You need more in your life than me and this farm."

"Next year I'll go off to college and be with my friends again. Meanwhile, I have you. And my guitar. And my books. And your biscuits and pie. That's enough for now."

"Your books and your guitar...maybe you'll run off to Nashville and make it big, become another Travis Tritt. You're always hiking in the woods or fooling around in the garden, so maybe you'll become a forester, or an agricultural consultant like your father. Or a college professor. You have so many books. How did your classes go today?"

"All right," Travis replied, taking in swift succession a big bite of the meat, then a forkful of half-runners, then a bite of tomato-topped biscuit. "I won't like Physics or Geometry, 'cause I don't like math. I think I'm kind of dyslexic that way. But American History will be cool, especially when we get to the Civil War stuff."

"You can tell them about your Civil War ancestor, son. My grandfather Isaac. He was a Rebel artilleryman, you know. You and he look a lot alike. Dark hair, dark eyes. The Black Irish blood."

"Yes, ma'am. Daddy showed me pictures of him down at the courthouse, at those Confederate veterans' reunions. Mmm mmm. This is all so good."

Nanny chuckled. "I love to watch you eat. You're like your father. A farmhand's appetite. Whatever little girl you do end up marrying, I sure hope she knows how to cook, or we'll all be in trouble. What other classes do you have?"

"Latin. I love it. We learned some words today, and we read a little about Rome. And I have English Literature. We're going to read more Shakespeare."

"Your daddy was always good in English. He called today while you were at school. They've settled into their apartment, and his job starts tomorrow." Nanny shook her head and sighed. "Mercy, I can't believe they're in Germany. So far away. Why couldn't Earl stay in America and do his consulting? You want more meat?"

"Yes, ma'am," said Travis, lifting his plate. "It was a great opportunity, Daddy said, and they'll be back next spring. How are they liking Berlin?"

"Pretty good," Nanny said, doling out another chunk of beef. "Earl's making good money, which will sure help your college fund, and Frances is all excited about being able to visit galleries and attend operas and other sophisticated city events." Nanny chuckled. "With that Virginia Tidewater blood of hers, she always has been a little too fine for West Virginia. They miss you, honey. I know they wish you'd gone with them."

Travis forked up a potato, rolled it in gravy, popped it into his mouth, and chewed. "Mommy wishes I'd gone. Not Daddy, I bet. He and I fight all the time. Everything's always about him—*his* projects, *his* interests. He never asks me what I'm into, what I want to do. It's all about what I can do for him, and what I do's never right or never enough. 'That's good for a start, but...' is his standard line."

"I know he can be critical, Travis, but he does want the best for you. Don't you miss him at all?"

Travis rolled his eyes. "Yeah. I guess. I sure miss Mommy."

"You should have gone with them."

"Then you'd have been alone, and I would have worried about you all the time. You can't keep this place up by yourself."

"I could have hired someone, honey. I don't want you to lose out on opportunities because of me."

"Hired someone? Waste of money," Travis snorted, sprinkling pepper on his food. "I'd rather be here with you on the farm. I don't want to live in some foreign city. Cities scare me. I want to finish high school here."

"You're a country boy through and through, that's for sure," Nanny said, fetching Travis a second biscuit. "And you know your daddy loves you. You and he are just too much alike to get along."

"He sure doesn't show it. I don't think he loves anyone," Travis said, reaching for the bread-and-butter pickles.

"Travis! That's an awful thing to say."

"All he thinks about is himself."

"Well, his father, Earl Senior, was like that. You got a little touch of that yourself, now don't you, son?" Nanny carried her emptied dishes to the sink. "Then again, I guess we all do. The Lord knows Earl Senior was selfish as they came till he found Jesus during the last months of his life. He used to drink so bad. And he had a terrible temper."

"That where Daddy gets his temper, huh?"

"Yes. And where you get yours. How Earl and I used to fight."

"I remember," Travis said, sopping his plate with the last bit of biscuit. "I was there the time you threw that bowl of wilted lettuce at him. Talk about tossed salad. And that time at the Christmas party at the Old Homeplace when he chased Cousin Kimmy and tried to hit her over the head with his banjo. That was really scary."

"Mercy, don't you forget anything? You've always been so smart. Just like your Daddy. I remember when your parents left you here for me to wean from the bottle..."

"I know this story. And you told me that you'd given my bottle to the little lambies 'cause they needed it more."

"Yes. And then the next time your parents brought you by, you told me..."

"I said, 'Nanny, you told me a fib. I saw those lambs in the pasture. And they couldn't have used my bottle, 'cause they don't have hands. They can't hold a bottle with their hooves.'"

"Wasn't that precious? Too smart for me. Too smart for Summers County. You've always been so good in school. I'll bet you'll be valedictorian this year."

Travis shrugged. "Maybe. I can't do basketball layups, but I can make A's. The kids at school call me 'nerd' and 'bookworm.'"

"They're just jealous. With those grades, I'll bet WVU will pay you to attend. Ready for some pie?"

"Yes, ma'am." Travis leaned forward, eyes eager. "Could I have a little piece of each?"

Travis's bedroom was stuffy with late-summer humidity, despite the fan he'd set in the window to provide him with an artificial breeze. It was nearly midnight. Nanny, as was her habit, had gone to bed hours ago. Travis sprawled on his sheets in his underwear, reading ahead in his English textbook. None of his teachers had ever mentioned that many of Shakespeare's sonnets were written to another man, but widely read Brenda had. She'd coached Travis in some queer literary history before she left for college, introducing him to works by Sappho, Shakespeare, and Whitman, plus paperbacks by Patricia Nell Warren about contemporary gay life and novels by Mary Renault about men wanting men back in ancient Greece. "Shall I compare thee to a summer's day?" Travis read aloud, wiping sweat from the crease between his chest and belly.

Faint lightning illuminated the window; thunder grumbled in the distance. Travis closed the textbook and pulled a padded envelope from his desk, one he'd received a week back. Inside it was tucked Bill's letter, plus a pink stone. Opening it, he reread her angular scrawl.

8-28-1990

Hey, there, Baby Butch,

Well, Brenda and I are college students. We have a room to ourselves in Arnold Hall, which is sheer heaven. It's so nice to be so far from Hinton, in a town where Brenda's father isn't around to have us spied on, the bastard. We're both working in the dorm cafeteria. Classes aren't bad. I love my karate class. The next time someone calls me a queer, I might just kick his ass. (You'd think the sensei—that's the teacher—was cute. Hairy chest and big red mustache. You should take the class when you get here.)

The best thing is this. There's a gay bar just downtown. It's called Foxfire. We've been several times, even though we still aren't old enough to drink. Lots of people dancing. Most of the guys are too fey for you (our favorite is a drag queen we call Miss Jerry; he looks like Suzanne Somers when he dresses up), but there are a few you'd like. They're sort of like you, with boots and denim jackets and beards. One of them, Bob, is a truck driver—Italian, dark features, leather jacket. He looks mean but he's a real teddy bear. I described you to him, and he's eager for you to come visit.

We have a couple of new friends we met at the bar: Cin is a butch from DC, and Laura is a classy lady who's quite a flirt. And Farron, he's a painter. Plus we hear there's a gay student group on campus, so we might attend their meetings.

Laura's a pagan, by the way, a feminist Wiccan. I told her about your interest in witchcraft and how much you wanted a boyfriend, and she gave me this stone for you. It's rose quartz, she says, and it's meant to attract love. Carry it in your pocket. I hope you meet some wonderful guy soon. You deserve it.

There are loads of gay folks here. It's so cool to be someplace that's so different from back home. No sanctimonious little dipshits like those morons in Hinton High's Bible Club. Do well in school this year and get that scholarship. We can't wait for you to join us!

Sorry so short. Got to do some laundry.

Your Buddy Bill

PS. Brenda says Hi. She misses cooking for you and says she has some new recipes to try on you once we get our own apartment. Spanish and German. Exotic!

Travis refolded the letter and slipped it back into the envelope. The stone he warmed in his hands. *Rose quartz. Love charm. Horned One, send me someone,* he thought, addressing his favorite Wiccan deity. He pictured the god, grinning and handsome, with glowing eyes, a hairy body, an erect penis, and stag horns sprouting from his brow.

Rising, Travis slipped the stone into his backpack and locked his door. He stood before a long lamp-lit mirror, studying his body and wondering if another guy would ever find it attractive. The boy facing him was six foot one, with green eyes, an oval face, shaggy shoulder-length auburn hair, and a close beard of the same color. His shoulders were broad and freckled, his fuzzy arms sporting a farmer's tan. His chest and belly were chunky, dusted with a sparse coating of hair. His legs were even furrier; Brenda used to call him her little Pan as a joke, which appealed to his pagan sensibilities. Still, he wished he were hairier, or thinner, or muscular, like the guys he admired on TV, or the country boys he saw driving around shirtless in their pickups all summer, or the jocks at school showing off their buff bodies in shorts and tank tops during after-school events.

Sighing, Travis flipped off the fan. Gift of the coming storm, a cool breeze streamed through the screen, and lightning flashed again. The thunder in its wake was louder, closer. He peeled off his underwear and stretched out atop the double bed. For a few minutes he flipped through his journal. Ever since Nanny had given it to him for his sixteenth birthday, he'd been recording ideas, images, and fragmented lines of verse, most of it inspired by good-looking boys at school and the desire they'd engendered in him. When he compared Shakespeare's sonnets to his own attempts at writing poetry, his heart sank. *None of what I write holds together. It's musical and sort of pretty, but it isn't real. And how could it be? I've never really been in love.*

Flipping off the bedside lamp, Travis closed his eyes. He thought about the subjects of so many of his journal entries, the guys at school he wished he could touch. He recalled Robbie Bowles's glossy dark hair, how white his smile was in Latin class. He pictured last year's student teacher Mr. Manley—so aptly named—with his big chest swelling against his shirt in math class. He remembered scruffy Mike Woodson, in Phys Ed back in tenth grade, the way his furry torso and muscled arms moved as he played Shirts and Skins. He remembered Mike down by the Bluestone Reservoir last summer, swimming half-naked in the green water, sunning on the rocky beach, giving Travis a sip of his Boone's Farm and then a brief ride on his motorcycle, Travis's arms around his waist, Mike's belly hair tickling Travis's palms.

Aroused, Travis moved on from memory into the confusingly perverse fantasies he most savored, running through a mental catalog borrowed from television he'd watched as a kid. First, a cowboy was surrounded by villains. Next, a beefy detective climbed from a pool in nothing but Speedos, wet brown hair plastering his torso. Travis joined the action. He grappled with the hapless cowboy, wrestled with the bushily mustached detective. The cowboy and the detective became the same man, one whose big muscles and wild struggles were no match for Travis, who overpowered him, tied him to a chair, and knotted a rag in his mouth.

Travis pulled a Kleenex from the box beside his bed and switched off the light. There was no one there to touch him, so he touched himself. He kissed his imaginary prisoner, loving the man's gagged protests. Outside, the thunder boomed again, and rain started its soft shushing on the windowsill.

CHAPTER TWO

It was a sunny Friday afternoon in Hinton, West Virginia, the only town of any size in Travis's home county of Summers, set very scenically along the New River beneath the looming Allegheny Mountains. School had let out, and kids eager for the weekend congregated along the long block of the high school, waiting for their respective buses.

Across the street, avoiding the crowd, Travis sat, leaning against the trunk of a maple tree, enjoying the cool September air and crystalline light. The Misfit Maple, he called it. It was where the outcasts and the asocial usually waited—his acquaintances, Emo Anita and Goth Goddess Ella, and other heavyset, brainy types like himself—but he was alone that day. He scrawled a letter to Jean in his notebook and wondered what sort of tasty meals his grandmother would make him that weekend.

That coming Sunday would be the autumnal equinox, so after his grandmother retired, he planned to light a few candles and celebrate the balance of light and dark. Nanny claimed to worry about his soul since he refused to attend Forest Hill's duo of churches with her, so he kept his Wiccan books hidden and always conducted his solitary rituals in his room after she'd gone to bed. As far as it came to his two secrets—his paganism and his attraction to other boys—he figured what Nanny didn't know wouldn't hurt her. *I remember what happened when Brenda came out to her father,* he thought, wincing. *All hell broke loose.*

A car stereo thumped by, followed by a ruckus of voices across the street. He turned, grimacing, resentful that his concentration had been shattered. There, just down the block, were tall, curly-haired athlete Brent Vass and his crew of townies, in their neat shirts and khakis, teasing a group of girls who were making irritated faces but obviously enjoying the attention. Again Travis thought with pleasure of how Brenda had doused Brent with pop.

He'd turned his attentions back to his letter, wishing he weren't so sensitive to noise and thinking about how sweet it would be to get back to the farm's relative silence, when he heard his name called.

"Hey, Ferrell, long time no see."

Brent and his fellow jocks were approaching. All five wore black and orange letter jackets, their smooth faces plastered with grins.

Travis closed his notebook, zipped it into his backpack, and stood. Ever since he'd realized he was gay, groups of straight boys made him nervous. When he thought about what they might do if they knew his secret, if they knew what he thought about in his bed alone at night, he grew a little nauseated. Poor Martin, a slender, effeminate boy he used to have some classes with, had been so harassed by Brent and his kind with shouts of "Queer!" and "Fag!" that he'd dropped out of school. Only Travis's bulk and relative masculinity, he knew, had kept him from being recognized for what he was and treated to a similar fate.

Trying to appear nonchalant, Travis looked for the school bus out of the corner of his eye, hoping it would show up before the little pack of townies got any closer. *If only Bill or Jean were here to back me up.* He'd felt vaguely unsafe ever since his butch buddies left town.

"Hey, guys," Travis said, forcing a smile. As much as he wanted to snarl, "Fuck off!" he could hear his mother repeating some old maxim about attracting more flies with honey than vinegar, and besides, he was outnumbered. "How was your summer?"

"Great. My dad took us all to the beach. What'd you do this summer? I bet I know."

Travis crossed his arms across his chest and tried to look amused. "Yeah? What's that?"

"Oh, putting up hay. Feeding chickens and pigs. You know, redneck things."

"Well, I do live on a farm," Travis said, flushing.

"Oh, we know. And you sure dress the part," replied Brent, looking Travis up and down. "Jean jacket. Dirty boots. Baseball cap. Flannel shirt. That messy hippie hair and beard. I can see you on *The Dukes of Hazzard*, slopping the pigs and making moonshine."

"Nothing wrong with being a country boy, or so my daddy says." Travis cleared his throat, mustering a crooked grin. Images of *Hazzard* stars John Schneider and Tom Wopat shirtless took shape in his mind and then dissolved. "I'll take that as a compliment." Part of him wanted to run, and part of him wanted to punch Brent in the jaw.

"I'll bet you will. I'll bet you're a big fan of the Duke boys. At least that's what Rhodetta told me."

"Rhodetta?" Travis lifted an eyebrow. "Rhodetta McNeill?"

"Yep. The pretty little president of the Bible Club. She's formulated a hypothesis, as they say in science class." Brent took a step closer. "She thinks she's figured something out about you."

"And what is that? She doesn't know anything about me."

"Well, we all think you're a Satanist, of course, since you don't go to church and say you believe in evolution. But that's not all. When's the last time you went out on a date?"

"Not...long ago. Why do you care?" Travis stomach clenched.

"Well, Travis, look. The boys here and I, we've pretty much had better things to do than pay attention to you. But Rhodetta's been studying you since last spring. You know how she likes to sniff out sin. She pointed out to us that the only folks anyone ever saw you hanging out with last year were dykes. That big lumbering Bill Walker and that big ferocious Jean Bugg. And that snooty little bitch Brenda Martin. So what kind of guy doesn't date girls but hangs out with dykes?"

Oh hell. Oh, no. Choking back fright, Travis clenched his fists, suddenly regretting that Bill never gave him any tips on how to fight. "Don't call Brenda a bitch."

Brent took a step closer. "Don't tell me what to do, Forest Hill trash. I can't believe it. You're a redneck *and* a fag. What a great combination. A big old hairy boy like you a cocksucker? Where's your tutu and tiara?"

"Up yours, Brent," Travis growled, his temper rising. "The only reason you call Brenda a bitch is 'cause she gave you a Pepsi shower. I sure wish I'd been there to see that. She should have kicked you in the balls. Me, I wish that Pepsi had been horse piss."

Brent swung, punching Travis in the mouth. Dazed, Travis staggered back against the maple tree. His father used to take a belt to him every now and then when he was a mischievous child, and he used to wrestle with Bill some, but he'd never been struck in the face in his entire life. The pain and fear flooding him shifted within the space of a few stunned seconds to rage. He lunged at Brent, only to be seized by two of Brent's friends and pulled backwards. Brent punched him in the belly. Travis doubled over. The boys holding his arms threw him to the ground.

"Stupid queer," Brent said, looking around to check for witnesses. "You should know better than to mess with us. Hey, guys. Here comes my mother's van. Let's get out of here."

Travis watched, teeth gritted and belly aching, as his attackers jogged down the block. Legs shaking, he got to his feet and felt his face. Already his lip was swelling. How was he going to explain this to Nanny? *If I tell her what happened, she'll want to know why I got in a fight. She might even call Brent's mother. And Brent's mother might ask Brent why he punched me. And Brent might share with his mother his opinion of my sexuality. Got to lie. Got to lie.*

The Forest Hill school bus rounded the corner. Wiping blood off his mouth, Travis snarled, "Right on time." He pulled on his sunglasses, cocked his WVU baseball cap over his eyes, and, face hot with humiliation, joined the line of students at the curb.

"It's nothing, Nanny. Really. It's nothing," Travis grunted as his grandmother applied peroxide. "I was just scrapping with friends. Some of us guys were fooling around, teasing each other, learning how to wrestle. Don't make a big deal about it."

"Wrestling?" Nanny tsk-tsked. "Like those big brutes on TV? Y'all ought to be more careful. Elbowed in the mouth. Lord. You could have lost a tooth. You're all swollen up. I should call the principal."

"No! Please don't. I'm fine." Travis managed a pained smile. "Guess I'm wilder than you thought, huh?"

"Wild's nothing to be proud of. If your mother were here—"

"She'd be all concerned about what folks thought. I know, I know. She wants a gentleman for a son, not a redneck brawler. Well, she isn't here. You won't tell her, will you?"

"We'll see. Right now, I'm going to make us some chicken and dumplings for dinner. That should be easy to chew. Oh, your poor mouth."

"Umm, dumplings sound good. Do you need any help? I have loads of homework, but..."

Nanny waved him away. "You go on and study. I'll fetch you when things are ready."

Travis grabbed up his backpack and headed upstairs. Being alone in his bedroom, free of the need for a false façade, was a relief. For a few minutes, he tried to focus on his Physics textbook, but he was feeling too much to think. *Brent. That bastard. That **bastard**. I can't believe he hit me. Damn him. And I didn't hit him back. I didn't know how to fight. Who knows how many people saw it all? Folks will think I'm a weakling and a coward.*

Travis slammed the textbook shut and threw himself on his bed. *And now I have a reputation as a queer. Exactly what I prayed would never happen. "A redneck and a fag," Brent said. Now I might get my ass kicked at any time. Damn it. I might end up like poor little Martin, harassed and tormented and run out of school.*

Travis stretched out, clasped his hands behind his head, and closed his eyes. He tried to imagine himself as a skillful, brave, and muscular warrior, taking grand vengeance against Brent and his cronies, but all he could think about was being cornered, surrounded by jeering classmates, called "Fag" in the halls of the high school, or punched and kicked by packs of bullies. He was about to crowd out these fears with another attempt at studying when the hallway phone rang.

"I'll get it," Travis shouted, bounding out of his bedroom, eager for any distraction. "Hello, Ferrell residence."

"Travis? Are you all right?"

"Anita? What's up?" Travis said, surprised. Though he and Anita had long chats at school, she'd never called him at home before.

"I just heard about it. About what happened. I can't believe it. That fucker Brent Vass punched you?"

"Oh, great," Travis groaned. "Soon the news will be all over town."

"So it's true?"

"Yeah, it's true. How'd you hear?"

"From Ella. Missy Meadows told her. Missy was waiting for the Forest Hill bus like you. She saw the whole thing. She told Ella your mouth was all bloody when you got on the bus."

"I'm all right, Anita. Don't worry about it. And please don't tell anyone else." Travis cleared his throat. "I'm kind of embarrassed. I tried to fight back, but his buddies held me."

"Have you ever been in a fight before?"

"Naw. Never. Guess I've been pretty sheltered. I just realized today that I don't know how to fight. And now I really wish I did. I wish I were strong, so I could kick Brent's ass if he ever messes with me again."

"I can't really see you as a karate master." Anita giggled.

"Me neither." Travis heaved a rueful sigh. "I'm about as coordinated as a newborn calf. I was terrible in Phys Ed."

"You have bulk, though."

"Flab, you mean." Grimacing, Travis pinched his belly's spare flesh.

"Well, toughen up. Get all athletic and then tear that bastard Brent up. You could start lifting weights at that new gym."

"New gym? I hadn't heard of it. Where is it?"

"It opened out in the West End a few months ago. It's in that old Laundromat across Temple Street from Coolheart Hollow Road. Right beside the garage that Mr. Woodson runs."

"Mr. Woodson? Mike Woodson's father?"

"Yum, Mike Woodson. The sexiest boy in Summers County. Yeah, Mike works in his father's garage after school and on weekends. With all the muscles he has, maybe he could give you some tips about weight-lifting."

"Yum, Mike Woodson" is right, Travis thought, recalling again the sight of Mike's bare chest down at the reservoir. "Well, okay. Thanks for the advice, Anita. Maybe I'll ride into town with Nanny tomorrow, since she has another beauty appointment, and check the place out."

"Good luck. And if you see that stud Mike, tell him 'Hi' for me."

CHAPTER THREE

Saturday afternoon, and the little office of Woodson's Garage was unstaffed. Taking a seat, Travis waited for a few minutes, flipping through *Sports Illustrated* and admiring photos of baseball star Mark McGwire, his big arms and red goatee. Never having thought that patience was a virtue worth cultivating, he soon left the office and stepped tentatively into the open door of the garage proper.

"Hey. Anyone in here?" he said shyly, peering into the dimness, breathing in heavy aromas of oil and gasoline.

There was a scraping sound, then someone rolled out from beneath a jacked-up car. "Yeah, yeah, just a minute," growled a deep voice. It was Mike Woodson, the boy Travis had so powerfully and so often admired in the past. He was dressed in filthy overalls atop a grease-smeared white muscle shirt. Mike got to his knees, looking annoyed. When he saw Travis, though, his face softened.

"Hey. What you doing here?" Mike stood, brushing off his butt. "Travis, right?"

"Uh, yeah. Travis Ferrell. We had some classes together a few years back, and, uh, you gave me that motorcycle ride once. Last summer at the reservoir."

"Right. That was fun. I miss that bike. My dad had to sell it."

"That's too bad. I never see you around anymore. How you been?" said Travis, extending his hand.

"Real greasy," Mike said, holding up a blackened palm. "Don't think you want to shake."

"I don't care about grease. I shoveled manure last weekend."

"I guess we're even then." Mike extended his hand and the boys shook hard.

You're one of the best-looking guys I've ever seen, Travis thought. Mike was shorter than Travis—five foot nine to Travis's six foot one—and, like Travis, a high school senior, but already Mike looked and acted like a man, with his muscled frame, full black beard, strong jaw, messy bangs falling over his brown eyes, and chest hair pouring over the top of his dirty muscle shirt. Some of Travis's fondest memories of tenth-grade Phys Ed, a class he'd otherwise hated, were of watching Mike's athletic prowess on the basketball court and in gymnastics and furtively studying his soapy nakedness in the locker-room shower after class.

Travis dropped Mike's hand and stepped back, trying not to stare and make his longing obvious. "Man, you got a strong grip," he said, feeling a stirring in his shorts and hoping it didn't show.

"Thanks. So what you needing? And, gotta ask, where'd you get that fat lip?"

"Well, this fat lip's why I'm here. I heard y'all opened a gym next door in that old Laundromat."

"Yep, Buck did. You wanting to lift?"

"Buck?"

"That's my dad."

"Oh? You call your father by his first name? Man, my father would never tolerate that. Okay. Yeah, I got punched the other day, and—"

"And you don't want it to happen again?"

"Exactly. I wanna get stronger. Thing is...I've never lifted before. But, uh, you, uh, sure look like you do. So, could you maybe give me some advice?" Blushing, Travis tied back his hair in a ponytail. The thought of spending some time in close proximity to Mike was both thrilling and terrifying.

"Thanks for the compliment." Mike flashed a gleaming catfish grin and flexed his right biceps. "I ain't bad. Been lifting for a few years. Sure, I could give you some coaching. Weight lifting *and* some boxing tips. How about now? I'm about done here. How long can you stay?"

"Well, I rode to town with my grandmother, and she's at the hair dresser's. I got about an hour. I got some gym clothes here in my backpack."

"Okay. Great. Let me wash up some and put on some shorts. You want a Mountain Dew? Or a beer?"

"Your dad lets you drink beer?" Travis shook his head in wonder.

"Every now and then."

"How old are you?"

"I'll be seventeen this November," said Mike, brushing sloppy black bangs out of his eyes. "You?"

"I turned seventeen last month."

"Well, on second thought, Buck might kill me if I gave you one. Let's stick to pop. Wait in the office and I'll be right back."

"**I**s this right?" Travis asked, doing his best to keep his arm angled the way Mike had suggested.

"Yep. Good. These are called concentration curls. Keep your elbow against your leg now." Mike gripped Travis's forearm, adjusting it, and Travis shivered at the firm pressure of Mike's fingers. It was glorious to be so close to a boy so handsome and so mature, and twice as glorious to have a context in which the two might touch.

"Mmm. It hurts already. They're harder than they look."

"That's just twenty-five pounds. I do forty-five," Mike boasted.

"Wow. Really? This is how you got your arms so big?"

"Yep. They'll get your arms big and hard too if you keep at it."

The boys were the only ones in the gym since the Ward brothers from up Coolheart Hollow had finished their huffing and puffing work on the bench press and headed out, loudly proclaiming their desire for bourbon. Country music radio wafted through the high-ceilinged space, Garth Brooks singing "The Dance."

Travis sat on a padded bench, lifting the dumbbell, with Mike standing only inches from him. They were both dressed for a workout, Mike in nylon gym shorts and his oil-stained muscle shirt, Travis in a baggy tank top bought to hide the little curve of his belly and camo shorts that hung nearly to his knees. As was usual when Travis was near a boy he liked, he was frightened, anxious, rapt, and excited all at the same time. After working in the garage and then spending time in the gym, demonstrating lifting techniques to Travis, Mike's unwashed scent was strong. To Travis, the aroma was pure aphrodisiac, the manliest cologne on the planet. It aroused him so thoroughly he had to adjust his shorts when Mike wasn't looking. *Damn hard-on. Thank God I'm wearing briefs,* Travis thought.

"Okay, take a break," Mike said, thrilling Travis with a casual pat to his shoulder. "Another set of those, and then the preacher curl and then we'll try the bench press now that the Wards are gone. Those boys are pretty tough dudes. Their older brother is in the pen for selling Oxycontin. That's some nasty shit. Buck's office manager Michelle got hooked on it and started stealing from us, the little bitch. He fired her, she lost her kids, and then she ODed. Retard. Man, I mean, I like pot pretty well, but that shit, no way."

"You smoke pot?" Travis squeezed his sore biceps, eyes wide.

"Some. Not too much. Shit makes you stupid. I'd rather drink."

"Yeah? Other than that little bit of wine you gave me last summer at the Pits, and a few beers with my buddy Jean, I haven't had much alcohol."

"Fuck, buddy, you *are* sheltered." To Travis's delight, Mike slapped him on the back. "We'll have to share some CLC soon."

"CLC?"

"Canadian Lord Calvert. My favorite. Or, shit, even better, I could set us up with some moonshine one of these days. Buck has a good connection up Madam's Creek."

"Really? I don't know if..." Travis smiled, stretching out his arms the way Mike had taught him before the lifting lesson began. "You're kinda wild, aren't you?"

"Fuck, yes. The world's always out to tame you, buddy. Don't you know that yet? You gotta fight back. Fuck 'em, y'know?" Mike gifted Travis with another wicked white grin, then took a swig of Mountain Dew.

"You sure got a potty mouth," Travis said, grinning back. "Nanny would wash my mouth out with soap if I talked that way. Doesn't your father care?"

"Hell, ole Buck don't mind my drinking or my language. He's too busy with that new girlfriend of his. He's been a rounder since Mom died. Does my trashy language offend you?" Mike said, rolling his eyes.

"Naw. It makes you sound...tough, I guess. I kinda like it. Hell, yes, I like it."

Both boys laughed. "Well, shit, buddy, that's good to hear," Mike said, putting weights on a bar, then tightening the collars. "Enough of cussing; back to the lifting lesson. Preacher curl next. We'll start you small with twenty pounds, then work up. Watch while I do 'em."

Mike demonstrated, his pale arms bulging as he moved the barbell in swift arcs, with a casual ease that indicated how little twenty pounds were to muscles so well developed. Travis watched, transfixed at his companion's show of strength.

"Okay?" Mike dropped the barbell into its stand, then patted the bench pad. "Sit here. Arms here. Keep your back straight. Don't strain. Just do 'em as I did 'em."

Travis did as he was told, wincing as his arms shakily lifted the bar, hoping he didn't look too weak or incompetent. He'd been working in the garden quite a bit over the last few months, weeding and picking, but other than a few days helping a Forest Hill neighbor heft hay bales in June, he was unaccustomed to moving heavy weight.

"Yeah, you're gonna be sore tomorrow," said Mike, as if reading his mind, "and it'll be worse the day after that. But sore is good. Means you're getting somewhere. Means one of these days you'll be ready to kick some ass. So who punched you?"

Travis let the bar clatter into its rest. "Brent Vass. Yesterday after school."

"He's a prick. He thinks he's something since he's on the football team and since his family has bucks. You're as big as he is. Did you punch him back?"

"Naw." Travis finished his Mountain Dew, then started into another set. "I don't know how to fight. And he had friends with him. He hit me in the mouth, and when I went for him, they grabbed me and held me, and he punched me again. In the belly that time. I'm still sore."

Mike waited till Travis was done with his second set before replying. "That's enough for now. We'll get to the bench press here in a bit. Let's take a break. I want a smoke." He led Travis through the long room, past more benches and racked weights, and out the open front door, where they sat on the steps and looked out over Temple Street and the jumbled, shabby houses of the West End. Mike fumbled in his shorts and pulled out a pack of cigarettes.

"Want one?"

Travis shook his head. "Naw. Thanks. I don't much like 'em."

"Rather dip?"

"Naw," said Travis, feeling embarrassingly square. "I've tried that too. And chaw tobacco too. Didn't take to either."

"Man, you're a pure sort. You mind if I indulge?"

Travis shook his head. "Naw. Go for it." Out of the corner of his eyes, he studied Mike's hairy calves and forearms. Mike's aroma washed over him again, and suddenly he ached to wrap an arm around the other boy and kiss him on the lips. Then, imagining shock and disgust in Mike's face, envisioning Mike punching him in the mouth the way Brent had, he pushed the dangerous urge back.

Mike lit up and inhaled, then rested his elbows on his knees and let out a long, smoky breath. "Brent's kind, they always travel in a pack. I should know. I used to be part of it."

"Yeah, weren't you on the football team with them? I seem to remember hearing—"

"Yeah." Mike spat on the street. "I played guard. Quit last season."

"Why'd you quit? I heard you were pretty good."

"Long story. Got tired of the bullshit. Had some issues. Why'd Brent punch you?"

"He insulted a friend of mine. Brenda Martin, you remember her?"

Mike nodded. "Yeah. She seemed pretty smart. I always saw her with Bill Walker, right? Were they girlfriends? Everybody said so."

Mike's casual tone surprised Travis. "Uh, yeah. They were."

Mike shrugged. "Okay. Each to his own, I say. Go on."

No rant about sin or perversion? Wow, thought Travis before continuing. "Last spring, before Brenda graduated, Brent called her a dyke and she threw Pepsi on him."

"Nice."

"And yesterday, when Brent told me she was a bitch, I told him I wished she'd thrown horse piss on him instead."

"Beautiful." Mike took a long draw on his cigarette, then tossed the butt to the ground, stood, and stepped on it. "Well, the next time you run across that douchebag, I want you ready. You want to hit the bench press now? After that, how about the punching bag?"

"You bet," blurted Travis. "I want to get as tough and ferocious as you, man."

Travis followed Mike inside, transfixed by the curves of his companion's compact rump. Before commencing their exercise, both boys sucked down cones of cold water from the cooler in the corner. On the radio, country music paused long enough for an announcer to give an update on Operation Desert Shield.

"Hot in here," said Mike, pulling his muscle shirt over his head, revealing a well-defined chest and flat belly, both coated with glossy black hair. *Oh, my God,* thought Travis with dazed delight. *Thank you, Horned One!* Having cherished the sight of Mike naked or bare-chested before, in Phys Ed and on that idyllic day at the reservoir, it took all of Travis's good manners and self-protective defenses not to ogle Mike the way the jocks at school ogled the cheerleaders.

Mike added weight plates to the bench press barbell. Travis watched, feigning interest in Mike's activity while taking in the details of his companion's build. *Broad shoulders, small waist, round butt. God, that swaying in his shorts... I don't think he's got underwear on. He's just downright beautiful. I look like a slob compared to him,* thought Travis, his desire for Mike's body muddied with contempt for his own.

"That's two hundred pounds. Now spot me, buddy, and study how I do it," said Mike, stretching out on the bench. Travis positioned himself near Mike's head, ready to help if necessary. With a steady movement Mike lifted the heavy bar from its rests and lowered it to his chest. Travis, grateful for any excuse to look at Mike's body, watched his friend's hairy and substantial pectorals swell beneath the impressive weight. Mike did a set of eight, stretched out, swigged more water, then did a second set and then a third. Travis's face was carefully expressionless, but inside he was rapt and thrilled. He breathed in the rising aromas of Mike's armpits, and his eyes ranged greedily over Mike's navel and his small brown nipples, barely visible in that sea of black torso hair.

"Your turn." Mike coached Travis through three sets, the bar set at fifty pounds to accommodate Travis's novice status. Mike had to help him through the last four presses, urging him on with his deep baritone. By the time Travis was done, his arms were shaking and his chest was aching and tight.

"Good boy," Mike enthused as the guys stretched out their limbs. "Now the punching bag. Take off your tank top."

"Uhh. What?"

"I wanna see what we're starting with. You stick with me, and I'll have you well on your way to buff in another couple of months. Come on. No reason to be shy. We're all guys here, right?"

Travis nodded. Face reddening, he peeled off his tank top.

"Okay." Mike circled him, rubbing his bearded chin. "You're solid."

"I'm fat." Travis shook his head. Avoiding his reflection in the full-length mirror on the nearby wall, he stared down the room, toward the big windows in the front of the gym. He could feel his cheeks heating up as Mike scrutinized him.

"You've got some extra weight, sure. But you got lots of potential. Big shoulders. Thick-built. Hairy like me."

"Not half as hairy." Travis rolled his eyes. "You have...uh, a great body. I wish I were built just like you. I look like a flabby boy. You're already a man."

"Yeah, yeah. Keep that flattery up. Flex for me," ordered Mike, grabbing Travis's right biceps.

Grimacing, Travis did so.

"All right," said Mike, squeezing the meat of Travis's arm. "We got some work to do, but you got lots of potential, promise. Come by here after school Wednesday, and we can lift again."

"That'd be cool. But I'll miss my bus."

"Shit, I'll drive you home. You got to get on the weights two, three times a week to get anywhere. You sure you got some time for a boxing lesson today? I don't wanna make you late."

Travis consulted his watch and nodded. "Got about fifteen minutes till I gotta leave to meet Nanny at the beauty parlor."

"Good. Let's punish that punching bag," said Mike, fetching gloves and tape from a pile in the corner. "Just a few beginning tips today." Unrolling some boxing wrap, he took Travis's right hand in his and began wrapping it up. "This stuff'll protect your hands, and so will those gloves. Just remember, you gotta throw your shoulder into a punch, okay? One of these days, if Brent Vass comes after you, he's gonna get a big surprise."

"Sounds good to me," Travis replied, gazing into Mike's cocky grin and again fighting back the urge to kiss him hard on the mouth. Already he was looking forward to being alone in his bedroom that night, running his hands over hoarded images of the half-naked boy beside him.

CHAPTER FOUR

"**Y**ou sure have a lot of books about war," said Travis, examining Mike's bookshelf and trying to look relaxed.

"Yep," Mike replied, kicking off his sneakers. "Ole Buck was in the army, so I guess I come by the interest naturally. World War II's my favorite. And Vietnam."

Rain fell steadily over Hinton the last Saturday in September. After a third session together at the gym, the boys had headed to Mike's house for lunch. Now Travis sat on Mike's bed, thinking, *I can't believe we're friends now. I can't believe I'm in his home, in his bedroom. He sleeps here. Probably naked. Lord.*

Mike, as if reading Travis's thoughts, shucked off the black-and-orange Hinton High Bobcats gym shorts he'd worn to work out in, then his black T-shirt. "I'm gonna take a shower," Mike said, standing there in nothing but white briefs. "You can take one too, if you want."

Only if we can take one together, thought Travis, his eyes raking Mike's compact frame while he suppressed a mischievous grin. *Such pale skin and such black, black body hair. You're always stripping down around me, man. You're gonna drive me crazy. God, I wanna hold you hard. God, all the things I think and feel that I don't dare to say. I'm so tired of living in my head. I'm so tired of pretending to be someone I'm not.*

"Uh, no, thanks. I'll wait till I get home," Travis said, turning his back on the almost painfully arousing sight.

"Okay. Won't take me long. Then we can have that lunch you promised."

Travis waited till he heard the shower splashing down the hall. Then he picked up Mike's gym shorts and pressed them to his face. The crotch-musk of them was thick and rich. Travis breathed deep, heart pounding, groin stiffening. He carefully replaced them on the floor, then retrieved Mike's T-shirt, burying his nose in the moist pits, inhaling Mike's smell for long, excited moments before replacing them as well.

Curious, Travis ranged the room, examining the contents, half-consciously looking for clues to his new buddy's identity. As rough a background as Mike's appeared to be, Travis had expected vulgar images of naked models or porn actresses to plaster the walls, but instead he found three movie posters: *Indiana Jones and the Last Crusade*, *Die Hard*, and *The Lost Boys*. The latter had apparently been ripped in half and then taped back together, a fact that piqued his curiosity.

Travis picked up and put down a pack of cigarettes, a pile of Southern rock tapes, and a blue jean jacket. He peered into the open closet, finding there a scuffed pair of cowboy boots, a mud-caked pair of work boots, several pairs of sneakers, faded T-shirts on hangers, and a heap of old jeans, several with tattered holes in the knees.

Moving over to Mike's dresser, Travis patted the top of it, wondering what revelatory items it might contain.

We all have our secrets. I've got my hidden library of gay and Wiccan books. I'll bet Mike has piles of porn and a stash of condoms hidden in here somewhere, Travis thought, fighting the urge to open drawers and confirm his suspicions. *The high school's right across the street. Irresistible as he is, I'll bet he brings girls up here during lunch hour and gets frisky with them. Lucky hussies.*

The shower still sounded. Giving in to temptation, Travis eased a drawer open. White gym socks. He closed it and opened a second. Thermal undershirts and a half-emptied fifth of Lord Calvert, the whiskey Mike had mentioned at the gym. He closed it and opened a third. *Oh, man.* Travis stared in dull awe at the collection of white briefs. He ran his fingers over the fabrics, wanting suddenly to steal a pair as a souvenir.

The sound of rushing water stopped. "I'm done," Mike shouted from down the hall. "Sure you don't want a shower?"

"Naw," Travis yelled. Guiltily, he eased the drawer closed. He sat on the edge of the bed. Bending, he gave Mike's pillow a quick nuzzle. He rose, paced in a circle, then went to the window and watched the rain descend.

Travis was the picture of innocence, flipping through Mike's books, when his friend strode in, towel around his waist, black hair gleaming with wet. "That felt good," Mike said, dropping the towel and gifting Travis with a few seconds of bewitching nakedness before pulling on fresh briefs, a pair of jeans, and a clean T-shirt.

"Cool posters. I like all those movies. But what happened there?" Travis asked, indicating the torn *Lost Boys* image with his thumb.

Mike scowled. "Buck's what happened. He came up here one night after two many six-packs and tore it off the wall. He said the guys looked like fags. We got into a pretty nasty shouting match, each of us threatening to kick the other's butt. Afterwards, I thought, 'Fuck him. It's my room, not his,' so I taped it back together and put it back up."

"Man." Travis cleared his throat, embarrassed for Mike's sake. *My parents may get on my nerves a lot, but they'd never threaten me.* He changed the subject fast. "Uh, you, you like Stephen King too, huh?" He held up a copy of *Carrie*.

"Hell, yes. I'm a horror buff. Wait till you see my Godzilla collection."

"Really?

"Really. I got all the models when I was a kid."

"You into comics? I'm a big Marvel fan. *The Avengers. The X-Men.*"

"Used to be. Then Buck made fun of me and told me to grow up. So how about that lunch? I'm starved."

"You bet. Me too."

The guys headed down to the kitchen. There, Travis fetched a big paper bag he'd placed in the fridge before their workout. Mike dug paper plates and plastic ware out of a drawer, poured some iced tea, and grabbed a few paper towels to serve as napkins.

Outside, they took their seats around a rusty table on the front porch. Rain beat down, rilling off the eaves, dripping off the fan-shaped leaves of twin gingko trees. Across Fifth Avenue stood the cinderblock high school gym. Down the block were Temple Street and the Episcopal Church, then the long slope of the town descending to the railroad tracks, where a CSX train was rumbling by. Across the New River, Freezeland Mountain rose into gray sky, looking like a cross-legged giant with Hinton at its feet.

Mike leaned back, hands clasping the back of his head, grinning with anticipation as Travis unpacked the Tupperware containers filled with lunch goodies Nanny had prepared for them earlier. "Potato salad. I dug the potatoes myself, just last week. Deviled eggs. And fried chicken. And fried apple pies."

"Goddamn. What a haul. I'm glad we're buddies," said Mike, snatching up a chicken leg.

"Feeling's mutual," replied Travis, biting into a deviled egg.

For a few minutes, the boys ate in silence, looking out into gray sheets of rain.

"Jesus, this is good," Mike mumbled in between bites of pie.

"I picked those apples too. Now you understand my gut," Travis said, pinching the little roll of flesh around his waist and making a rueful face.

"Hell, yes, I do. Buck can't cook, and neither can I. If I lived with your grandmother, I'd get damned fat."

"I think you look great the way you are."

Mike chuckled. "Yeah? Thanks. A few girls have thought so."

Travis bent his head and rubbed his forehead, suppressing a grimace of self-disgust. *"You look great?" God, Travis, so stupid. I might as well have said, "Man, you're hot. Let's get it on." If I don't watch myself, he's going to be calling a fag like Brent did.*

"I mean, well, you're really in shape, and, uh, and thanks again for the weight training."

Mike reached across the table and softly thumped Travis's arm. "Three times in the gym, and I can already see a little difference."

"Yeah, I can feel it." Travis flexed his biceps and smiled sheepishly. "I wish I were athletic like you. Remember tenth grade? You were as good in Phys Ed as I was bad. I couldn't climb that rope or do a pushup or layup to save my life, but you were great at all of it. I used to watch you on the horse when we did gymnastics and wish I could move like that. "

"Thanks." Mike gave Travis a lazy grin. "I've always been good at sports. Not so good at other subjects."

"So why don't I ever see you at school? We used to have classes together."

"It's 'cause you're smart and I'm dumb," said Mike, finishing off the pie.

"Huh? You're not dumb."

"You're taking all those college-prep classes. I'm in the vocational track, bud. Most of my classes are in that Career Center down toward Brooks. You're studying English, Physics and Latin, and I'm studying Vo-Tech stuff like Shop and Car Mechanics."

"Oh. Okay. I didn't realize that. So you don't plan to go to college?"

Mike snorted. "I don't have the brains for college. Not the academic type. I'm a C student at best. Plus, hell, even if Buck had the money, and he don't, he wouldn't spend it on my schooling. Now cars, I know cars. I'm gonna stay here in Hinton and work in the garage."

Travis nodded. "Well, at least you know you're good at something and you'll have a job. Me, I don't know what kind of job I'll end up with. Only things I'm good at are reading books and digging potatoes."

"Shit. Smart as you are, you could do anything. Lawyer, doctor, teacher, farmer. So how big a farm y'all got?"

"Before Daddy got that consulting job overseas, we did right much. Grew all the basics: corn, potatoes, carrots, broccoli, cabbage, and so on. Made maple syrup one year. Raised pigs one year. I have a soft heart when it comes to animals, so eating that sausage was hard. We had a couple horses for a while. Skittish things, so unfortunately I never really learned to ride. Still have cows. The garden's smaller this year, but Nanny still put up a lot. Her basement is full of pickles and—"

"Oh, *hell*. Sorry to interrupt. Here comes Buck."

A big red Ford pickup—twice the size of Mike's—descended the steep slope of Fifth Avenue, slowed, then pulled into the narrow driveway beside the house. From it emerged a beefy man in mechanic's clothes. He slammed the truck door and climbed the stairs. Buck was a little taller than his son, with a solid frame, a beer gut, a gray-and-brown buzz-cut, a stubbly face, and a sour expression.

Travis rose, extending his hand. "Howdy, sir."

"Guys," Buck grunted, walking past them without a glance and entering the house, letting the screen door slam behind him.

"I would have introduced you, but I can tell he's in a foul mood." Mike took a swig of iced tea and stared out into the rain. "He's in a foul mood a lot."

"So, uh, your mother. How long's she been gone?"

"A long time." Mike fetched a cigarette from the pack on the table and lit it. Propping his feet up on the porch railing, he inhaled, then released first a smoke ring and then a stream of blue-gray smoke. "Died when I was ten. Cancer. Buck never got over it. He's been using other women as a bandage for years, but I don't think that helps much."

God, you look sad. Man, I'd like to hug you hard. "Wow. When you were ten? I can't imagine. I'm guessing you never got over it either," Travis said, putting the emptied Tupperware back into the bag.

"You're right about that." Mike scratched his belly and lowered his voice. "Buck and I were both big fucking messes for a long time. I guess grief drove us apart instead of pulling us together." His voice dropped lower, just above a whisper. "For a while, he pulled a lot of binges. Used to come home piss-drunk and beat on me."

"Oh, damn," Travis gasped. "Really?"

"Yep. Then I grew up, hit the gym, got my arms hard, and had a few roughnecks down on Third Avenue teach me some street fighting. Next time Buck tried to beat me, I gave him a helluva black eye. He got the hint. Never hit me again. Then he started dating, and I pitched a fit and tore up the house a few times. We hardly spoke for month and months."

"And now? How do you two—"

"Hold on." Mike stiffened as Buck's heavy steps sounded inside the house. "Here he comes again."

Buck threw open the screen door and strode out, a six-pack of beer in his hand. "I'll be over at Janet's tonight. You need anything to eat, there's pizza in the freezer."

"Sure, Buck," Mike said, knocking the ash off his cigarette.

The boys waited till Buck had pulled back out of the driveway before resuming their conversation.

"He's a charmer, ain't he?" Mike shrugged. "Well, anyway, things evened out. Now we just kinda tolerate one another. He lets me do what I want, and I think he appreciates the help in the garage. And hell, Mom's gone and ain't coming back, so I guess he deserves some kinda love life. At least with Janet around, he ain't so damn mean."

Mike took another long drag off his cigarette and smiled at Travis. "Speaking of which, what about you, farm boy?"

"Speaking of what? What about me?"

"Got a love life?"

"A love life? Me?" Travis said, face turning pink.

"Touched a nerve, huh?" Grinning, Mike ground out his cigarette in an ashtray on the floor. "Sorry, stud. Didn't mean to embarrass you. We'll have that conversation some other day. What about your family, man? Got any siblings? You get along with your parents?"

"No siblings. Daddy and I argue a lot. Everybody says we're too much alike. He's brought me up to love the outdoors and reading, but we're both pretty stubborn and we both want our way, I guess. It's all about him, you know? Mommy and I are pretty close. She's big on manners. Wants me to be a Southern gentleman, not a hillbilly. Both of them have pushed me to focus on my studies and get good grades."

"So what's the story? Why you living with your grandmother instead of them?"

"No story," Travis replied. "Nanny—that's Daddy's mother—has been living with us for the last couple of years. My father got a consulting job overseas, in Berlin, and they left in late August. I wanted to spend my last year in high school at home and help Nanny with the garden."

"You got a chance to go to Germany and didn't take it? Crazy. I'd kill to travel some. Don't you wanna get out of this town?"

"You just told me that you're planning to stay here after we graduate."

"Yeah, but I'm a grease monkey like Buck," said Mike, giving his head and then his ribs a simian scratch. "You, *you* got a future."

"I think you're great, Mike. Stop putting yourself down."

"Man, you're bossy, Mr. Scholar. Say something in Latin."

"Oh, hell. Now you're teasing me?"

"I'm not teasing you." Leaning closer, Mike gently fingered Travis in the ribs, causing him to giggle.

"Cut it out," Travis yelled.

"Wow. You are *so* ticklish. I love it."

Mike gave Travis's ribs another dig, causing him to squeal with laughter.

"Stop!" Travis pulled away, swatting at Mike's hand.

"Cute," Mike said, desisting. "I'm serious. Teach me something."

Travis looked Mike in the face, admiring his bushy black eyebrows, deep brown eyes, and long lashes. "*Amo, amas, amat,*" he blurted.

"Nice. Sounds exotic. You could be Caesar. If Caesar had hippie hair," Mike added, tugging at Travis's ponytail.

"Stop it! I'm not a hippie," Travis said, with a nervous glance at his watch. He grabbed the bag of Tupperware and stood. "Look, we better get going, okay? Nanny wants me to dig more potatoes this afternoon. And pick the damn Japanese beetles off the roses. And gather some green tomatoes to fry for dinner."

Mike smacked his lips and poked Travis in the side before standing. "Fried green tomatoes. Haven't had those in years. One of these days you gonna invite me to dinner, right? Your grandmother's cooking reminds me of my mother's."

"Sure. We can arrange that." Travis took a deep breath, gathering his courage, then continued. "Y'ought to stay over some weekend night. I got a spare bed in my room. And I want to play you some guitar. I'm pretty good." *Any excuse to see you in nothing but your briefs,* Travis thought, remembering the gloriously hirsute spectacle in Mike's bedroom earlier that afternoon.

"Yeah, we should definitely do that. Sounds fun. Okay, lemme hit the toilet and then we can head out."

Mike disappeared inside. Travis waited on the porch. *Thank you, Old Ones, for such a handsome friend,* he silently prayed. Gazing up at the surrounding mountains, he extended a hand into the rain, caught water in his palm, and lapped the cool moisture up. In a few minutes, Mike returned, jingling his truck keys.

"So what did they mean?" Mike asked as the boys strode down the porch steps.

"What?"

"The Latin words you just used."

"Oh. Uh. They mean, 'I love, you love, he loves.'"

"Yeah?" Mike winked. "I'll have to remember that. How do you say 'I love you'?"

"Uh. *Te amo.*"

"Sweet. Might come in handy sometime."

"You gonna use that on one of your girlfriends, I'll bet," Travis said, climbing into the musty truck.

"Shit. Ain't had a girlfriend since I quit the team. How about some Marshall Tucker for the drive? 'Fire on the Mountain' is one of my favorites." Mike pushed in a tape, and the wail of pedal steel filled the cab. "One good thing ole Buck gave me was a taste for Southern rock."

CHAPTER FIVE

Travis didn't board the school bus after classes were done. Instead, he sat with Emo Anita beneath the Misfit Maple, enjoying the warm mid-October afternoon, gazing up into the amazing burnt orange of autumn's leaf blaze. Mike was due to come by at any minute, and Travis was profoundly eager to see his friend again.

"So why are you hanging around?" asked Anita, combing out her rich brown hair. She was a large girl with a plump, pretty face, full lips, and a creamy complexion she highlighted with subtle makeup. "Don't you always take the Forest Hill bus?"

"Mike Woodson's going to pick me up," said Travis, veiling his excitement inside a casual tone of voice. Most of his energy, most days, seemed to be spent on hiding his true feelings, pretending to be someone else. Anita and Ella were pretty cool girls, but they were straight, and he'd never gathered sufficient courage to come out to them. They might have been understanding if they knew, but neither was very good at keeping secrets.

"Mike Woodson? Oh, Lord, that sexpot? You lucky bastard. I've had a crush on him for years. I even asked Ella to cast a love spell on him, 'cause I'd love to get hold of him. No such luck. I don't think she's quite the Wiccan priestess she thinks she is. When did you start hanging with him?"

"About three weeks ago. That was good advice you gave me about the West End gym. Mike's been helping me lift weights and learn to box. He's coming by here in a little bit. We're gonna work out some, then he's gonna drive me home."

Anita lifted a dubious eyebrow. "Travis the bookworm turning big bad jock? Well, I *have* noticed you getting more buff, but I guess I was too polite to ask how. Your chest and arms are looking pretty good."

"Thanks for noticing," Travis replied, blushing. Avoiding her gaze, he fumbled a leather cord from his backpack and tied his unkempt hair back in a ponytail. Open admiration from girls both pleased him and frightened him. The pleasure came from the unexpected luxury of feeling physically attractive to someone, anyone. The fear came from the certainty that he would have no idea what to do if a girl wanted him to engage in bodily intimacy with her.

"That busted mouth you got has turned you macho, huh? I heard that dolt Brent has been saying stuff about you. That you're a fag. That über-religious little bitch Rhodetta has been saying the same thing."

For a split-second, Travis contemplated telling Anita the truth, but the tone of her voice when she said "fag" made him think better of it. Instead, he scowled.

"Yeah. So I hear. To hell with them. They don't know jack-shit about me. Mike's gonna teach me how to handle myself if they bother me again."

"Your grandmother doesn't mind you spending time with Mike? Hot as he is, he's got kind of a rough reputation. Like his father. Kinda trashy, like a lot of those Vo-Tech kids."

"Naw, Nanny's fine with him, though she hasn't met him yet. I think she's just glad I have a buddy."

"You *have* been kind of a recluse this year. We could spend more time together if you want." Anita winked, adjusting her blouse to better emphasize her large breasts.

"You live in Pipestem. I live in Forest Hill. Kinda hard to get together. Plus we gotta keep our grades up, right? For those scholarships," said Travis, trotting out his usual excuses. He just couldn't relax and be himself around straight kids, plus he'd been a little afraid of Anita ever since she tried to get sexy with him at the Pipestem State Park pool a few summers back.

"I guess." Anita made a pouty face. "Isn't Physics boring? And that holier-than-thou Mr. Adkins, the Bible Club sponsor. He teaches science but doesn't believe in evolution. Don't you get sick of being around so many stupid kids, Travis? Retards! We're the ones with the brains. We're the superior ones. Why do they get to run the school? Why do they get to be so popular?"

"Good question. And speaking of retards," said Travis, gesturing with his thumb. "There's a pair of 'em now, right across the street."

Anita turned and glared. "Oh, damn. Rhodetta, that pinch-nosed skeleton. And her greasy pet toad, Franklin. Well, ugh. They're heading over here."

"I proclaim those honest-to-God shit-eating grins," Travis whispered to Anita, steeling himself for another encounter with the aggressively pious.

The pair approached. Rhodetta McNeill was a bony girl wearing an old-fashioned, prim-looking, polka-dotted dress that Travis thought would be more appropriate on someone of his grandmother's generation. As for Rhodetta's companion, Franklin Grimmett, Travis had held him in contempt for years, not only because of his pushy evangelizing but because of his unfortunate looks. The boy had an acne-cursed complexion pale as curdled milk, a prominent spare tire of a gut, and a wispy attempt at facial hair that made Travis even prouder of his own beard. Franklin wore penny-loafers and a polyester outfit of mismatched checkers and clashing colors.

"That poor boy must be colorblind," Anita muttered. "Look at that shirt. As my father used to say, I'd like two of those: one to shit on and one to cover it up with."

Travis choked back a guffaw. "Oh, my God. I've got to remember that line. Quiet. Here they come."

"Why, hi, y'all," piped Rhodetta. "Franklin and I saw y'all over here and thought you could do with some witnessing. We're so worried for your souls."

"Oh, God," Travis groaned. "Really?"

"You said, 'Oh, God'?" Franklin stared at Travis with a mixture of disgust and curiosity, as if he were a fetal pig in need of dissecting. "But you don't believe in God, do you? That's the problem."

"Now, Franklin, be polite," ordered Rhodetta, adjusting her large rhinestone brooch. "Here, y'all. Read these tracts. Please." Pulling little booklets from her purse, she offered an orange one to Anita, a pink one to Travis. "Your salvation depends upon it."

Anita waved away the proffered pamphlet. "Stuff it. I have better things to read, thank you."

Travis took the tract and stared at it. The cover was half black, half pink. In the pink half was set the silhouette of a man with one hand on his hip, the other hand held up, the wrist cocked in an effeminate manner. About him floated several reproductions of the Greek letter Lambda, which Travis recognized, thanks to Brenda's coaching last year. It was, he knew, the sign for gay liberation. On the black half was set the title in white letters, *The Gay Blade.*

"The sin of Sodom Christ hates most of all," intoned Rhodetta, gazing down at Travis with sad eyes.

"Sorry, Rhodetta. I don't need this. Pink's not my color." Travis shook his head and handed the pamphlet back. Rising to his feet, he considered further responses. *I can't say "Go screw yourself" to a girl. If I don't say I'm straight, they'll assume I'm gay. But if I say I'm straight, I'll be a liar and a coward. And if I'm brave and tell the truth, my life will become a living hell, just like poor prissy Martin's turned into.* "Just go away," he sighed, looking down the uneven brick street and praying for Mike's truck to appear. *Where are you, Mike? Get here fast.*

Anita seemed less conflicted. She too rose. "You know, folks," she said evenly, hauling her backpack onto her shoulder, "I think I know why you worry so much about the afterlife. You're so damned ugly that there's no hope for a fulfilling life in this world, so you've got to hope for heaven instead. Franklin, your pimples belong in the Guinness Book of World Records. And look at you, Rhodetta. Stick girl. You've got as many sexy curves as the two-by-four you have stuck up your ass."

Rhodetta's façade of polite evangelism and pious concern cracked. "You fat whore! How dare you?"

"Dare?" Anita sneered. "I suggest you get out of my face, or I'll snatch you bald-headed. Someone needs to clean up that rat's nest on your head."

"Now, ladies," Travis murmured, palms sweating. Confrontations always made his stomach churn.

"They're abominations, Rhodetta. Damned souls. Let's get out of here," said Franklin, tugging at Rhodetta's ruffled sleeve.

"Rat's nest?" Rhodetta shook him off. "I'll have you know I have my hair done at Bobcat Beauties. I'd suggest you do the same, but you can't afford it, can you, you poor thing? All that long, stringy hair. You're just so common. Vicky told me that you blew Bobby Lilly underneath the football stand."

"Oh, Lord," Travis grunted. He'd heard that rumor, and he was envious. Bobbie Lilly was nearly as handsome as Mike was, in a blond-haired and blue-eyed kind of way. "I thought you were a Christian, Rhodetta, always going on about God's love. Ugly talk like that isn't exactly loving, is it? My grandmother tells me that Christ—"

Anita interrupted, smiling sweetly. "You heard I blew Bobby? Maybe I did. You jealous? With a face and body like that, you'll die a virgin."

"I'm saving myself for marriage," Rhodetta sputtered. "You, you'd do it with anyone, I'll bet. A boy would have to be desperate to climb on that lard ass of yours. The white-trash queer and the beached-whale Whore of Babylon. Y'all make quite a pair."

Travis mentally shuffled through the photocopied list of Shakespearean insults Brenda gave him before she left town. He'd settled on "Get thee hence, mooncalf!" for Franklin and "Your virginity breeds mites, much like a cheese" for Rhodetta, when, to his immense relief, Mike's truck pulled up. It was a beat-up black Ford pickup with a white capper, what Mike affectionately referred to as his "Fucked-Up Old Run-Down Dodge," and it was blaring Lynyrd Skynyrd.

"Hey, folks. What's going on?" Mike turned down the music and pulled off his sunglasses. His face was hard, as if he could already guess. He was dressed, as usual, in a casual, manly way that Travis found frustratingly hot: cowboy boots, camo pants, and a white A-shirt that displayed his muscled arms and chest hair.

"Not much, man. Let's head on out," Travis blurted, shouldering his backpack and heading for the truck cab, more than eager to escape.

"I'll tell you what's going on," Anita said. "Rhodetta called me a fat whore and Travis here a white-trash queer."

"Oh, yeah?" Mike cut the engine. "And did you tell 'em to fuck off?" He flashed Anita one of his broad catfish grins, a snowy gleam framed by the midnight-black of his beard.

"No. As a matter of fact, I didn't." Anita smiled back.

"Good. Then I will." Mike turned his brilliant smile on Rhodetta and Franklin. "Y'all fuck off."

"You can't talk to us like that, Mike Woodson." Rhodetta pursed her lips. "I know what kind of nasty man your father is. A whoremonger and a drunk."

Franklin added his two cents. "Yeah. He'd screw a snake if he could hold its head still. I heard he—"

"I said, fuck OFF!" Mike shouted, throwing open his truck door and making as if to step out.

"Stay away!" Rhodetta shrieked.

"Leave us alone!" Franklin squealed.

Rhodetta bolted across the street, with oily-faced Franklin close on her heels. Soon they'd veered around a corner of the high school and disappeared.

"Oh, my *God*. Thanks for the show." Anita thumped the hood of Mike's truck. "You scared the shit out of them."

"No problem, pretty lady. Sometimes my rough-n'-tough reputation comes in handy."

"Flatterer. Keep it up."

"I call it as I see it, ma'am. You need a ride?"

Anita's face brightened. While Travis was doing his best to hide his admiration for Mike's physique, Anita was under no such compunction. She gave Mike a long, bold look and ran a finger along the truck's passenger-side mirror as if she were stroking Mike's thigh.

Dammit. Straight folks have it so easy, Travis thought. *The percentages are all against me. He's probably looking at her breasts and wishing I'd just go away.*

"Well, my bus should be here any minute, but...sure. It's a pretty day with all the leaves changing. You don't mind driving me home? I live all the way up Pipestem."

Travis, peeved at the thought of having to share Mike's company, pointed to the truck seat. "It'd be pretty crowded, folks."

"Cozy, not crowded. Yes, brave defender, let me mount your steed."

Mike, sniggering, put on his sunglasses. "You got the kinda mouth I like. Get on in, y'all. We'll have us an Anita Sandwich."

Great. They're going to start groping one another any minute now. Travis squeezed in after Anita, trying to remember his manners. He told himself that Mike was straight and single, and so was Anita, that they were both his friends, that he ought to be happy for them if they hit it off, but all he could do was sulk, stare out the window, and pretend to admire the autumnal colors. Mike and Anita shared small talk as they drove out of town, across the New River, and up toward Pipestem, a remote area in the southern end of the county.

"So you're in Vo-Tech, right?" Anita said, snuggling against Mike. Between her curvy size and Travis's well-fed country-boy bulk, it was indeed a tight fit.

"Yep. And you're one of those brains like Travis. College-bound." Smiling, Mike brushed black hair from his eyes. "Travis here's into Latin and stuff. What about you?"

"Science. Engineering. I want to go to MIT."

"MIT, huh? Y'all want a cigarette?"

"Naw," Travis grunted, feigning interest in the structure of the Bluestone Dam as they drove by it.

"Sure," Anita replied.

"They're in the glove compartment. Light one up for me and help yourself to one."

Anita did so. Both of them puffed.

Travis grimaced, leaning into the window's flow of clean air. "Those things are gonna kill you," he groused, pretending to focus now on the crumbling sandstone road cuts as they skirted the reservoir.

"Yep. They surely will," Mike said. "Yes, indeed. So what's MIT?"

"What's MIT?" said Anita. "Don't you know what that is?"

"Nope. Can't expect much of us dumb Vo-Tech boys, ma'am. Though we are good for driving away dildos and dildettes like Franklin and Rhodetta. And fixing your cars."

"False modesty. You were a football star, Mike. I've always thought you were super-cool."

"No star." Mike chuckled. "But thanks. I envy folks like you and Travis. Y'all got lots to look forward to. So what's MIT? The backwards and the ignorant want to know."

"It's the Massachusetts Institute of Technology. It's up in Boston."

"Boston? You wanting to move up there to Yankeeland, huh? Live among the bluecoats?"

"Bluecoats? You're as bad as Travis. Forget the Civil War." Anita bumped her shoulder against Mike's. "Lord, yes, I want to live in Boston. And get out of this Podunk place. You ought to visit me there. I'm going to have a fabulous salary and a fabulous wardrobe and go out to fun night spots and museums."

"I'll bet those Yankees all have horrible manners," Travis growled. "Nanny said she was up there during World War Two, and they didn't even have biscuits. And the traffic was terrible."

"I'll bet you'll have a stable of big-city boyfriends," Mike said, exhaling smoke.

"Like you have a harem of girlfriends. I've heard all about you, Mike Woodson. That charm has broken many a heart." Anita gave Mike's bare arm a squeeze and giggled. "All those muscles. You're a Romeo and a rounder like your daddy. You're a bad boy. Downright dangerous."

"What maiden could resist, right?" Mike frowned. "Don't believe everything you hear, Anita." He took a last draw off his cigarette before stubbing it out in the ashtray. "So how much farther to your place?" he asked, before turning on the tape deck and cranking up the volume.

Anita waved from her porch and blew dramatic kisses as the boys drove back down her gravel driveway. Before Mike reached the main road, he stopped the truck long enough to fetch a beer from a cooler behind his seat. He popped it open, took a sip, then wedged it between his thighs.

"Drinking and driving?" said Travis, eyes on the mountainside.

"Yep. I'm a bad boy, remember?"

Mike steered the truck back onto the road toward town. For a couple of miles, the boys were silent. "This bird you cannot change," sang Skynyrd on the tape deck.

"You've been mighty quiet," Mike said evenly, eyes on the road. Reaching over, he turned the music down.

"Yeah. I get that way sometimes. The cigarettes bothered me."

"First time I've heard that."

"I just don't like 'em in a car."

"Uh huh. I'll keep that in mind."

Mike took a long swig, then handed the can to Travis. Seeing no other cars on the road, he followed suit before handing the can back. The beer was cold and bitter on his tongue.

"So what'd Anita say wrong? One minute you were flirting with her, and the next minute you got all grim and cranked the music up. It was kind of rude. You know she likes you."

Mike sighed. "Yeah, I do. And I wasn't flirting with her...exactly. I was just being nice."

"Looked like flirting to me. Are you into her?"

"What's it to you?"

I'd rather you be flirting with me, that's what. "Nothing, I guess. I just... don't want you to lead her on. She's kind of lonely. Most guys don't give her the time of day 'cause she's plump. Plus she's so smart most of 'em are intimidated."

"I don't want to lead her on either. Flirting's kind of a habit. I didn't mean anything by it. I'm not into her that way. Women are way too much trouble."

"So why'd you go sour all of a sudden?"

"It's just all that shit she started to say, about me being a heartbreaker...it was a little close to home, okay? I have some regrets, Travis. Stuff I'd just as soon not talk about now. Can we drop it?"

"Sure," said Travis. "I didn't mean to push."

For a few minutes, the boys drove in uneasy silence.

"I guess we're both in piss-poor moods," Mike said. "You still wanna lift?"

Travis hesitated. Then he thought of Mike's arms bulging during biceps curls, and desire banished his peevishness. "Sure. Yeah. You bet. Why not?"

"Okay. Exercise might do us some good. I know the punching bag will. So, look." Mike paused. "Anita said Rhodetta and Franklin called you a queer. Is that true?"

Oh, no. Oh, no. "Yeah," Travis said, staring out at passing woodland. The angry jealousy he'd been feeling shifted suddenly into a bellyache of fear. He could feel Mike's eyes on him, but he was unable to return his friend's gaze.

"Any idea why?" Mike's voice was soft.

"I-I guess because I was such good friends with Jean, Bill, and Brenda."

"They *were* pretty obvious." Mike chuckled low in his throat. "Me, I wouldn't want to pick a fight with either of those butches. Either of 'em might whip my ass."

"Hey! They...were good friends to me. I really miss them."

"Man, I wasn't talking shit about 'em. I'm serious. Those girls were tough. I admired that. I don't have any problem with them. If they're friends of yours, they're friends of mine."

Travis turned, finally meeting Mike's eyes. "Really?"

"Really. I may be a redneck, but I ain't no asshole." Mike tapped Travis's shoulder with the side of his fist before returning his attention to the tortuous road.

"That's good to hear," Travis said, taking a long look at his friend. *Damn, what a relief. Thank the gods you feel that way. Understanding* **and** *hot. Camo and cowboy boots...the army look and the cowboy look together? Wow. Right up my alley.* "I mean, they should be able to love who they want, seems to me."

"Yep. Guess so." Mike took another swig of beer, then offered Travis the can. "More?"

"You're a sot, aren't you? Seems like you're always drinking."

Mike shrugged. "Takes the edge off. You want more or not?"

"Hell, sure, pass it over," said Travis. He took a few sips, then a swallow. *Speaking of being a sot, I'm besotted. Damn. That's the word. Besotted,* Travis thought, gazing out over the glitter of the reservoir. *Boy, you're beautiful. Boy, am I in trouble. No good can come of a crush on a straight guy. You may say you're cool, but if you knew what kind of things I do to you in my dreams, you'd probably beat me senseless.*

Mike drove back over the New River into town and down Temple Street into the West End. "So did you tell 'em off?" Mike asked, parking his truck in a side street beside the gym. "Rhodetta and Franklin?"

"Didn't have to. Anita tore them up. Besides, my mother always said to just ignore folks like that. She says all they want is attention, and if you ignore them, they'll go away."

"More?" Mike lifted the beer can again.

"Naw, thanks."

Mike knocked back the last of the beer, crumpled up the can, tossed it behind the seat, and then, to Travis's surprise, patted him on his denimed thigh.

"Friend, I hate to contradict your mother, but she's wrong. Believe me, I know. Ignore 'em, and they'll keep on being pricks and pick on you. Kick 'em in the ass, that's how you get 'em to leave you alone."

CHAPTER SIX

"**D**on't y'all hike too long," Nanny said, cutting Crisco into flour. "It's looking like rain. Food'll be ready around six."

"I really appreciate the dinner invitation, ma'am," Mike said, his voice deep and eager. "I know it'll be good, since I've already tasted your fried chicken and fried apple pies."

"That little lunch I sent down the other day? Glad you liked that, son. I've been cooking since I was a little girl."

"You're baking a pecan pie, right, Nanny?" Travis pointed to the bag of nut meats and bottles of corn syrup set out on the kitchen counter.

"Yes, son. Plus, since it's gotten chilly, we're having stuffed cabbage. That's what's in that pot on the stove. An old Hungarian woman from the coalfields gave me that recipe. You like cabbage, Mike?"

"Yes, ma'am. I like everything. Since Mom died, Buck...ah, my dad and me, we mainly eat fast food, since I never learned to cook and Dad can't cook worth a...a whit. Thanks again for inviting me."

"Well, you're welcome. You boys get on now, and leave me to it. Travis, put out some hay for the cows while you're out there. And when you get back, would you fetch another jar of lime pickles from the basement? And a jar of apple butter too. For the rolls I got rising."

"You bet," said Travis. "We'll be back in time for dinner, promise. No way I'm missing your homemade rolls."

Mike pulled on his olive-drab army coat, Travis his black hoodie, Levi's jacket, and Mountaineers baseball cap, and they headed out the door. Outside, October was nearing its end: the sky overcast and gray, the breeze chilly, and most of the leaves fallen from the trees. Hands in their pockets, the boys passed the exhausted garden, mulched with bags of raked leaves.

"I appreciate you watching your language around my grandmother," said Travis as they climbed over a metal gate into brown-grass pasture. "'Worth a whit' isn't exactly a Mike Woodson phrase. 'Worth a shit' is."

"Got to admit my mouth's a little nasty. I don't spend much time around women."

Hard to believe. I heard you were quite a lady's man there for a while, back when you were on the team. What's changed? Why'd you get all grim when Anita called you a heartbreaker? "Well, anyway, thanks for the good manners. I think Nanny really likes you."

"Nice to know. It's real pretty here. I hope I can come back."

For a few minutes, they strode the pasture slope in silence. Travis remembered last night's fantasies, how he'd chained bare-chested Mike to the wall of his father's garage, gagged him with an oil-grimed cloth, beat his back till he cried, then freed him, held him in his arms, and comforted his bruised and sobbing friend with kisses. *I must be crazy. Why does such stuff turn me on? Am I gonna grow up to be a serial killer? I wouldn't hurt Mike for anything.*

"Look there," Travis said, with one hand shifting his erection in his pants, with the other pointing out the scarlet leaves of a shrubby plant. "That's staghorn sumac. You can make a kind of lemonade with the berries. And that tree, see the bark? That's a black walnut. See the leaf scars?" Travis pulled a limb down and pointed to a twig. "Like little clown faces. Nanny collects the nuts, dries them, cracks them, and picks out the nut meats. Really tasty in banana bread. But the hulls can stain your skin for days. The other kids used to make fun of me when I came to school with brown hands. Used to call me 'Nigger Finger.'"

"Yeah, Buck uses that word sometimes. I hate it. Downright trashy, that's what Mom used to say. Some of my best buddies when I was on the team were black. You know Eugene Robinson?"

"Sure. He and his sister Wilma are great. She's really smart; we have some classes together. I love it when she sings at assemblies. She's always been really sweet to me, and so has Eugene."

"Yeah, Wilma's pretty cool too. Well, when I tried to bring Eugene home for lunch one day, Buck about had a heart attack. Retard." Mike spat into the pasture grass.

"Man, that must be hard. I'm lucky that way. Nanny is probably the biggest fan of Martin Luther King in all of Summers County. And when Daddy caught me using the N-word when I was a kid, shouting it at some tramp downtown with a bunch of other kids, he took a belt to my butt. I learned early to be respectful. Hey, look there," Travis exclaimed, pointing. "Now that's broomsedge. Means that the soil is acidic. If you see redbud, on the other hand, the soil's probably lime-rich and alkaline."

"How do you know all this stuff?" Mike shook his head. "You're amazing."

"Amazing? Me? No one's ever said that before. Except for Nanny."

"Well, she's right. You are."

"T-thanks, man," replied Travis as they reached the top of the slope. "You...are too. You're kind of like a, well, a role model of mine. So, anyway, here's the view I told you about. That's Peter's Mountain, there in the distance. That cleft there, that's where the New River cuts through, and—"

"Role model? Me?" Mike interrupted Travis. "I ain't nothin' but trouble. You're smart as hell, and all I can do is fix cars."

"Naw," said Travis, knowing even as he spoke that he might be going too far, revealing too much. "You're smart too. You're...a real man. You show me how to be a man. You, you're strong and you're tough, but you're...kind. As, ah, handsome as you are, you could run with the popular crowd, but you don't."

Travis cleared his throat, plucked a stalk of fluff-seeded broomsedge, and fiddled with it. "You're like a, a sort of solitary warrior, and you stand up for misfits like Anita and me even though you don't have to. You've been really nice to us. That kind of protectiveness...that's the way I want to be. The kind of man I want to be. Strong. Heroic. I want to be like you, Mike."

"Heroic? Me? Wow." Mike chuckled. He soft-punched Travis's arm, then gripped his biceps. "Well, farm boy, you're coming along. You really made that punching bag swing today. Brent better watch himself around you."

"Well, he *has* left me alone lately. Don't know why, but I'm glad."

"It's those new muscles of yours, man. Let's stop here for a bit. Great view." Mike sat down on a fallen log, and Travis joined him.

"So, Travis. I wanna ask you something. Something important. I could offer you a drink first," Mike said, patting his jacket pocket. "Got a flask in here. That CLC I told you about."

"Don't think so. I figure going back to Nanny's house with booze on our breaths would be pretty dumb. She hates liquor since my grand-daddy drank so much."

"I got some Certs."

"Better not. So what you want to ask me?"

"Uh, well. We're friends, right?"

"Yeah. And I'm glad. I haven't had a good guy friend since Richard, and he left town back when we were in the ninth grade."

"So we can be honest with each other?"

"Yeah... Sure." Travis tensed, his mouth going dry. *Uh oh. Now what? All of a sudden I wish I **could** take a swig of that flask.*

"Well, some guys in Shop today were talking about you. Calling you queer. I told 'em to shut up, and they did. Told 'em all that shit is lies. But then I got to thinking. Look, *are* you gay? 'Cause if you are, it's no big deal. My cousin Eddie, he lives out in San Francisco, he's a few years older than us, and...he's gay. And he's cool. So, look, Travis, if you're gay, just tell me. I'm okay with it. Really."

Travis stood. He stared out at the distant blue-gray line of Peter's Mountain. He opened his mouth and closed it. "Mike," he said, then stopped. "Oh, hell," he groaned before turning and walking away.

"Hey!" Mike followed, grabbing Travis's right arm and turning him around. "Hey, buddy. Don't run off. Look, just tell me. I need to know."

"And why is that?" Travis snarled, shaking Mike off. "Afraid I'll rape you? Afraid you'll get the same reputation I have?"

Mike grinned. "Is that why you've been wanting to get stronger? So you can become a rapist?"

"Yep," Travis exclaimed. "The Redneck Rapist of Summers County. Should go down in the West Virginia history books, like the Hatfields and McCoys. And the Mothman. Yeah, I'm a real predator, all right. Downright dangerous."

Travis snickered, and Mike guffawed. "Look, Travis, you can trust me. Just be honest with me, and then I'll be honest with you."

"How about you first?"

"Naw. Naw."

"Why not?"

Mike scratched his black-whiskered chin, then laid a hand on Travis's shoulder.

"'Cause, my friend, I think you're braver'n me. I think Bill and Jean and Brenda taught you that."

"Me braver than you? You're full of it. Okay, come on. That's the barn down there near the pond. I got to put out some hay. We can talk there. I think it's about to rain anyway."

Drizzle shushed on the barn's tin roof as the boys climbed up into the loft, then stretched out, side by side, cozy and comfortable in the hay.

"I think I'll take that drink," said Travis. "Long as I get the Certs later."

Nodding, Mike pulled the flask from his pocket, screwed off the lid, took a swig, and handed it to Travis.

"Thanks." Travis took a long sip, then handed it back. "Damn, it burns," he said, licking his lips.

"It's supposed to. Go on. Please?" Mike urged. "I swear you won't regret it."

"All right. Here goes." Travis stretched his legs, cupped his hands behind his head, lay back, and stared at the ceiling. "Yeah. I'm gay."

Mike heaved a sigh. "Okay. Good."

"Good? You're glad to hear this?"

"Yep. Go on. How did you, when did you realize..."

Travis shrugged. "I've been having feelings for guys since I was little. A buddy of my father's, Mr. Wolford, a tall guy with curly brown hair and a beard. Guys on TV...Westerns, cop shows, you know? Then I met Bill and Brenda, and we got to talking, and they must have recognized a kindred soul. Brenda lent me some books. Gay novels. I read 'em and I, I guess I recognized myself in 'em."

"Do your parents know? Or your grandmother?"

"Lord, no. My parents are pretty liberal, but my mom's really hoping for grandchildren, and Nanny's kinda religious and is always talking about what kind of woman I'll end up marrying, so... Plus I'm afraid what happened to Brenda might happen to me."

"And what was that?" Mike took another sip.

"Oh, Lord," Travis groaned. "Because Bill was so butch, Brenda's father got suspicious about why they were spending so much time together. He had some coworkers follow them and figured out they were lovers. Things got real nasty. He threw Brenda out. She spent her last year in high school living with an old lady out Greenville Road and supporting herself with odd jobs. How she's paying for college, I don't know."

"Sounds pretty damn rough, all right. So who else you told?"

"Just Bill, Jean, and Brenda. And now you. Not Anita or Ella. They gossip too much."

"Have you...been with a guy before?"

"Me? Naw. Never. Christ, in this county?" Travis heaved a bitter laugh. "The only guy I've known for sure was gay was that poor little prissy Martin, and he sure wasn't my type. You remember what happened to him."

"Yeah. Yeah, I do. Which sorta leads into what I wanna tell you."

"What?" Surprised, Travis rose on one elbow, peering at Mike through the gloom. "Did you know Martin?"

"Not really. I'll tell you all that in a minute. So, you ever been with a girl?"

"Huh uh. You're looking at a true-blue country virgin here, Mr. Woodson," Travis sighed, plucking hay from his hair. "Sally Richmond and I did some kissing down an alley just back of your house once—you know where that big dillweed patch used to be? That was back in ninth grade. I thought I had a crush on her, 'cause she was so smart, but that kiss convinced me otherwise. How about you? Surely you've had lots of girls, considering your reputation."

"A few." Mike mustered a faint smile and took another drink. "There's a reason for that reputation."

"I'll bet. Pass that flask back over here. I need me a little more of that. A reason, huh? I'm thinking it's 'cause you're a handsome horn-dog ladies can't turn down. Am I right?"

"It's not as simple as that," Mike said, handing over the flask. "Finish it. There ain't much left. You think I'm handsome?"

As usual, Travis felt constrained to think one thing and say another. *You're the handsomest man I've ever seen. God, I want you bad.* "Good Lord," Travis snorted. "Fish for compliments much? Have you looked in a mirror lately? Cocky as you are, you *know* you're good-looking."

Mike laughed. "Thanks. You are too, but we'll get to that. Well, here's my story, and none of it's pretty." He lay back in the hay and closed his eyes. "You remember Randy Lowry?"

Travis downed the last of the whiskey, then leaned back against a bale, eyes fixed on Mike's face. "Sure. Big guy. Shaggy blond hair, blond beard. Built like a wrestler. A year older than us. Graduated last June. He always intimidated me, got to admit. What about him?"

"We were on the team together. Randy and Brent were the ones who gave Martin the most trouble. And Randy's the reason I left the team."

"Wow. Really?"

"Yeah."

"How did he... What happened?"

Mike opened his eyes and rolled over, facing Travis. "This is hard to say. Damn, I should have brought another flask."

"Go on, Mike. You can trust me," said Travis, scooting closer. The bereft look in Mike's dark eyes made Travis want to hug him, but he settled for an encouraging look.

"The reason Randy was so goddamn mean to Martin, the reason he was always talking about how much he hated fags was...Randy was kind of a fag himself."

"What? That big studly guy? I don't believe it. How do you know that? Are you sure?"

Mike gave a low laugh. "Oh, I know. I'm sure. I'm *real* sure."

"But how? How do you..."

"How do I know? I know because, every chance we got, for about four months, Randy was fucking me."

Travis froze, his mouth agape. "*You?* Fucking you?"

"Yeah. Me. Fucking me."

"Holy hell," Travis gasped. "You have got to be kidding me. You? Are you—?"

"Gay? Naw. Not exactly. Maybe bi. I like sex with girls all right. I like their bodies, not so much their company. I just don't fall in love with 'em. Or I haven't so far. I like the company of guys a helluva lot more."

"So you were...in love with Randy?"

"Oh, God, yes. Crazy about him. Talk about being 'young, dumb, and full of cum.' Couldn't live without him. Wanted him on top of me all the time. Christ, he was *fine*. So much bigger'n me, with those yellow whiskers and all that muscle, fuzzy golden hair all over his body. I still think about him. He was my first."

"So what happened?" Travis rasped, feeling vaguely faint with shock and disbelief. "And why'd you leave the team?"

"This is where it gets ugly. Fuck, I could use a smoke."

"In a barn?"

"Guess not. So, after a few months of meeting in secret and having some incredible sex—better than anything I've had since—just about the time I decided I wanted a life with him, he just went to shit. Couldn't deal with the fact that he was fucking another guy. That's when he started baiting Martin. Guess he thought that being nasty to the obvious queer would guarantee that no one would ever accuse him of the same perversion."

Mike rubbed his temples and grimaced. "I was having problems too. I mean, Buck brought me up to be tough, but there I was, whenever Randy and I could arrange it, with his dick in my mouth or up my ass...and me loving the big hairy weight of him on top of me. So I freaked too. Shit, I was a guy in love with a guy, and I didn't know how to handle it. And I was scared, 'cause if Buck had found out, he would have beat the hell out of me. He *hates* queers."

Mike closed his eyes again, brushing black bangs from his brow with the back of his hand. "One time I helped Randy and Brent pick on Martin. Chased him down an alley screaming nasty shit. I felt so bad after that—a liar, a hypocrite, y'know?—I never did it again, though I should have stood up for the poor guy. Instead, I decided I had to prove to myself I wasn't queer. So...fuck, fuck, fuck! So stupid!"

"Oh, Lord. What?"

"Well, I decided I was going to screw as many chicks as I could. And guess who I started with?"

"Uhhhh... Who?"

"Randy's sister, Rachel! She thought I was hot, and I saw her around some when Randy and I hung out, so she was convenient. First girl I'd ever been with, and I got her pregnant right off the bat. Buck was pissed, 'cause he had to pay for the abortion. Randy found out and beat me up, and I guess I don't blame him. We'd pretty much broken up by then, since he was so scared of getting caught. But that didn't stop me. I slept with five more girls, led 'em on, pretended it was more than sex. Gail, Ruth, Bobbi, Theresa, Cindy. I was a pig. I used 'em. I let 'em down bad."

Mike paused to wipe his eyes. "Damn, it's dusty in here. So, finally, I thought, 'What the fuck am I doing?' and started worrying about more abortions and maybe STD's, and so I stopped screwing around. And I couldn't bear to be around Randy any more, so that's when I quit the team. I was so relieved when he graduated and went to Marshall on that football scholarship."

"Does anyone else know all this?"

"The only person I've told, other'n you, is my cousin Eddie. He came out to the family a few years back, right after he graduated, and when his parents threw a fit, he moved to San Francisco. He writes to me every now and then."

Rolling onto his belly, Mike rested his chin on his arms. "I fucked up big-time, Travis. So there you go. That's why I'm so glad to hear you're gay. 'Cause at least I got someone around here to talk to. And now so do you."

"That was a great meal, Mrs. Ferrell. Especially the pie. Thanks for inviting me," said Mike, pulling on his coat.

"Glad you liked it, honey. You were sweet to help Travis with the dishes. You're welcome here anytime." Nanny patted his hand before heading into the living room and turning on the TV.

"I'll walk you out," Travis said, tugging on his own jacket.

"You got a good life here, farm boy," said Mike as they reached his truck. It had stopped raining, and patches of fog swathed the surrounding hills. "Real nice place. And your grandmother's a sweetheart. Plus damn fine eats. Can I come back sometime?"

"Sure. Glad you could join us. And glad we could talk," Travis said. "That was quite a surprise." *My God, I can't believe a guy as butch as you has made it with another guy.*

"For both of us, man. For both of us." Mike bumped Travis's shoulder with his before climbing into his truck. "Okay, I better get home before Buck starts thinking I'm hanging out with whores down on Third Avenue. Though, come to think of it, a super-stud reputation is a damn fine way to conceal the truth."

The truth that Randy Lowry was up inside you...just like I'd like to be. Man, what I'd give to have been in his place. He didn't deserve that privilege. "Want to come up here for Halloween?" Travis asked. "We get lots of kids with some pretty amazing costumes. Nanny always makes a great stew for Halloween, and some kind of pie."

"Tempting...but naw. Sorry. I promised my cousin Darlene I'd go to a party with her. I think the only reason she wants to go is to piss off her mother. Aunt Drema is super-religious and thinks that Halloween is Satan's holiday."

"Well, I guess I'll see you...when?" *You're just now leaving, and already I'm aching to see you again? Bad sign. I've read* Wuthering Heights. *I know how badly this can end. You die somehow, and I end up grieving forever.*

"How about lifting on Wednesday? I can pick you up after school."

"Sure. That'd be great."

Mike lit a cigarette and turned on his tape deck. Alabama's "Song of the South" started thumping.

"See you Wednesday. You're gonna be one ferocious bumpkin by the time I'm through with you." Giving Travis a wink, Mike backed up and drove off, spinning wheels spitting gravel.

Damn tease, Travis thought. *Flirting with me like you flirted with Anita. You know I want you. As hot as you are, everyone does. Man, what would life be like if...if everyone wanted me?*

Travis stood in the cold, watching Mike's truck disappear around the corner. Restless, he strolled toward the garden and into it. He passed between rows of dying corn, the papery rustle of their autumn-dry leaves reminding him of how badly they needed to be shocked. He stood there, stroking the rain-wet stalks, studying stars through gaps in the dispersing clouds, and thinking of Mike's solemn face in the barn loft.

God, he sleeps with guys. This is a dream come true. What are the odds that a guy I want so bad is bi? But, Lord, what if he's not into me the way I'm into him? He may find me no more attractive than he does Anita. I'm so damn plump. Who'd want me? How could a guy as hot as he is ever want me? And how can we just be friends with me wanting to touch him and kiss him every time we're together? Oh, man, I just want to get him naked and hold him in my arms and comfort him and help him forget all his regrets.

Neck craned, Travis tried to calm himself by picking out constellations—Ursa Major, then the Pleiades—but their luminous grandeur didn't make his anxieties feel any smaller. Hands chilled, he finally went inside, said goodnight to Nanny, and went to bed early. It took him hours to fall asleep.

CHAPTER SEVEN

Halloween evening, little monsters of every shape and size descended upon the Ferrell farm. Children made Travis nervous—their erratic movements and shrill voices had always disturbed him—but this night, his favorite holiday, the pagan festival of Samhain, he enjoyed the variety of outfits the trick-or-treaters wore despite their clamor. A series of pink princesses appeared, plus Batman, a few Ninja Turtles, and several Bart and Homer Simpsons. A couple of the young fathers escorting their kids had handsome beards or goatees that caught Travis's eye. In between "bouts of brats," as Travis liked to put it, he and Nanny enjoyed beef stew and biscuits. When the official hours for trick-or-treating were over, they blew out the candle inside the Jack-o'-lantern perched on the porch and had warmed-up slices of butternut squash pie with Cool Whip. Weary, Nanny went to bed early.

For a few hours, Travis sprawled on the living room couch and read homework assignments, but as usual, his thoughts drifted toward Mike. *Where is he right now? Flirting with girls at that party he said he was attending, no doubt. Wonder if he's got a costume on? Probably drinking and smoking and getting wild. Wish he were here instead. Glad I'm not there, around a bunch of noisy folks I don't know. Wish I could be more comfortable around strangers, but I'm not. I'll never be as relaxed, confident, and charming as he is. If he ends up with a man, it'll be some hairy beauty like himself, not some fat and awkward rube like me.*

Done with his homework, Travis indulged in a second slice of pie before heading up to bed. There, he changed into his cold-weather sleeping duds—thermal undershirt and boxers—before lighting a candle on the dresser. He lay back beneath the bedcovers, studying the flame, trying to forget Mike and concentrate instead on the season.

The Celtic New Year, he thought. *When the Green Man's vegetation fades, and the Lord of the Hunt takes his throne. When the Crone walks the night, and the veil between the living and the dead parts.* He thought of his ancestors conducting rituals around bonfires and among standing stones, feasting and celebrating the Old Gods. *I wish I lived then, not now. Among the Celts or Vikings. In England or Scotland or Ireland or Iceland. Among big hairy pagan warriors. Not in this Baptist-blighted county with all these damned preachers and simpering Christians.*

Travis sighed. *Well, I can't be at Stonehenge, but I can still do a little ritual.* "Dread Lord of Shadows, God of Life, and the Giver of Life..." *How does that invocation go?*

Rising, he headed for the closet. He was sorting through his secret stash of gay and witchcraft books, looking for *A Witches' Bible Compleat,* one of his favorite volumes, when the phone rang in the hall.

"Oh, hell, who's calling this late?" Travis muttered. His alarm clock said eleven fifteen. Nanny had been in bed for hours.

Bolting into the hall, he snatched up the phone. "Ferrell residence. Hello?"

"Hey, man! How's it hangin'?"

"Mike? What's up?" Afraid of disturbing his grandmother, Travis carried the phone back into his bedroom and closed the door behind him.

"Partyin'. How's your Halloween?"

Travis could barely make out Mike's words. The ruckus in the background—loud voices, pounding music—made clear that the party was in full swing.

"Uh, good. We had some cute trick-or-treaters and a nice meal. Wish you'd been here, but it sounds like you're—"

"Yeah, havin' fun. Some damn good 'shine here. And my buddy Eugene brought some pot. Ain't smoked that shit in ages. What you dressed as?"

"I didn't dress, Mike. I stayed at home, remember? We just gave out candy and—"

A female voice interrupted, sounded closing to Mike's end of the phone. "Come on, honey, let's dance. I wanna *dance*."

Mike yelped and guffawed. "Don't be pinchin' my butt, you tramp. Sorry, Travis. Tammy's gettin' a little wild. Anyways, just wanted to check in. Y'awt to dress up as a lumberjack. You'd make a good lumberjack."

"You have a costume?" Travis said, imagining his friend clothed in various skimpy or romantic outfits. *Hercules in a loincloth? A bare-chested gladiator? A knight in shining armor? A cowboy? A Viking? A Hell's Angel?*

"Yep. Rebel soldier. Dammit, stop it, Tammy."

"Come *on*," the girl whined. "I love this song."

"Better go, farm boy. Happy Halloween. I'll drink some 'shine for you."

Before Travis could reply, Mike hung up the phone.

Travis woke at three A.M., used the bathroom, crawled back into bed, but couldn't sleep. He kept imagining Mike in a Confederate uniform, with some seductive girl on his knee, a girl he kissed and fondled, a girl who unbuttoned Mike's gray jacket and caressed the hair on his chest.

Every time I see or talk to him, he stirs my mind up into a crazy whirl-pool. I still can't believe he's bi. He's lucky he's so butch that he can pass for straight...like I did before Rhodetta and Brent caught on. What kind of life is he going to have in Hinton as a mechanic, having to hide half of who he is all the time? Will he get married? Would he even still want men if he settled down with a girl? Will he start sneaking around like those guys I hear about who leave their phone numbers in the bathroom stalls of rest stops? If we were together, maybe we could move away someplace. Go to college, be around other gay guys. Get our degrees, buy some kinda log cabin in the hills, make love every night by the fireplace.

Travis rolled onto his side, patted his fuzzy belly, and sighed. *As if he'd want to be with me the way he was with that big, sexy Randy. Damn, the two of them together?*

Again, Travis touched himself, wallowing in fantasy. Brawny-armed Randy, his big chest coated with golden hair, wrestled Mike down onto the bed and tied his hands behind him. He crammed a rag in Mike's mouth, greased up Mike's butt, lay on top of him, spread his legs, and brutally entered him from behind. Mike struggled and gasped, but soon his muted protests and cries for help had metamorphosed into moans of pleasure as Randy rode him fast and hard.

Travis's self-induced spasm of sticky pleasure receded rapidly. Soon he'd returned to his brooding. *Mike said getting fucked by Randy was the best sex he'd ever had. As if I could please him the way Randy did. All I know about sex is how to jack off. Randy's such a big jock that his dick is probably huge, way bigger than mine. Mike may be bi, but no way he'd want me after having such a built-like-a-brick-shithouse athlete. Man, he'd be creeped out if he saw me like this, my own stuff in my hand, if he knew how I just jacked off to fantasies about him getting tied up and screwed. Maybe I'm sick in the brain.*

Shaking his head, Travis fetched a Kleenex from the bedside table and cleaned himself up. For a short time, he sat in the dark on the edge of his bed, fiddling with mournful chords on his guitar in an attempt to slow his speeding thoughts. Returning his guitar to its case, he strode over to the window and looked out over the darkened landscape. The moon, nearly full, had slipped out from behind the remaining clouds.

Damn it. I wish I didn't want Mike. I wish I didn't want men. Desire makes me feel so vulnerable. If I were straight, I could live anywhere I wanted and be myself. I wouldn't have to keep secrets and hide who I am. I don't want to leave my family and the farm. I don't. But I have to. There's no way to be gay here. My family would be so disappointed if they knew. Nanny would think I'm a sinner. And guys like Brent would be hounding me everywhere. I've got to leave. I've got to leave.

Climbing back into bed, Travis curled up, his arms wrapped around a pillow, his chest tight with a deep sadness. He nuzzled the pillow, pretending it was Mike's bare back. Finally he fell asleep.

CHAPTER EIGHT

"Happy birthday," Travis said, his auburn beard framing a happy smile. "You ready to celebrate at Kirk's? The meal's on me. I'll be ready in just a second."

Mike grinned, leaning against the line of lockers, arms crossed upon his chest, while Travis stuffed textbooks into his backpack. In the long hall of the high school's south wing, kids bustled by, ready for another weekend.

"Big spender, huh? Sure. After Kirk's, if you got time, how about we take a drive down to Sandstone Falls? It ain't that cold for November. We could take a hike before I drive you home. You could tell me all about the trees and the weeds, the birds and—"

"Oh, no. Look who's coming," Travis groaned, staring down the hall. "It's Brent. I hope he doesn't get nasty."

Mike turned, his face stiffening. "He damn well better not. I'll handle him," Mike growled beneath his breath. "You just stand back, buddy."

The sleek athlete walked up, a buxom blonde on his arm. "Mike Woodson. How you been? You remember Linda?"

"Yep. How you been, Linda?" Mike managed a thin smile.

"Just fine," Linda said, beaming. "You look great. We sure miss seeing you at the games. Why'd you drop out?"

"Long story," Mike replied with a frown.

Brent nodded. "You were a good guard, Mike. We'd love to have you back. Why're you hanging out with this loser?" He cocked his head at Travis. "He's a fag. Haven't you heard the rumors?"

"Yes, I have. So what? What kind of moron pays attention to rumors?"

"Are you calling me a moron, my man?" Brent released Linda's arm and took a step forward.

"Mike, let's just leave, okay?" Travis slipped his backpack over his shoulders and adjusted his baseball cap on his head. "He's not worth the trouble."

Mike balled up his fists, glaring up at the taller boy. "Travis and I are buddies. You cross him, you cross me." His voice was low and hoarse.

"Buddies? Or something else?" Brent sneered. "Girlfriends? I'll bet you both have frilly panties on right now. Which one of you is the girl in bed? Travis, I'll bet."

"You. Shut. The fuck. Up. Or I'll kick your ass."

"You? I doubt it."

"You think you can take me?" Mike snarled.

"H-hell, yeah." Brent rolled his eyes. "Little man."

"Don't fucking think so." Mike took a step forward. "You may be taller, but I'm stronger. You leave us the hell alone. Or I'll break your face. If I hear you've been picking on Travis here...there's gonna be hell to pay."

Brent took a step back, face crimson. "You wouldn't be so damn brave if my buddies were here."

"Your buddies?" Mike's mouth curled in mockery. "Hah. You ball-less wonders always travel in packs. Git on. Git on now. Git on back to your parents' pretty house in Bellepoint."

"Trash!" Linda spat. "Dirty and dumb."

"Come on, Linda. I'll deal with this fool later." Brent grabbed his girlfriend and hustled down the hall.

"What a brave boy. And to think we used to run together." Mike gave Travis another of his charming smiles. "Luckily, I got better buddies now. Okay, big guy. How about those hot dogs you promised me?"

"Let's sit out here," Mike said, shouldering through the door onto Kirk's patio, the orange tray in his hands heaped with food. "Easier to talk."

The friends took a table by the railing. Below, the New River swirled by, high and muddy with November rains. Across the water, Hicks Mountain rose sheer, gray, and leafless. For a few minutes, they dug into their early dinner, their only sounds scattered groans of pleasure.

"Yum, hot dogs with everything. Fries. Some of my favorites. Thanks, man," Mike said, crumpling up the empty wrappers, then leaning back and sipping his Coke. "You didn't need to pay for this."

"Least I could do for your birthday. I made some extra money last summer picking strawberries and helping folks put up their hay. Plus, uh…" Travis pulled a paperback from his backpack. "I got you this. Since you like war books. I know you're into World War II and Vietnam, but I figured you might enjoy this one too. It's about the Civil War. I read it last year, and it's really good."

"*I Rode with Stonewall?* Nice. Thanks."

"I hope you like it. I read a lot of Civil War stuff. My grandmother's grandfather was a Rebel artilleryman. With Lowry's Battery."

"Lowry. Argh." Mike frowned. "Makes me think of Randy. Yeah, Buck's always said a Woodson ancestor of ours was in that battery too. Apparently I share the guy's birthday."

"So, November ninth. That means you're a Scorpio. Mars rules that sign. No wonder you're a fighter and enjoy reading about war."

"You take that stuff seriously?" Mike asked, crunching ice.

"I'm sort of into the occult, I guess. Scorpios are notoriously lusty too."

"Well, that explains a lot." Mike patted his denim-covered crotch. "Took me a while to keep my prick in my pants, as I've already told you. The big ole thing might get me in a lot of trouble some day."

"Super stud, huh?" Travis sniggered. *Man, oh man, you are such a tease.*

"Yep. So what sign are you?"

"August eighth. Leo. We're supposed to be creative and ambitious."

"Sounds about right. I bet you'll write books and travel the world before you're done."

"I do want to travel. To England to see Stonehenge. To Greece to see the Parthenon. To Rome to see the Colosseum and the Pantheon. There are photos of them in my Latin textbook."

"Bet you'll miss the mountains, though. Buck said when he was in the army he about died from homesickness."

"Yeah, my parents say the same thing. They like Germany, but they sure miss West Virginia."

"I'll tell you one thing they don't miss. That ugly thing. Don't know why the town let 'em build it," Mike said, jabbing a thumb toward the huge yellow "M" looming against the sky on the far side of the river. "Must be four stories high. Spoils the view. Only good things about McDonald's the coffee and the toilets."

"I agree. I guess Nanny's cooking has spoiled me, because I think most fast food is pretty nasty. But, yeah, other than that stupid colossal 'M,' Summers County sure is pretty," Travis replied. "The mountains, the river." Sitting back, he propped his boots on an empty chair. "About half of me wants to get to college and about half of me wants to stay here. Except you can't really make a living these days by farming, and there aren't many jobs around. There aren't even many positions on the railroad anymore."

"Tell me about it," Mike said, pulling out a cigarette and lighting it. "I'm just glad I have a job with Buck, as much as the guy gets on my nerves. I'm guessing you'd be a lot better off in college. You're counting on a scholarship to WVU, right? My little straight-A buddy."

"Nerdy, huh? Kind of easy to get good grades when you don't have much of a social life."

"Speak for yourself, Brainiac. I'm guessing there's gotta be some gay life up in Morgantown."

"There is." Travis sat up, eyes bright. "That's why I want to go to WVU. My friends there have already gone to the gay bar, plus there's a student group on campus that sponsors events. Coffeehouses and parties and readings. All sorts of stuff. Can you imagine?"

"Hard to. Mighty different from here. All the damn Baptists spouting off about sin."

"You could go to college too, Mike," Travis suggested. "You don't have to stay here. Wouldn't it be great if we could go to WVU together?"

"Don't have the money. Don't have the grades." Mike heaved a matter-of-fact shrug. "I'm a mechanic, pure and simple. Plus I like this town, despite all its down sides. I don't want to leave what I know."

Travis sucked on his straw, rolled the Dr. Pepper around on his tongue, and swallowed hard. "I get that. I really do. Moving to a city scares me. But if you're bi..."

"Different from being gay. That's gotta be damned hard no matter where you are. Much as I like a little brawl every now and then, I'd get tired of the constant hassle. Maybe I'll settle down here with some girl. A lot easier than being with a guy."

You with a girl? What a waste. Oh, God. I don't even want to picture that, Travis thought, turning to gaze out over the turbid river. "Yeah. You're lucky you have a choice."

"I guess. You're lucky you got brains and some parents that'll help you pay for an education. So what are you gonna major in?"

"I'm going to double-major in Forestry and English, I think. I like books as much as I do the outdoors."

"A forest ranger or an author. That's how I see you."

Travis smiled. "I'm flattered. Actually, I have written some poetry. I had a ferocious crush on Robbie Bowles last year and I wrote a few poems about him."

"Yeah? He's a pretty handsome dude. So, we haven't discussed types yet. What's your type?" Mike blew out a smoke ring, then a second, then a third.

"Oh. Well." Travis paused.

"You're blushing again," Mike stated. "Cute. You're so easy to embarrass." Reaching over, he poked a forefinger in Travis's ribs.

"Cut it out," Travis protested, giggling. "Okay, my type. I like real masculine men. With muscles. I like beards. Dark beards. And hairy, like Tom Selleck."

"Yeah? Kinda like me?"

"God, what an ego you have," Travis blurted, blushing harder.

"Uh huh. And are you a Top or bottom? You do know what that means, right?"

"You're such a cocky bastard. Yes, I know what that means. How would I know which I am? I haven't had sex."

Mike blew another smoke ring. "Yeah. But you have fantasies when you jack off, right? So are you topping or being topped in 'em?"

"Mike! Man, you'll just say anything, won't you?"

"Why not? Ain't that what friendship is? Talking about real things? Important things?"

Travis snatched up a stray fry and bit into it. "Well, Mommy would say that such talk is vulgar..."

"And she ain't here, is she?" Mike scratched his side and smiled with that easy confidence Travis had so come to love. "Just us, buddy. So tell me."

"Since you're so frank, why don't you tell me?" Travis said, leaning forward and resting his elbows on his knees. "What's your type?"

Mike cleared his throat, his expression suddenly serious. "Okay, shy boy. I'll tell you. I like bigger guys, taller guys. Beefy. A little chunky. Randy had a combo of fat and muscle I really liked. Butch, yeah, but gentle too. Some guy who looks like he could get wild in bed with you, get all rough and sweaty, and then hold you real sweet afterwards. I like beards too. I like blonds and dark-haired guys about the same. Honestly, there's only been a handful here in Hinton who have really turned me on. Robbie Bowles, your favorite, yeah, he's nice-looking, though a little too pretty for me unless he's got some stubble. Davey Smith—you remember him?—lean and lanky, with those bushy, honey-colored sideburns. Steve Burroughs, up Jumping Branch. That boy has quite the set of biceps. And Randy, of course." Mike sighed. "Randy was just fucking beautiful."

"O-okay," Travis stammered, admiring Mike's easy honesty and aroused once more by the thought of Randy topping Mike. "Yeah, those guys are all pretty handsome. So, uh, how'd you and Randy end up...first doing it?"

"Figured you'd ask me that sooner or later. We were both drunk as hell in his father's basement den. I passed out. Came to only to find my pants down around my ankles and Randy's greasy finger stuck up my ass. We got to tussling around. He held me down, put a hand over my mouth, and screwed me. He was a lot stronger, so he sort of forced me. Or I let him think he did. Shit, I wanted it as bad as he did. Can't rape the willing, right?"

Oh, my God, that's hot. "And you liked that? Him screwing you?"

"Damn right I did. For a while, I was ashamed, and then I thought, 'What the fuck? Why should I feel ashamed just 'cause other folks think I should?' You gotta live your life the way you please. Right?"

"Yeah, that's what my daddy says. So you're a bottom?"

Mike shrugged, stubbing out his cigarette and lighting another. "Always a bottom with Randy. He's the only guy I've ever been with. With some other guy, who knows? I think I could go either way, depending on the guy, what the other guy wanted."

"Doesn't it...hurt? Getting, uh, you know."

"Screwed? Yeah. Some. At first. But then, if you use a lotta lube, and if the guy's doing it right, it starts to feel good. Mighty good. If y'ever top a guy, y'need to go slow and easy for a while." Mike gave his friend an exaggerated wink. "'Course it all depends on how big you are. I'll bet you're like me. Hung like a horse." Mike gave Travis a wicked grin.

"I'm not telling you *that*," Travis rasped, feeling heat spreading over his cheeks and arousal tautening his pants. *God, if you only knew how many times I've made love to you in my mind. I'm going to cream my jeans if you don't shut up.* He cocked his arm and made a show of checking his wristwatch. "So, look, we better head out. Nanny's expecting me home soon."

"Not so fast, farm boy. You didn't answer my question."

Travis stood. "What question?"

"Asshole. You know. You top or bottom in your jack-off fantasies?"

"I don't, uh—"

"Jack off?" Mike smirked, sucking on his cigarette. "Bullshit. Someone said that ninety-nine percent of guys jack off, and the one percent who say they don't are lying."

Travis thought of last night's lengthy fantasy, in which he'd forced Mike onto a bed, bound him belly down, taped his mouth shut, and made ardent love to him for hours. "Oh, L-lord. Okay. Top. I t-top," he stuttered.

"Yeah? A sweet-faced boy like you? Rough or gentle?"

"Both. God, would you stop?"

"God, is your face red. Beautiful."

"Glad you're satisfied," Travis growled, dumping the trash on his platter into a rubbish bin before loping toward the parking lot. "You gotta know everything, don't you? Now let's get going."

"Wanna drive down Sandstone Falls like I said?"

"Not today. Forest Hill instead. Nanny has a birthday surprise for you."

"Great." Mike jiggled his keys. "Dessert, I hope."

"Yes. Cake. German chocolate. You said it was your favorite, right?"

"Hell, yes. I haven't had a homemade German chocolate cake since Mom died."

The boys strode to the truck and climbed in. Mike slipped the key into the ignition, then turned. "Travis?"

"Yeah?" Travis looked out the passenger-side window, studying the sheer hillside across the road, trying to calm himself. *I'm in too deep here. I'm feeling too much. Don't I always feel too much? I want him even more now that I know he's slept with another guy. And bottomed for him.*

"I'm sorry I embarrassed you. I just want to get to know you, okay? Don't you like talking about, well, sex stuff?"

"I guess I'm not used to it. I didn't really talk about stuff like that with Bill and them."

"Okay. I'm sorry if I went too far. But I just want to tell you...this has been the best birthday I've had since Mom died. Buck never does much for it...though he bought me a bottle of Mad Dog last year, when I turned sixteen." Reaching over, Mike grabbed Travis's left hand and gave it a brief squeeze. "Thank you."

"W-well, sure, Mike," Travis stuttered, stunned by the fond gesture.

"Okay, buddy," Mike said, starting up the truck and turning his gaze to the road. "Let's get that cake."

CHAPTER NINE

"**I**'m sorry I have to leave, boys, but it sounds like Mr. Houchins has taken a turn for the worst, and I know Mizz Houchins would appreciate having me there. You boys sure you'll be all right without me?"

Nanny stood by the kitchen door, overnight bag in her hand. Outside, night was falling, and early December flurries dusted the lawn.

"Yes, ma'am," Mike said from his sprawled comfort on the couch. He, like Travis, was dressed in jeans, thick boot socks, and a thermal undershirt. "We'll be fine. I'll take care of ole Travis here."

"All right. Don't forget the pie. I'll call in the morning and let you know when I'll be home. Should be around noon. There's sausage in the fridge and biscuits in the freezer for y'all's breakfast," Nanny added before bustling out.

"Take care of me?" Travis said, from Nanny's favorite rocking chair before the TV. "I'm older than you are."

"Yeah, yeah." Mike winked at Travis, then closed his long-lashed eyes. "But I'm stronger. And meaner."

"True. I won't argue with that. Okay, how about you take care of me and I'll take care of you?"

"Sounds like a deal. That's what buddies are for. Guarding each other's backs." Mike rubbed his belly and groaned contentedly. "Man, I'm full. Best brown beans, chowchow, and cornbread I've ever had."

"It was all pretty tasty. *Golden Girls* is about to come on. You want to watch it?"

"How 'bout you play your guitar for me instead? You keep promising me you will, but you haven't yet. Anita says you're really good."

"I'm all right."

"What kinda stuff you play?"

"Some old seventies folkie stuff, a little country, some of that Southern rock you like. Hold on."

Travis fetched his guitar from the bedroom, sat on a footrest, and tuned up. For a long time, the only sounds were the wind scratching at the eaves, Travis's shy baritone, and his quiet fingerpicking as he moved through one of his melancholy favorites, "Who Knows Where the Time Goes?" then tuned to open G for Joni Mitchell's "Morning Morgantown" and "The Circle Game."

"You asleep, Mike?" Travis asked, pausing to retune for a Bob Dylan song.

Mike grinned, eyes still closed. "Naw. Just been a busy day. Got to admit I'm a little tired after this morning working in Buck's garage, then us lifting in the gym and splitting wood here and hiking down to the pond. It was fun skipping pebbles over the ice. Keep on playing. I love the seventies stuff. You're really good."

"Thanks. I'm glad you like it." Travis strummed softly through "I Shall Be Released," then stopped long enough to add wood to the Buck stove. He hesitated, studying Mike's reclining form. *Man, I hope Mr. Houchins will be all right, but his illness sure is sweet timing. Gives me more time with Mike alone.* Pulling an afghan off the back of the couch, Travis spread it out on top of his friend.

"Thanks, man," Mike opened his eyes only long enough to give Travis a fond wink before closing them again, rolling onto his side, and snuggling into the soft fabric. "You treat me like a king. Talk about Southern hospitality."

"That's how my family's brought me up. Now here's an old one, 'The Water Is Wide.'"

Travis sang softly, eyes ranging from his Yamaha's fretboard to Mike's peaceful face. Mike listened, nodding occasionally.

"Pretty. Oh yeah. That's a sweet tune," Mike murmured as soon as Travis was done. "Thanks, man. Thanks for all of this."

"Well, sure. No big deal."

"But it is. I don't think you realize how much it means to me to spend time here with you. It's so warm and cozy, and the food is always so good. You and your grandmother have been really great to me. For a long time, after Mom died, I felt like I didn't really have a home, but now at least I can borrow yours. It's a real refuge, man. A 'shelter from the storm,' to use your man Dylan's phrase."

"Glad you feel that way." Travis studied Mike, wanting badly to brush away his black bangs and kiss him on the brow. "We love having you here. You know that. You're always welcome. You ready for that cherry pie? With ice cream? I made it myself. Sort of. First pie I ever baked. Nanny showed me how. I figured it was time I learned."

"Really? You baked a pie for me?"

"Uh, yeah. For us. You don't get all of it."

"You're gonna make some guy a great husband. You blushing again?"

"How did you know?"

Mike snickered. "'Cause I know you, big guy. How about you play me 'Free Bird,' and then we'll have that dessert."

The cherry pie was great," Mike enthused, tossing his backpack on the smaller spare bed set in a corner of Travis's room. In the background, Joan Baez, turned down low, sang "Sweeter for Me" on Travis's little tape deck. "Though I really shouldn't have had two pieces."

"Glad it came out, though, yeah, I'm a little stuffed too," Travis said, staring out into the night before pulling the drapes. "It's still flurrying some."

"So many books." Mike knelt by Travis's bookshelf, fingering the spines. "*The Iliad* and *The Odyssey*. *Oedipus Rex*. Plato. *Wuthering Heights* and *Jane Eyre*. *Flora of West Virginia*. Civil War, Civil War, Civil War. And all these vampire novels. Great."

"My occult books and gay books I keep in here," said Travis, pulling a box out of the closet and opening it.

"In the closet. Perfect." Mike chortled.

"Yeah. I know. Appropriate. I just don't want Nanny seeing them and asking questions. This one's *Maurice*. It's kind of a classic. This one's about Alexander the Great's lover," Travis said, holding up *The*

Persian Boy. "Brenda introduced me to quite a few gay novels before she graduated. Reading them really helped me deal with the fact that I wanted guys."

"Alexander the Great was gay?" Mike asked, black eyebrows arching.

"Yep. Swear to God."

"Good to know. He was a real ass-kicker, right? One of the things that pisses me off the most is that folks assume if you're attracted to guys that you have to be a sissy."

"Yeah, I hate that too. These here, by Patricia Nell Warren, and this one by Felice Picano, and this one by Andrew Holleran, and this one by Edmund White...all really great. Some of the characters are outrageous, sharp-tongued queens, like Sutherland in *Dancer from the Dance*—I don't want to be one or sleep with one, but I'll bet they'd be great friends—but some are strong, butch guys like you."

"You're getting pretty butch yourself, bud. Look at those arms."

Sheepishly, Travis flexed. "I had a good teacher. You want to borrow any of these? I think you'd really like *The Fancy Dancer*. The love interest rides a motorcycle. You remind me of him."

"Sure. I'll start with that one. Speaking of reading material, I got a couple of surprises for you." Mike unzipped his backpack. "You ain't gonna believe this," he said, pulling out a slick magazine and offering it to Travis.

Travis stared. His mouth dropped open. The word "BEAR" was plastered across the cover in big letters. Beneath that was the black and white photo of a handsome man, with dark hair and a dark beard. He was wearing a Levi's jacket just like Travis's. It was unbuttoned, and beneath, the man was shirtless. Travis stared at the man's chest and slighted rounded belly. Both were plastered with fur.

"Isn't he *hot*?" Mike said.

"Oh, man. He sure is. Is this—?"

"Gay porn, farm boy. Gay porn."

Grabbing the magazine, Travis flipped through the pages of photographs and text. Bearded, hairy men sprawled naked, proudly displaying erect penises. A few, including the cover model, were teasingly arranged to show off their butt-holes, as if in invitation. Travis ran his eyes over a story, catching words like "semen," "cock-sucking," "thick beard," and "Fuck the shit outta me!"

"Where'd you get it?" Travis sputtered, both shocked and aroused.

"Cantrell's store, there at the bottom of Beech Run."

"What?"

"Sorry. I'm shitting you. Those Cantrells are mad-dog Baptists through and through. Naw, my cousin Eddie sent me some stuff from San Francisco. The guy on the cover's Jack Radcliffe. Don't he look a little bit like you? An older version?"

"You're crazy. He's so sexy. I'm just a plump nerd who's lucky enough to grow a beard."

"He's bigger and hairier, but I think y'all look a lot alike," Mike said firmly. "And stop putting yourself down. You're looking pretty good these days. If you went to San Francisco, all those bears would eat you up."

"Bears? So what are bears?"

"That kinda guy," Mike said, tapping the cover. "A few weeks back, I got a letter from Eddie telling me about 'em. There are all kinds of guys in Frisco who call themselves bears. They're butch, and burly, and hairy, and bearded. Like us, Travis. They're not into thin pretty boys, they're into men like themselves. Eddie says that you and I are cubs."

"Cubs? Really?"

"Yep." Mike soft-punched Travis in the arm. "A cub's a young bear. So you could be a cover cub for *BEAR* magazine."

Travis's face colored with another of his customary blushes. "Naw. I think you should be. As nice-built as you are."

"Yeah?" Mike lifted his arms and flexed. Beneath his thermal under-shirt, his biceps and pectorals bulged. "Want me to pose for you?"

"You're always posing for me. You're such a show-off," said Travis.

"Mike Woodson, centerfold stud." Mike laughed. "We could pose together. Wouldn't the good folks of Summers County like that?"

Naked? Pose together naked? God, yes. That'd be paradise. "True." Travis snickered. "Nanny would have a conniption fit."

"And ole Buck would break my neck. Anyway, I've been dying to show you this magazine. I got it last week but was afraid to bring it to school. You can keep it for a while. Nice jack-off material, huh?"

"I don't wanna talk about—"

"Yeah, yeah. So bashful," Mike said, folding his arms across his chest. "Look, you're always complaining about your little belly, so I just wanted you to see that some guys would find you really hot. You got the beard, you got the bulk, you got the chest hair. You don't have to look different for some guys to like you. When Eddie told me about the bears, I thought of you, thought hearing about 'em would make you feel better about yourself."

"It does, actually," Travis admitted. "Thanks."

"That ain't all. Eddie sent me some other stuff," said Mike, removing a newspaper from his backpack. "There's this. *The Bay Area Reporter*. Figured you'd enjoy reading about gay life in Frisco. And this." Mike pulled another magazine from his backpack and handed it to Travis. "This one's *Drummer*. Eddie says this is his favorite porn magazine. It's pretty kinky, so it might be a little too much for you."

Another shirtless man posed on the cover. He was bearded, wearing a black leather cap and black leather pants and holding a whip. His chest was hairless but well developed, the muscles accentuated by a contraption made of leather straps and steel rings. Travis flipped through a few pages, then, fascinated by the images, sat on the edge of his bed. "Wow," he murmured. "Amazing."

Mike sat beside him. "Like it, huh?" He bumped Travis's shoulder with his own. "It's kinky but it's pretty hot. I like that leather look. I figured you'd be shocked, innocent as you are."

"I guess I am a little. But, yeah, I like it."

For a few minutes, Travis, dazed, thumbed through the magazine. Articles about leather bars and sex toys alternated with drawing and photos: a movie still of a guy being whipped; a muscled man tied to a chair; a cowboy with a dog collar around his neck kneeling at another man's feet; a gagged captive hung from rafters, clamps applied to his nipples. *Oh, my God, it's the stuff I fantasize about,* Travis thought, light-headed.

"Some pretty wild shit, huh? Eddie goes to a leather bar called the Eagle. You ever seen anything like this?"

"No. But I've read about it. Brenda gave me a novel last year that had a gay couple in it, a cop and his lover, who were into S&M. *The Beauty Queen*, based on all that mess Anita Bryant stirred up back in the seventies. The cop, Danny Blackburn, was pretty cool. Not at all the stereotype of the effeminate queer. I related to him." *And how many times have I reread that love scene and jacked off?*

"You can hold onto that mag too. Bet you'll get some good use out of it. Just don't get the pages stuck together. That's quite the hard-on you got there."

"Mike!"

"You're so easy to fluster, Cubbie. See? New nickname for you. Hey, if it turns you on, it turns you on. Nothing wrong with that. I like it pretty well myself. How you think I'd look in a leather vest?"

"Pretty handsome." Travis turned away, hurriedly adjusting himself.

"Great. Maybe after I'm done modeling for *BEAR*, I can do the same for *Drummer*."

"You'd have to wear a dog collar for that one." Imagining the delicious combination of Mike's nakedness and black leather, Travis got even harder.

"Right. Think of the fan club. Wanna be president?"

"Heh-ullll." Travis smirked, drawing the satiric syllables out. He slipped the magazines and newspaper into his underwear drawer. "Next you'll be talking about becoming a porn star. You think you're such a super stud. You need a nickname too. Think I'll call you Studly."

"Studly? Love it. Okay, I'm beat," said Mike, retrieving toothbrush and paste from his pack. "I'm gonna get ready for bed. You can stay up and read if you want, but you mind if I hit the sack?"

"Naw, that's fine. I'm tired too."

"You wanna get up early and track some deer? I got my rifle in the truck."

"How about we sleep in and I make us breakfast instead? I'm not much on killing things."

"What kind of country boy are you? Don't you like venison?" Mike teased. "Be right back."

When Travis returned from brushing his own teeth, Mike was sprawled on the smaller bed wearing nothing but white boxers and a sleepy smile.

Damn tease, Travis thought. *All that black belly hair. Those big pecs and that flat belly. The bastard has the perfect body.* Turning his back on Mike, he hurriedly changed into a baggy pair of gym shorts and an over-sized tank top.

"You sleep in all that?"

"Yeah. Anything wrong with that?" Travis pulled loose his ponytail and shook his hair free.

"Just looks uncomfortable. Ball-binding, y'know. These shorts are a courtesy," Mike added, snapping his waistband with a curved thumb. "I usually sleep naked."

"Of course you do. You're always taking your clothes off around me."

"And that bothers you?" Mike folded his hands behind his head, giving Travis a fine view of his densely furred armpits.

God, I want to climb on top of you. "No. Well, sort of," Travis said, thankful for the concealing bagginess of his shorts. Crossing his arms, he frowned. "You're just so cocky and proud, like you know how handsome you are. You're always showing off. Letting me know how strong you are."

"I thought you liked my strength."

"I do. It's just... You're so well built you make me feel fat. Sometimes I wish I were you, not me."

"Oh, hell," Mike snorted. "Don't wish that. You're not fat, Travis. Well, a little. I prefer the word 'burly.' But I like that. I like that bulk of yours. And, like I said, you've really hardened up in the last few months. Your chest, your arms and shoulders. You might not like your body, Cubbie, but I do. You're strong too."

"Naw. Not like you."

Abruptly, Mike sat up. "You're getting there. Wanna arm-wrestle?" he said, giving Travis another maddening smile.

"No. No, I don't."

"Why?

"Because I'd lose."

"Maybe. But you're strong, I tell you. I bet you could pick me up." Mike slipped off his bed and stood. "Come on, big guy. Try it."

"Stop teasing me, Mike." When Travis turned toward his bed, Mike grabbed his arm.

"I wasn't teasing you. Now, *this* is teasing you." Mike jabbed Travis in the right side.

"Hey!" Travis giggled, recoiling. "You know I hate that."

"Hell, you don't hate it." Mike jabbed him again. "You love it."

"No. No, I don't. Stop!"

"Ain't gonna stop." Mike poked Travis's belly-swell.

"Cut it out." Travis grabbed for Mike's hand, but Mike evaded him, only to dig his fingers into Travis's left side.

"You bastard." Convulsing, Travis grabbed Mike's wrists. The two boys staggered around the room, laughing and struggling. They bumped against Travis's desk and fell onto Mike's bed. Mike heaved hard, tipping Travis over onto the floor. Travis grabbed Mike's forearm, dragging him down with him. They rolled around, Mike on top, then Travis, then Mike, then Travis, then Mike.

Finally, Mike stopped struggling, and Travis heaved himself atop his friend. "Got ya now," he wheezed, forcing Mike's wrists to the floor on either side of his head and locking Mike's legs together with his own. By then, both boys were panting and red-faced. *He's hard,* Travis thought, feeling Mike's stiffness against his own. *Oh, my God, he's hard too.*

"You win. You win," Mike gasped. "You are one ferocious Cubbie."

"Liar. You let me win," Travis said, shaking long hair out of his eyes.

"I sorta did. Where'd you learn to wrestle like that?"

"Bill. She was good."

"You're not bad yourself," Mike said. "So you know what you do now?"

"Uhhh, no." Travis licked his upper lip and stared down into Mike's brown eyes.

Mike pressed his groin against Travis. "This is when you say, 'I won't let you up unless you kiss me.'"

"What?" Travis asked, disbelieving.

"God, do I have to do everything?" Mike leaned up, kissed Travis on the lips, then lay back, grinning.

"Mike?" Travis gasped, loosening his grip. "Are you—?"

"Oh, my God. You're dense." Mike pulled his arms free, only to wrap them around Travis and hug him. "This is where you kiss me back, big guy. If you want to. Do you want to?"

"Oh. Oh, yes. Oh, yes." Head reeling, Travis pressed his bearded lips to Mike's and kissed him hard once, then twice. Mike's tongue flickered along Travis's upper lip, then probed his mouth. Travis followed Mike's lead, pushing his tongue between Mike's lips and loving the silky feel of his friend's mouth. After long minutes of their eager kissing, Mike began rubbing Travis's erection beneath his hand, and Travis's body began to shake.

"Easy, guy. Easy," Mike said, kissing Travis's whiskered chin. "You're trembling. Are you scared? Don't be scared."

"I, uh. No, I just..." Travis shook even harder.

"Don't you wanna do this? Don't you want this?"

"Oh, yes. I do. I want it bad. I, uh, want *you* bad."

"I feel the same, man. Been flirting with you for weeks now, hoping you'd make a move."

"M-Mike," Travis said, willing his body to stop shaking but failing completely. "I don't know *how* to make a move."

"Well, I do. You're *sure* you want this?"

"Y-yes. Y-yes. Real bad. I've wanted to b-be with you like this *so* bad. For so long. I swear. I don't know why I'm s-shaking so bad. I can't stop."

"Just relax, Travis. Just relax, buddy. I wanna love on you. That all right?"

"Y-yes. I-I want to make...m-make love to you too. But, but I don't know how."

"I'll show you. We'll start slow, take our time. We got all night, Cubbie. Let's get your shirt off now."

"O-okay. Okay."

With Travis's help, Mike pulled off the tank top. Once Travis was bare-chested, Mike slid down his body. He nuzzled Travis's armpits, stroked his chest hair, flicked his tongue over his nipples, then began sucking them gently as he rubbed Travis's erection.

"You have such a great chest," Mike muttered, squeezing Travis's left pec while he lapped at his right nipple. "Does that feel good?"

"Oh! Oh, yeah," Travis gasped, gripping Mike's shoulders. "That's great. Oh, man."

Moving lower, Mike lapped the hair around Travis's navel, then reached down and tugged at Travis's shorts. Trembling, Travis lifted his hips and Mike slid the garment off.

"Wow. Nice. I wanna suck you, Cubbie," Mike whispered, brushing his bearded chin along the tip of Travis's penis. "That all right with you?"

"Y-yeah. Yeah," Travis muttered, his voice low and shaky. He closed his eyes, stroking Mike's hair as his friend gave him a few soft licks, then took him into his mouth.

CHAPTER TEN

"**S**till a few flurries," Mike said, climbing back into Travis's bed after a trip to the bathroom. Travis extended his arm, and Mike curled against him, his head on Travis's shoulder, one arm flung over Travis's chest. Travis hugged him hard.

"I can't believe this," Travis murmured, running his fingers through Mike's black chest hair. "That was amazing."

Mike snickered. "All three minutes of it. Man, you were ready to shoot, weren't you?"

Travis flushed. "I'm sorry. I-I was just so... I just... I couldn't control myself."

"*I* was the one in control, Cubbie. I played you like a fiddle, huh? Or like a skin-flute." Mike snickered again. "No problem. Glad you liked it. Randy always said I gave the best head he'd ever had. He never could hold back either, once I really got going on him."

"You were wonderful. I've wanted this for so long."

"Yeah?" said Mike. "Me too."

"Really?"

"Hell, yes." Mike snuggled closer still. "I hoped the tickling would lead to wrestling and then the wrestling to something more."

"So you—?"

"Seduced you. Yep."

"Miraculous. That you could want me."

"No more of that stuff." Mike rubbed Travis's belly. "Or I'll start tickling you again."

"Okay, okay. How long have you been...wanting to be with me like this?"

"Since last summer. That day on the bike. I'd never really noticed you that much in Phys Ed, but I did that day at the reservoir. You'd filled out, grown your beard, gotten these tasty, beefy, furry pecs." Mike kneaded Travis's chest and sighed. "Such a sweet, shy smile. You were adorable. I loved the feeling of your arms around my waist."

"I loved it too. You were so lean, so hairy. Touching you, it was a fantasy come true."

"Like tonight?" Mike grinned, fondling Travis's limp penis.

"Oh, yes."

"So how long *you* been wanting this, Cubbie?"

"Oh, man. Since we had Phys Ed together. I used to watch your muscles move, used to study you in the locker room, in the shower. I thought about you all the time."

"Yeah? Did you...think of me when you were jacking off?"

"But of course, Lord Studly," Travis groaned. "Is that what you want to hear?"

"You bet. What kind of fantasies?"

"Ummm. Holding you. Kissing you. Topping you. Some of them... were sort of *Drummer*-style."

"Yeah? Rough and kinky?"

"Well, uh, a few."

"You're blushing again? We're lying here naked, after I just sucked you off, and you're embarrassed?" Mike grabbed Travis's head and kissed him hard. "Please. We can do kinky sometime. We can try whatever you want."

"So we're doing this again?" Travis kissed Mike back, his chest swelling with delight. "Really?"

"Hell, yes. You want to, right?"

"Lord, Mike. Yes. Whenever we can."

"Good to hear. In fact, I ain't done with you tonight. You came, but I ain't yet." Mike rolled onto his side, facing Travis, and nudged his hard-on against Travis's thigh.

"Will you...show me? How to make you feel good?" Travis grasped Mike's erection.

"You bet. And I got some lube in my backpack."

Travis's eyes widened. "You mean, y-you mean...?"

"Yep. You can fuck me." Mike rubbed the curve of Travis's belly. "I love to come that way, with a big guy inside me."

"Oh, oh, man." Travis's penis stirred again. "But...I've never...been inside a guy before. Is it...can it be, well, you know...dirty?"

"Sometimes. Randy was real squeamish about that, so he stole one of his sister's douche bottles that I used to use beforehand to squirt warm water up my ass. It's in my backpack. I can clean myself out if you'd like."

"Yeah. Yeah, that'd be good. Wow, you came prepared. Guess you were pretty sure that you'd be able to..."

"Get in your pants. Yeah. I had a pretty clear sense of that." Mike's grin was even cockier than usual. "You were always telling me how well-built I was...and then on my birthday you told me what kinda guys turn you on."

"Guess I was pretty obvious. I'm not slick and suave like you."

"True. You're a rube, all right. Cutest rube I ever sucked off. Okay, lemme get clean for you. It'll only take a few minutes."

Mike made as if to slip off the bed, but Travis grabbed his arm. "Wait, Mike. So what about condoms?"

"Yeah, I guess we should have that talk." Mike patted Travis's hand, then rolled onto his back. "So, you're a virgin, right? Or you were." Mike smacked his lips and wiped his mouth.

Travis giggled. "Yeah. I was till about ten minutes ago."

"Till I sucked it right outta you. Me, on the other hand... As you know, I've had some experience." Mike rested his forearm over his eyes. "Randy fucked me a lot when we were together, and he didn't use condoms. And then I screwed those girls, and I only used condoms once or twice. After that, I got real paranoid about STD's, got convinced my dick was itching, so I begged Buck to take me to the health department and get tested. Everything was negative, thank God, though I believe ole Buck has thought of me as a womanizing super stud, to use your phrase, ever since. Better he thinks that than know the truth."

"So we're both clean."

"Yep. And thank God for that." Mike, sighing, ran his fingers through his hair. "In his letters, Eddie's been telling me about all the guys he knows in Frisco who are sick or dying. It sounds terrible. Look, Travis, I brought condoms, and we can use 'em if you want. If you wanna fuck me without condoms, that's cool, but we both gotta swear to be honest if we're ever with other guys. If you ever get with someone else, then you gotta use condoms with me."

"Someone else? I don't want anyone else. Do you?" Frowning, Travis propped himself up on one elbow. "Was this just sex? Am I just another...what's that expression? Notch on your bedpost?"

"Calm down, Cubbie," Mike said, grasping Travis's hand. "I don't want anyone else. I swear. And this isn't just sex. Can't you tell I care about you a lot?"

"Yeah. I guess I can. It's just that this is my first time and you..."

"I've been around. Yeah. I can see how that would worry you. But screwing all those girls, that was me freaking out. I didn't care about 'em. And Randy, well, I was in love with him. I ain't no whore."

"But you might meet a girl. At Kirk's last month, you said that being with a guy is too hard."

"'Might, might.' You might meet another guy. You're going to college next year, and I'm not. Already I'm hating the thought of that. I mean, I don't own you, obviously, but I don't want you fucking around with a bunch of hot, preppy collegiate types bound for fancy careers like yourself, then come back home over Christmas Break and give me some big-city bug."

"I'd never do that. I'd be careful. I'm not stupid."

Mike laughed. "You're so innocent. Everyone's stupid when it comes to sex."

"I won't be. I'm different." Travis crossed his arms across his chest and turned his back on Mike. "I'll be smart."

"Um. I may just be an underachieving ex-jock with grease under my fingernails, but even *I* know there's smart here"—Mike tapped Travis's head—"and smart here"—he tapped Travis's chest. "And like I said, almost nobody's smart here," Mike added, squeezing Travis's dick.

"Maybe. Maybe. But I'd never take stupid risks. And why do you assume I'll sleep around as soon as I get to WVU?"

"Lots of kids run wild in college. I've heard all kinds of stories. Why should you be the one who's above temptation?"

"You're the wild one, not me. And what if you and Randy get back together while I'm away? You said you loved him. You said that he was great in bed. You said—"

Mike rolled his eyes. "*That* ain't gonna happen. Randy's up in Huntington now. I slept with his sister. He beat me up. That bridge is burnt for good. Man, you are one silly Cubbie."

"Don't laugh at me, Mike. That's one thing I can't stand. Don't laugh at me."

"Look, Travis, let's not fight," Mike said, wrapping an arm around his friend and kissing the back of his neck. "Ain't no use in worrying about the future. 'We got tonight,' as that old Kenny Rogers song goes. Okay?"

"Yeah, we do." Turning, Travis kissed Mike on the mouth. "I'm sorry I got mad. I love the feeling of your beard against mine. God, touching you is just wonderful."

"Feeling's mutual. Man, your arms have gotten so thick. So you ready to love on me some?"

"Oh, yes. Just tell me what you want." Travis's hand ranged over Mike's chest, then pinched a nipple.

Mike groaned. "That's a good start. Yep, yep. Now suck on 'em. Good. Harder. Yep. Yep. That drives me crazy."

Travis made love to Mike's chest for a long time, while Mike gasped and writhed beneath him. "Can I, uh, taste you now?" Travis said, stroking Mike's hard-on.

"Go for it, big guy. Just do what I did."

Bending, Travis gave Mike's erection a tentative lick. "You're juicy down here," Travis said, sampling the glisten welling from Mike's glans. "Ummm. Not bad." Positioned himself on his belly between Mike's thighs, he nibbled Mike's cockhead, then took his buddy's penis in his mouth.

"Easy. Watch the teeth. Yeah. Use your lips as kind of a sheath. Yep. There you go. Yeah, that's good. Man, you're a natural."

Travis huffed, gagged, and sucked, responding to Mike's whispered suggestions, at last achieving a rhythm. In only a few minutes, Mike pushed him away.

"Whoa, I'm close. Hold on. Lemme clean out." Rolling off the bed, Mike grabbed his backpack and left the bedroom. Travis lay there, warm with anticipation. *This is happiness,* he thought, *knowing that I've never wanted anything more and that soon I'm to be given all I desire.* He heard rushing water down the hall, then splashing. Finally, the toilet flushed.

Mike returned. He dropped his backpack on the floor, then climbed back onto the bed and handed Travis a tube of lube. Turning, Mike got down onto his elbows and knees. Travis stared in wonder at his friend's ass. He ran a hand over the pale, hair-dusted cheeks. That a boy so desirable would kneel before him in submission and offer himself this way was almost too incredible to comprehend.

This is the best night of my life. "God, you're beautiful," Travis sighed, his face flushing with rapt gratitude.

"Start with a finger," Mike muttered. "And go real slow."

Travis woke to dim dawn, one arm around Mike, Mike's muscled back pressed against his torso. Travis pulled Mike closer, kissing his freckled shoulders. Fervently, he began fondling his chest, then stroking his penis, then fingering his butt. Under this onslaught of attention, Mike woke.

"At it again, huh?" He gave a low laugh. "Think I've created a monster."

"I think you have. Was I...did I do it right?"

"Oh, yeah. A little too fast at first, but once you slowed down, yeah."

"I'm sorry. You were so warm and tight inside, I kind of lost control." Travis kneaded Mike's furry pec and pinched his nipple gently. "I always seem to lose control when you're around. Did I hurt you? You winced some."

"It hurt at first. You're pretty big, and I haven't been fucked in a long time, so a little pain was bound to happen."

"I'm so sorry. Your dick wasn't hard part of the time. Did that mean..."

"Don't worry about my dick. Just 'cause I ain't super-hard sometimes doesn't mean I'm not into it."

"I'm sorry I finished before you could come. Are you sure you enjoyed it?"

"Yes. Yes, I did. Relax, Travis. Relax. Getting screwed by you was great."

"Yeah?" Travis took Mike's hand and kissed the back of it.

"Yeah. I swear."

"As good as Randy?"

"Yeah. Different somehow. But as good."

"Really? Was...Randy was so much stronger and bigger than me. Was his dick bigger than mine?"

"Travis, Lord."

"Was it? Was it bigger?"

Mike reached back and gripped his friend's half-hard cock. "Actually, no. Just 'cause a guy's big-built doesn't mean he's always big down there. My cousin Eddie's had plenty of dicks, and that's what he tells me. Your dick's bigger than Randy's, farm boy. That's one of the reasons it hurt."

"I'm so sorry I hurt you. I'll go slower next time."

"Stop apologizing. It's just our first time together, bud. We'll get our rhythm. It'll just get better over time."

Over time? Please, yes. I want to be with you again and again and again. Travis sighed, kneading Mike's chest hard. "Last night was wonderful. Being inside you was wonderful. Please, can we do it again? I'll go slow, so slow. I'll be real, real tender. Please? Please? This time I want you to come."

In answer, Mike ground his butt against Travis's groin. "You're a real wolf, ain't you? Sure. Go for it, farm boy. I'm all yours."

It was nearly noon by the time Travis climbed out of bed. Leaving Mike to sleep, he quietly closed the bedroom door. After a visit to the bathroom, he headed downstairs. The kitchen was bright with the white light of sun after snow. To be in that cozy house, with that warm, naked boy in his bed, and the world outside wintry and bleak, seemed to Travis like paradise.

Half an hour of breakfast preparations, and Travis bore a tray of food upstairs. He found Mike still asleep. He lay on his belly, one leg drawn up, one arm flung over his head, emitting soft snores. Travis set the tray on the dresser and opened the curtains, letting in a flood of light, but Mike continued to slumber.

Sitting on the bed's edge, Travis stroked Mike's tousled hair. When his friend didn't respond, Travis pulled back the quilts and sheet and gazed at his nakedness. *He's an embodiment of the God. This is religion. This is reverence,* he thought, ever so gently running his right hand over the sleeping boy's back, down his spine, over the fuzzy mounds of his buttocks. *Horned One, Lady of the Moon, thank you. Thank you, thank you.* Bending, Travis kissed an ass-cheek.

Travis was fondling the lube-moist hair in Mike's butt-cleft when he awoke.

"Damn. Again?"

"I was just looking at you. Wanted to make sure you were real," Travis said.

"You ain't plowin' me a third time, horse dick. My hole's all tore up." Mike rolled over, grinning sleepily. He rubbed his eyes and scratched his belly. "Gonna be walkin' crooked for a week."

"Oh, no. Did I hurt you again?"

"Not really. You're so easy to tease I couldn't resist." Mike gave his own butt a soft slap. "Just a little sore is all. No big deal. Comes with the territory."

"But you enjoyed it, right?"

"You keep asking me that. Couldn't you tell? The way I was grunting and groaning and thrashing around and begging you to pound me harder? Hell, I came, didn't I?"

"Thank God Nanny wasn't here. I guess we were both pretty loud." Travis chuckled. "I fear I come from a long line of horndogs. Look, I brought you breakfast."

"Really?" Mike stretched. "Damn, did I luck out. The cub plows me cross-eyed not once, but twice, then brings me breakfast in bed? Think I'm gonna be sticking with you for a while. Smells good. Whatcha got?"

Travis slid off the bed and fetched the tray. "Coffee. Sausage and scrambled eggs. Biscuits, butter, and home-canned strawberry jam. Made from berries I picked a few years ago."

"Great."

"I told you I'd take care of you. This is better than getting up early and deer-hunting in the snow, right?"

"God, yes."

The boys had wolfed down a biscuit apiece and were buttering up their seconds when Travis heard a door open downstairs.

"Sheee-ut. She said she'd call first," Travis blurted. Bounding off the bed, he locked his bedroom door.

"Travis! Honey, I'm home." Nanny's voice sounded downstairs. "Did y'all have breakfast?" Footsteps sounded on the steps.

"Here she comes. Get dressed." Snatching up the tube of lube, Travis lobbed it to Mike, then started scanning the floor for his gym shorts.

CHAPTER ELEVEN

What do you get your boyfriend for Christmas? Travis thought, following Nanny around the streets of Lewisburg, a wealthy town in adjoining Greenbrier County. The holiday was only a week away, and the stores and boutiques were colorful with seasonal decorations and packed with shoppers. *Is he even my boyfriend? Is it too soon to buy him a ring? Yeah, guess so, plus I can't afford anything like that. A shirt he can look sexy in? Or maybe some underwear. A book? I wish I had the guts to buy him a tube of lube. God, if all these people only knew what he and I did together, how he moaned when I slid inside him. I'm the luckiest guy in West Virginia.*

"Honey, why don't you wander around for a while on your own?" Nanny suggested as they entered Belk's. "I want to buy you some gifts here, and I don't want you around to watch."

"Yes, ma'am," Travis said. "How about I go to the bookshop and look for something to get Mike?"

"He doesn't seem like much of a reader to me, Travis. Are you sure?"

"He reads," Travis said defensively. "Mainly horror novels and books about war, but he reads."

"Well, how about we get him a nice shirt too?"

"That's a good idea. He wears flannel shirts and chamois shirts in chilly weather. Will you look for one? I don't know much about clothes."

"Well, I do. I love to shop, even though I rarely get to." Nanny eyed the racks in the Women's section. "Mercy, some pretty dresses. I just may have to treat myself. You go on now, honey. I'll find something for your friend. And then you and I can get a nice lunch."

Travis left Nanny browsing among Belk's women's clothes. Furtively, he entered the Men's section, where he examined the underwear selection. *Damn, Mike'd look great in these,* Travis thought, snatching up a pair and taking them to the payment counter. *If Nanny sees 'em, I'll tell her they're for me.*

Pleased with his purchase, already imagining Mike dressed in nothing but the briefs, Travis left Belk's and headed up the street to the bookshop, a tiny place fronted with limestone. There he weighed his options. *I've already got that tasty book that Bill sent me to give him, but another won't hurt. Lots of Stephen King books*—The Eye of the Dragon, The Dark Half—*but I'll bet he already has them all. Not many books on Vietnam. Ah, here we go.*

Travis took *A Poet to His Beloved* off the shelf. A collection of W.B. Yeats's early love poems, it was a handsomely produced gift volume, a copy of which he already owned and had read several times. He browsed through poems he'd known for years, stunned by how his passion for Mike had given the verse new and deeper meanings. *Yeah. Wow. That's how I feel about Mike.* **That's** *what that line means. Yeah, I gotta get this for him. I'm still too shy to say things like this to him, but maybe Yeats can do it for me. I can read him poems in bed. That'd be really romantic.*

When Travis rejoined Nanny, she'd chosen a slate-gray chamois shirt. Travis stroked the soft fabric. "That's great, Nanny. Thanks. He'll really like it." *He'll look like Paul Bunyan in this,* Travis thought. *It'll show off the hair between his pecs, and it'll be mighty fun to take it off him next time we get frisky.*

"Now don't peek in here. Some of those presents are yours," said Nanny, handing him a heavy shopping bag. "Ready for lunch?"

"Yes, ma'am. I'm starved."

They stepped out onto the sidewalk. The wind was brisk, though the day was sunny. A few dead leaves skittered by their feet. "Let's head up to the General Lewis Inn," Nanny suggested. "It's very historic and has fancy cuisine. I love their crab melts and their French onion soup. They might have a nice fire going. Did you know your parents spent their wedding night there?"

"No, ma'am. That soup sounds good. And so does—"

"Faggot!"

Travis froze, fists clenched. An adolescent boy shouted it again—"Faggot!"—as he chased another boy across the street between slow-moving cars.

"Nasty-mouthed child," Nanny said, shaking her head. "If his parents don't watch out, he's going to get run over."

I hope he does, the little bastard. Every time I hear that word, I hate it more. Lips curled, Travis glared at the two boys as they bustled to the end of the block and vanished around a corner.

Christmas afternoon was sunny but very cold. The boys' breaths hung steaming on the air like pale banners as they strolled through the leafless woods of Pipestem State Park and down to Long Branch Lake. Both were dressed for a winter walk, in jeans, wool sweaters, toboggans, heavy jackets, and hiking boots.

"Thanks for letting me spend the holiday with y'all," Mike said. "Ole Buck was all hot to take his lady friend to Gatlinburg for the Christmas festivities, and you can be sure as shit I didn't wanna go, and you can be just as sure he didn't want me to go."

"I wish my parents could have come home, but they're determined to save as much money as they can. Must admit I miss them, even Daddy. Still, it's great that you and I can spend Christmas together, though the Winter Solstice means more to me. It's all about the birth of the Sun," said Travis, pointing to the sky, "not the Son, as far as I'm concerned."

"You and your exotic paganism." Mike chuckled. "Well, I love the shirt you got me."

"Nanny picked it out, but I paid for it. I love my hunting knife. Great gift," said Travis, patting his left hip. "I got a few more things for you back in my room that I didn't want Nanny to see."

"Yeah? Actually, I got a surprise for you too."

"Tonight, after Nanny goes to bed, how about we have our own little gift exchange?"

"Cool. What's for dinner, by the way? I'm famished. Eating delivery pizza seems pretty piss-poor after being introduced to the Ferrell family cooking."

"You'll just have to wait and see."

"Tell me, dammit."

"Baked ham. Homemade bread. Deviled eggs. Sweet potato casserole. Green bean casserole. And fruitcake. Most fruitcake you get is nasty, but Nanny's is real good. She flavors it with bourbon, of course. Only use she has for liquor."

"Sounds super."

Travis patted Mike's shoulder. "You stick with me, Studly, and you're going to have a belly like me."

"No problem. I love your belly. Especially with all that brown hair on it. Damn, Travis, don't you know by now how much I love...how you look. I'd really like to hold your hand right now," Mike said, wiping frost crystals from his mustache, "but I guess we better not."

"Yeah, someone might see. So annoying. Straight folks get to be all over each other all the time—Hinton High's full of PDA's—but we have to sneak around."

"That's the facts, Cubbie. Didn't you read that stuff in the *Bay Area Reporter* about gay bashing? If shit like that could happen in big cities, you can be damn sure it could happen here. We may both be strong, but muscle ain't nothing against a gang of guys, especially if they got knives or guns or two-by-fours. And being out in the woods like this..."

"Yeah. It's like *The Scarlet Letter*. The forest represents freedom from society's rules, but if someone caught us together out here—"

"Books, books, books. You and your literary references. But I know what you mean. Someone could end up dead. Yeah."

"Makes me want to carry a gun," Travis said, face grim. "At least we got our hunting knives." He patted his left hip again. "I think it's super cool that we have matching knives. Might have to take me out a homophobe or two."

"Da-yum. What happened to that shy, wide-eyed guy who came into the garage this past September and asked me about lifting weights? You're getting downright fierce." With his elbow, Mike jabbed Travis in the side.

"Don't you start tickling me again. Well, I don't know what happened to him. To me. I guess that...getting as, uh, fond of you as I've gotten, it just pisses me off that we could be in danger if some asshole saw us touching or knew we were fucking. I mean, we aren't hurting anybody. Why can't folks just live and let live? Pricks. If anybody tried to hurt you, I'd kill them, the motherfuckers."

"And what happened to that well-spoken kid who called me a potty-mouth, huh? And said talk about sex was vulgar? So we're just 'fucking'? 'Am I just another notch in your bedpost?' Isn't that what you said?"

"You're always giving me a hard time." Travis soft-punched Mike's arm.

Mike returned the favor. "I thought you liked it hard."

"Vulgar!" Travis scanned the woods before giving Mike a quick hug. "You know what I mean, Mike. Of course it's not just sex. It's making love. Making love. And that polite kid, well, he met you. And he changed in all kinds of ways."

For a few minutes, they were silent. The wintergreen of the lake glimmered through the dull trunks of leafless trees as the boys neared the bottom of the hill.

"Little sip?" Mike pulled out his flask. "It'll warm you up."

"Sure. What is it?"

"Applejack. A buddy of Buck's made it."

Curious, Travis took a swig. "Not bad."

"Take it slow. It's strong."

The friends took turns pulling on the flask as they made their way closer to the lake. At last they stood on the shale-crumbly bank. Bright sun glinted off the water. Mike pulled out sunglasses and put them on. Travis followed suit.

"So," Travis said, looking not at Mike but out over the water. "Are we dating?"

Mike turned to Travis and grinned. Then he too gazed out over the lake. "Lookee there. I think that's a hawk of some kind. Dating? Yep. Yep, I do believe we are. That all right with you?"

"Hell, yes. Hell, yes." Travis flashed Mike a happy grin, gave his hand a quick, hard squeeze, and then the boys continued their hike around the lake.

"Thanks again for the pretty scarf, Mike. Don't y'all stay up too late." Nanny shuffled toward the stairs.

"Thank *you* for this sweatshirt, ma'am." Mike lounged on the couch, watching a muted football game on television. Travis sat on the floor near his friend's feet, picking out "Silent Night" on his guitar. Like Mike, he was dressed in cozy sweats and boot socks.

"Travis, honey, would you clean up the dessert plates? I'm exhausted."

"Sure. You get on to bed."

"I'll make y'all buckwheat cakes in the morning. With that maple syrup your daddy made and some Jimmy Dean sausage."

"How about *I* make the buckwheat cakes and you sleep in?"

"The batter's already made and in the fridge. Besides, you know I can't sleep in. I'm up at five thirty every morning."

Travis made a face. "Better you than me."

"I worry about her," Travis said, once his grandmother had ascended the stairs. "I can tell she's slowing down. I haven't lost anybody close to me yet, and I can't imagine life without her."

"I know the feeling. Felt that way about my mother. And now you."

Travis stared. "Y-yeah?"

"Yep," Mike said matter-of-factly. "Scary. 'Cause I remember how it hurt to lose Mom."

"You aren't going to lose me, Mike. I'm not—"

"Going anywhere? But you are. WVU. Didn't you just get good news about that scholarship? Full tuition waiver, right?"

"Yeah." Travis strummed a dissonant chord, then put his guitar in its case and edged another log on the fire. "But I don't have to go."

"Bullshit," Mike said, rising. "You're going, or I'll kick your lily-white ass. You're going, even if you do end up dropping me for some slick scholar with a trust fund and a big dick."

"Mike, damn it. Stop talking like that."

"Just teasing, Cubbie. Let's get those dishes done."

"So how about those surprises you promised?" said Mike, sitting on the spare bed.

Travis locked his bedroom door. "Here you go," he said, pulling three paper bags from a dresser drawer. "Sorry. I can't wrap presents very well. When I do, they look like some halfwit or the Frankenstein monster did it. Kinda like my pie crusts."

"I'm crazy about your pie crusts," said Mike, grabbing the bags. "Give 'em here." He rummaged in the first. "Oh. Nice." He held up a package of skimpy black Calvin Klein briefs.

"You said you might end on the cover of *BEAR* or *Drummer*. Now you're prepared. Besides, I'll bet your butt is going to look glorious in them."

"I'll give you a show here in a minute. But first..." Mike removed a hardback book from the second bag. He peered at it. "*A Poet to His Beloved?*"

"It's poetry. An Irish writer named Yeats. We've read him in school."

Mike flipped through it. "*You've* read him in school. We're in different tracks, remember? Not much call for poetry in Vo-Tech."

"Oh. Yeah, I guess not. Well, it's really good stuff anyway."

Mike scanned a page. "Hm. Sorry to say this—I know you said you've written some poems—but I don't really get most of it. Buck says poetry's for sissies."

"Excuse me?" Travis pursed his lips.

Mike put the book on the bed. "You're sooo sensitive. I wasn't saying you were a sissy, Travis. Relax. I just meant, well, poetry might sound pretty, but what good is it?"

"Poetry's really important, Mike. It's been around for a long, long time. I mean, back in ancient Greece, Homer was writing about wars, and Sappho was writing about love—lesbian love. There's still love and war in the world, right? So it's relevant. It records how folks thought and felt, what they went through—whether two thousand years ago or last week—and when I read it, it helps me understand my own emotions—my...heart, I guess—and that makes me feel...less alone. It sure helped me when I realized I was gay. Brenda gave me poems that Shakespeare and Whitman wrote about other guys—"

"Shakespeare? Shakespeare was gay?"

Travis grinned. "Not exactly. But he wrote loads of love sonnets to a man. And Whitman...he was definitely gay. And a bear, from what I can tell from photos. 'When I Heard at the Close of the Day' is amazing. A whole bunch of poems in a collection he called *Calamus* seem to be gay. Plus," Travis continued, pointing to the Latin textbook on his desk, "some of the Roman poets we're reading in my

Latin class, like Catullus, wrote love poems about guys. Not that the teacher mentions those poems, but Brenda tipped me off. Even Virgil in *The Aeneid* and Ovid in *Metamorphoses*—those are long poems I've read in translation—mention relationships between men."

"Wow. Sounds like we got more in common with those old guys from Greece and Rome than I ever woulda guessed. Still, I think I'll stick to horror novels."

"Look, you like country music, right?"

"Sure. I love it."

"Song lyrics are poetry too. You're not just listening to the melody, are you? You're paying attention to the words."

"Yeah, that's true."

"And the words move you, right? They make you angry, or sad, or happy?"

"Yeah. That's true too. Look, Travis," Mike said, kneading his forehead, "I guess I'm not being completely honest with you. The thing is, if I took this book home, Buck would make fun of me if he saw it. He makes fun of me when he finds me reading anything, but poetry...I'd really catch it. How about I leave it here? You can read me some of it next time I visit and explain what that Yeats guy is saying. I ain't no scholar, you know. I don't think I'd make heads or tails of it without you around to help me."

"Oh. Okay." *Shit, I should have gone for the Stephen King books.* "I'm sorry you don't like the book. I guess it's kind of a stupid gift."

"I like it. I just think I'd like it better if we read it together. Speaking of stupid gifts, I can't believe I got you that dumb knife."

"What? I told you I love the knife."

"Nice of you to say, but what the hell are you going to do with a knife in college? Menace your teachers? I should have bought you books. Or something you could use up there."

"No, Mike. No. I have enough books. The knife makes me feel... butch and tough. It'll remind me of you, of all our walks in the woods. And if I'm a forestry major, it'll come in handy."

"If you say so."

"I do. Now check out that last gift. You'll like it better than you did Yeats, I'll bet. It's, uh, poetry of a more bodily sort."

"Feels like another book. Now, Travis, like I said, I ain't no scholar."
Looking dubious, Mike pulled the third gift from the bag. "Oh, man.
The Joy of Gay Sex? Where the hell did you get this?"

"Bill sent it to me from Morgantown." Travis smiled proudly. "I've
told her a lot about you, and I guess this was her way of saying that
she approved. The book's kind of for both of us."

"I like this woman already. Wow," murmured Mike as he flipped
through it. "Tasty illustrations. And what's this?" he added, pulling a
folded piece of paper from the book.

Travis blushed. "Uh, some page numbers listing a few of my favorite entries. And a little scene I wrote, stuff we might do. Some...stuff
I'd like to try. Only if you're into it, though. Just suggestions."

Mike laughed. "I love it. And there's a card too." He read out loud.
"'You are cordially invited to share New Year's Eve with Travis Ferrell at Bluestone State Park in a romantic woodland cabin.' Wow. Really?"

"Yep. So you only have about a week to study up," Travis said, tapping the cover of the book. "Unless you have other plans for New
Year's Eve."

"Uh, wait for the ball to drop and watch Buck and his girl get drunk
and snuggle on the couch? I think I *much* prefer Bluestone. How'd
you arrange this?"

"It's my Christmas present from my parents, along with a couple
of sweaters and a slew of socks they had Nanny buy me. They felt
so guilty for not coming home that they agreed to pay for a night at
the cabin. I told them that I wanted to spend New Year's Eve with a
buddy of mine. They said no alcohol, no pot, and no girls."

Mike guffawed. "Don't need the last two; might have to have just a
little of the first. So your grandmother doesn't care if you're not here
for New Year's Eve?"

"She goes to bed so early she's never up till midnight, and she doesn't
drink champagne, so New Year's Eve is just another night to her. She
said it'd be fine."

"Great. I can't wait."

"You going to pose in those briefs now?" Travis said, eyes gleaming
with lusty impatience.

"In a minute, you horny hillbilly. Time for your surprise. I've already hid it in your closet. See if you can find it."

Travis rummaged excitedly through his clothes. "Ah. Here it is. Oh, man, Mike, I love it." He held up a black leather vest on a hanger.

"For my little studly Cubbie. Try it on."

Travis did so, beaming.

"Beautiful. Fits you just right."

"It does. How could you——?"

"Afford it? Remember all those days I told you I couldn't lift with you? I was working extra for Buck at the garage. Figured this would be the perfect gift for a baby leather bear."

"I love it. Thanks so much," Travis said, doing his best to swagger. "But Nanny thinks black leather means bikers, and she thinks bikers are trashy."

"Hell. Now she'll think I'm a bad influence."

"Naw. I'll tell her Bill gave it to me. Nanny disapproves of Bill anyway, since she's so butch. So how about that underwear?"

"Don't have to convince me. You know I love to take my clothes off and give you a show." It took Mike only half a minute to shuck off all his sweats and slip on the tiny briefs.

"How they look?" Mike flexed his chest, then turned and wiggled his ass.

Travis stared, relishing the sight of so much pale, muscular skin and black body hair. "Ohhh, damn. I think I've just been hoist on my own petard."

"What?"

"Uhhh, I mean, blown up by my own bomb. I should have waited till Bluestone to give you those. Because I really want to throw you on the bed right now, but I can't, because Nanny's bedroom is right beside this one."

"I can be quiet, I swear." Mike's whisper was comically exaggerated. He squeezed the bulge in his briefs. "And I brought lube. How about you just finger-fuck me while I jack off? Just hold your hand over my mouth when I come."

"Damn, that sounds hot. Lord, you look good enough to eat. But, look, Mike, we better not. I'd feel really strange doing it while Nanny was here. Her eyes aren't so good, but her ears are fine."

"I get it." Mike nodded, flinging himself on Travis's double bed. "We can just cuddle. Or do I have to sleep in that spare bed?"

Travis slipped off his sweats, stripping down to his boxers. "Naw. If you promise to behave."

"If *you* promise to behave."

Travis mussed the spare bed to give it the appearance of having been slept in, then flipped off the lamp and joined Mike. They arranged themselves in one of their customary cuddle-positions: Travis lying on his back, Mike lying on his side with his head on Travis's shoulder, his fingers fondling Travis's furry belly.

"No way I'm letting you sleep in another bed," Travis said, tugging the quilts higher before pulling Mike close. "I never get to touch you enough."

"I feel the same. I think a lot of folks are touch-starved. And being here with you is sweet as hell, even if you won't use me hard and put me away wet."

"You're as much of a satyr as I am. That's one of the things I love about you."

Oh, man, I just used the L word, Travis thought.

To his relief, Mike let it slide. "Satyr? What's that?"

"One of those half-man, half-goat Greek things like Pan," said Travis, kissing Mike's forehead. "They were all horny. There are pictures of them, paintings on pottery shards, in my Latin textbook."

"Sounds like you as much as me, yeah." Mike chuckled. "Hairy-legged and horny."

"Pan was a forest god. Mike Woodson. Wood Son. Even your name fits. Roll over, please." Travis nudged Mike. When he did so, Travis pulled him closer, till Travis's hairy chest was pressed against Mike's smooth back. "You feel so good, Wood Son."

"Man, Travis. I love it when you hold me like this. When you spoon me from behind. I feel mighty safe."

"And I feel mighty protective," Travis replied, combing Mike's chest hair with his fingertips. "Like I'd take on all the world for you. Funny thing for a bookworm to say, huh?"

"You're sounding like a warrior, not a bookworm."

"Warrior? Me? You're the warrior. But, yeah, I guess...you mean so much to me that...I guess a guy gets to thinking warrior thoughts when he thinks about all there is to love and all there is to lose."

"Now you're sounding poetic. And the L word too? Wow."

Argh. This time he noticed. "Oh, I just...I meant..." Travis shifted nervously.

"Relax, big guy. I don't want any serious talks tonight. Let's just snuggle. I wish we could spend more nights together like this."

"I do too. And speaking of poetic, there's another kind of mythological creature you remind me of."

"Uh oh. Hercules, I hope?"

"Yeah, actually. But I had muses in mind. They inspire folks. I know you said you don't really get poetry, but, uh, I've been writing some poems about you."

"Yeah? Really?" Mike took Travis's hand. "That's pretty cool. I'll bet I'd like 'em a lot more than that Irish guy's. You gonna read 'em to me?"

"Uhhhhh. I don't know how good they are."

"Aw, come on. I wanna hear 'em."

"One of these days, maybe." Travis kissed Mike's shoulder and squeezed a fuzzy butt-cheek. "Let's get some sleep before I decide to rape you. Tomorrow, after breakfast, before you head home, would you help me split more wood? And feed the livestock?"

"Sure."

They fell silent. *Horned One, let me hold him like this for the rest of my life,* Travis thought. *He makes me so happy. Please let us have a future together.*

"Hey, Mike?" Travis nuzzled the nape of Mike's neck.

"Yep?"

"So what kind of life...can gay guys have? Do they get to big cities and sleep around like satyrs? Like, uh, horndogs? People are always saying that gay promiscuity spread AIDS. Or do some of them, uh, do they find another guy and settle down like straight people? Like my parents have? Living together and cooking meals and watching TV like regular folks?"

"Hell, Travis, gay folks are just people. My guess is some of 'em are rounders and some of 'em are romantics, folks who settle down.

Though Cousin Eddie sure gets around. I know that much. He picks up guys in gay bars. He's always writing me from Frisco, complaining about catching another case of the crabs."

"Catching crabs? Ack. Sleeping with some stranger you don't care about? Doesn't sound very appealing to me."

"Even if the stranger is really, really hot?"

"I don't think so. Maybe. I guess if I didn't have you, I might. Would you?"

"Maybe. As I've explained, I haven't always been real jewlicious in the use of my dick."

"Jewlicious?"

"Yeah. Isn't that right?"

"I don't think that's a word. Do you mean 'judicious?' That means showing good judgment."

Mike sniggered. "Yeah, judicious. Shit. I screwed up. A guy in the garage used that word the other day, and I asked him what it meant. I was trying to impress you."

"I'm already impressed, believe me, and your vocabulary has nothing to do with it." Travis patted Mike's rump and giggled. "Jewlicious? Does that mean 'sexy Hebrew'?"

"Guess so. One of those exotic New York City types."

The boys nestled closer, again falling silent. Travis, full of contentment, was nearly asleep when Mike sighed. "Travis?"

"Yeah?"

"Best Christmas I can remember. And I can't wait for New Year's Eve."

"Me too. Be sure to check out those pages in that book." Softly, Travis kneaded Mike's pecs. "I want to try some, uh, *Drummer* stuff. Okay? If you think you'd be into it."

Mike's only response was a snore. Travis kissed Mike's back and ran his fingers through his lover's hair, feeling as if he were the most blessed boy in the world.

CHAPTER TWELVE

Travis, dressed in jeans, a black-and-red plaid flannel shirt, and his new leather vest, peered with puzzlement out the front window. Instead of coming to the door to fetch Travis, as was Mike's custom, he'd parked his pickup out front and honked.

"*There's* Mike. See you tomorrow," Travis said, kissing his grandmother on the cheek before pulling on his coat, shouldering his backpack, grabbing his duffel bag and cooler, and bounding out the door into the light drizzle, the last afternoon of 1990.

"Have a good time. Behave!" Nanny yelled after him.

"Sorry I'm so late," Mike mumbled as Travis clambered into the truck. He stubbed out a cigarette in the ashtray. "Buck had a rush at the garage and made me work an extra hour. I shoulda called."

"No problem. I'm so glad to see you. I brought—" Travis stopped abruptly, staring at Mike's sullen face. His right eye was bruised and puffy, and his lower lip was split and swollen.

"How the hell did *that* happen?" Travis snarled. "Who did that you?"

"I don't want your grandmother to see me like this. I'm afraid she'll think you're running with the wrong crowd. I'll tell you what happened once we're on the road."

Mike had barely driven past the church at the crossroads when Travis asked again, his teeth clenched and his face flushed with rage. "*Who* did that to you?"

Mike turned down the Eagles music on the tape deck. "I'm really sorry. I wanted today to be perfect."

"*You're* sorry? I'll make somebody sorry. What happened?"

"On the way up here, I stopped at the hardware store to fetch something, and I ran across Brent Vass and that big dumb buddy of his, Jack Holt, in the parking lot. They started talking shit about you, I told 'em to kiss my lily-white ass, then Brent called me a fag, so I punched him." Mike shook out his right hand. "I was trying to break his nose, but I don't think I managed it."

"God, I wish I'd been there."

"Me too. As strong as you've gotten and as much as you've worked the punching bag, I think you could have helped me plenty. Anyway, then Holt swung at me. Caught me in the eye and then the jaw. Laid me out. I hit the asphalt hard. So much for me being a heroic Hercules. The big bastard's strong as shit. Twice my size and surprisingly fast."

"Then what happened?"

Mike rubbed his side and winced. "The fucker kicked me in the ribs and was about to do it again when some folks came out of the store and threatened to call the cops. We all three hightailed it out of there."

"Hell, Mike. Now, thanks to me, you have the same reputation I have."

"Thanks to you? *Please.* I knew what I was getting into as soon as you told me you were gay. I knew I wanted to be with you, and to hell with the consequences. Everybody knows everybody's business in this pissant county. You know that. Sooner or later, some rumor was gonna come around and bite us in the ass."

"Maybe..." Travis looked out the passenger window, where the Greenbrier ran deep and wide on its way to its confluence with the New River at Bellepoint. "Should we stop seeing one another for a while? Till the rumors die down?"

"Die down? Rumors last for decades in this town. Ain't nothing better to talk about. Not see one another? Fuck that, Travis. I'm crazy about you, and you make love to me so damn sweet, and you're heading off to college in August. I'm gonna see as much of you as I can, as often as I can, and let people talk."

"I just don't want you to get hurt."

"I don't want *you* to get hurt. And not seeing you would hurt me bad. Real bad. A lot worse than bruised ribs. Only thing is, if word gets back to Buck about this, and if he believes the rumors, and he may not since, after that abortion and that trip to the Health Department, he thinks I'm a pussyhound like him...well, if he believes 'em, he'll throw me out for sure. Probably try to kick my ass first. So I'm reserving your spare bed just in case."

"Spare bed? *My* bed. I wish I could sleep with you every night. I wish you *would* move in."

"Me too, man. But not like that. I'd lose my job in his garage, and then what the fuck would I do? Plus, as much of an asshole as Buck can be, he *is* my father."

"So what are we going to do?"

"We're going to be careful. We're going to keep seeing each other. Let's try to forget this for today, huh? We got that cabin to ourselves, out in the woods. What could be better?"

"How can I forget it with those bruises on your face? Those fuckers. I wish I could break their necks. I wish I could get even somehow."

"Me too. But I don't know what likelihood there is of that."

"They can't just get away with it. They need to pay for hurting you. They—"

Mike rubbed his head and looked away. "Look, Travis, just stop talking about it, okay?"

Something inside Travis quailed, hearing the annoyance in Mike's voice. "Dammit. All right, all right, I'll shut up."

The boys fell into a brooding silence. Mike drove them down through Bellepoint, over the bridge, up past the dam and along the reservoir. All around them, steep blue-gray mountains loomed, their tops concealed by low clouds. Just before the Bluestone River met the New, Mike turned right and they followed the tortuous road into Bluestone State Park. *The hills are so beautiful,* Travis thought. *Why are so many people in this county so mean? Why do they care how or who I love?*

"You wearing your vest under that jacket?" Mike asked.

"Yep."

"Bet you look good in it."

Travis shrugged.

"So, I finished those books," Mike said, eyes on the road. He shifted into second gear to make one of the sharp turns.

"You're trying to distract me, aren't you?"

"I am. I repeat: I finished those books. 'What books?' you ask."

"What books?" *Vass and Holt, goddamn them. God, I'm so angry. God, I wish I were ten feet tall. Or one of those X-Men mutants. I wish I had super powers or powerful magic. I wish I could protect you always. From all danger and all loss.*

"The Civil War book you gave me for my birthday. *I Rode with Stonewall.* It was great. Jackson was one helluva man. And *The Fancy Dancer.* That was good too. Cool to read something with gay guys in it. I could relate. I really remind you of Vidal Stump?"

"Yeah," Travis said. "All butch and handsome and dark-featured. All you need is another motorcycle and a black leather jacket."

"Yeah? I miss that bike. Oh, I brought the gay sex book."

"Yeah?" Travis's sour expression faded. "And did you read the assigned sections?"

"Yes, sir. I did, sir. I read the whole damn book, sir. And that scene you wrote, sir. All of which is fine by me, sir."

"Ummmmmm. Good boy." Travis reached over and patted Mike's thigh, then pointed ahead. "There's the sign for the cabins."

Mike steered the pickup up the slope and into the woods. The cabin was rustic-looking, one of four, and set well back from the other three. The parking spaces around the cabins were all empty.

"Looks like it's only us," said Mike, parking.

"Wow, this is perfect. Guess that means you can shout for help all you want, and no one will be around to hear you." Travis raised his eyebrows dramatically and tried to look tough.

"You did say you were planning to become the Redneck Rapist of Summers County. Considering the sections of that sex book you listed, I figure I'm about to become your first victim?"

"Afraid so. Prepare to be kidnapped." Travis scanned the forested surroundings, then leaned forward and gently kissed Mike's swollen mouth. "Except with you bruised up..."

"Hell, a few bruises ain't nothin'. I'm up for all those things you're wanting to try. Though you may just have to liquor me up before you overpower me," said Mike. "I got a jar of peach moonshine in the back. Prime stuff."

"I brought quite a few surprises too. Let's haul it all in and get a fire going."

By the time Travis and Mike had finished unpacking, a dense fog was filling the forest around the cabin and night was falling. In the little kitchen, Travis heated up the miscellaneous leftovers Nanny had packed for them: cabbage rolls, macaroni and cheese, and succotash. In the den, Mike got a fire going. When the food was ready, the boys sat on the couch before the blaze and ate, quietly and steadily, till every morsel was gone.

Mike pulled off his cowboy boots, loosened his belt, sat back, and groaned. "I'm stuffed again."

"No room for jam cake? With caramel icing?"

"Jesus, that sounds good. But I don't think I have room. Let's have it for breakfast."

"I brought fried apples for breakfast. And bacon. Plus I'm going to make grits."

"God, you country people sure know how to eat. Okay, I'll have that cake. Let's wait a little while, though. Want to try the moonshine in the meantime?"

"Sure. I guess. It'll be my first."

Mike rose, loped into the bedroom, and returned with a Mason jar. "It burns blue, so it's safe. I already tested it. Want a glass?"

"Naw. I want to look dangerous, redneck, and macho for you, man. Got to drink it from the jar. Hand it here."

"Go slow."

"I've heard that before." Travis gave Mike a salacious grin. "Music to my ears. Don't worry. I promise."

Mike snickered. "Satyr. I'm serious. This shit is even stronger than that applejack we had at Long Branch Lake. It'll knock you on your ass if you ain't careful."

"If it's that strong, should we even drink it at all?"

"Man, you ain't a real mountaineer if you haven't slurped some 'shine. Go on now."

Travis took a cautious sip. "Wow. Tastes like a cross between an orchard and the surface of the sun. Sort of like you. Fiery but sweet. Intoxicating." He took a second sip before handing the jar back to Mike.

"Oh, please. You're such a sweet-talking bastard." Mike took a swig. "I been reading some stuff about astrology. Said Leos love flattery. Sounds like they're good at using it too. Bet you've kissed the Blarney Stone."

"I haven't, but I'd like to someday. The Ferrells came from Ireland. Longford County. The family crest is hanging on Nanny's wall."

"Longford County. You'll make it there someday, I have no doubt. You have a big future in front of you, Cubbie." Mike took another big gulp of moonshine, then another. Coughing, he replaced the jar lid. "Wow, I'm feeling it a little already."

"You said to go slow, remember?"

"Ah, I can handle it. You're the novice."

"Just don't drink too much."

"Like Buck does? Is that what you mean? Worried I'll end up a mean ole liquored-up bastard like him?"

"That's not what I meant, Mike. I just meant— My grandfather, Earl Senior, used to get into the bourbon bottle, especially on holidays, and scare the hell out of us, so folks getting real drunk, that frightens me."

"Yeah, I get it. You're right. Gotta pace ourselves," Mike said, leaning against Travis and patting his thigh. "I'm so glad we could do this. Helluva fine way to end the year."

"I agree. Best Christmas gift my parents ever gave me."

"Best Christmas present ever, far as I'm concerned. You mentioned your grandfather and holidays and drinking too much? It was the same in our household. Every damn Christmas, ole Buck would get shit-faced, and then him and Mom would fight like cats and dogs. Then after she died, the holiday season didn't mean much. But this year, thanks to you... Man," said Mike, looking around the room, "what a nice place. I always wanted me a log cabin."

"Me too. Log cabin or farmhouse. Or maybe one of those fancy Victorians with a turret. Someplace way out in the woods or up in the hills, where no one else is around and you can live your life free. *Montani semper liberi*, right?"

"Now there's some Latin I actually know. I remember it from eighth grade West Virginia History. 'Mountaineers are always free,' right?"

"Right. And you call yourself dumb." Travis tousled Mike's hair. "You've had a traumatic day, buddy. Why don't you stretch out and put your head in my lap?"

Mike took Travis's suggestion. "Is this the start of the seduction and kidnapping?" he said, smiling up into Travis's eyes.

"Naw." Travis bent to kiss Mike's swollen mouth ever so tenderly. "Beat up as you are, maybe we should just cuddle."

Mike snorted. "I spent Christmas night with you just cuddling. Now that we're alone, I'm wanting more. I ain't that beat up. Besides, I read that whole damn sex book in preparation for tonight. Including the 'Bondage' and 'S&M' sections you marked. Hell, the reason I stopped by the hardware was to buy rope."

"Really? I brought rope too."

Mike laughed low in his throat. "Yeah? Great minds, right? Guess we'll have enough."

"Sounds like it." Travis caressed Mike's dark hair. "Okay, you got it. Let's take our time, draw it out. We got all night, right?"

"Right. We can sleep some other time. 'Y'can sleep in the grave,' Buck says when he rousts me outta bed early."

"Yeah. *Carpe diem*, and all that."

"More foreign stuff?"

"More Latin. It means 'Seize the day.'"

Mike squeezed Travis's hand. "You're so damn smart. You're gonna be a professor some day."

"Maybe. I can read some Latin but I can't fix things like you. I'm pretty useless. You're functional as well as decorative."

"Useless? My amazing farm boy? You're so cute it hurts. Especially in that vest. You look like one of those ferocious leather-masters in *Drummer*."

It was Travis's turn to snort derisively. "Hardly."

"It's true. Well, you look like a real young, shy version. You'll get there, I predict. Meanwhile, 'adorable' is the word…which, I know, I know, I've used before. You're fucking sweet as sorghum, and don't you forget it."

Travis rolled his eyes. "Sorghum's sweet, but it's dark and bitter too."

"That's what I like about it. What I like about you. You're complicated. So tell me more about *Carpe diem*, professor. Farm boy and professor, that's a cool combination."

"Yep. *Carpe diem*. So, a good example of the concept was a line by an English poet named Waller who said, 'Gather ye rosebuds while ye may.' It means that—"

"More poetry, huh? This grease monkey gets it, guy. It means, 'Suck all the cock you can while you can.'"

"I don't think it means to be promiscuous. I think it means to be passionate and—"

"And live intense and deep. I *get* it. That's the way you and I live when we're together. And don't worry. I ain't wanting to be promiscuous. I'd rather have one guy call me 'lover' than have ten guys call me 'stud.'"

"Really?"

"Really."

"'Lover.' I like that. So we're lovers?"

"You bet, farm boy," said Mike, giving Travis's hand another squeeze. "I ain't interesting in whoring around like Cousin Eddie. He used to do the I-64 truck stops like crazy, he told me."

Travis grimaced. "I've heard about those guys. Truck stops and men's rooms. Aghh. You're asking for disease or an ass kicking. Me, I prefer quality to quantity."

"Me too. That's why I'm here with you."

"Flattery again. Keep it up. Please. Anyway, Bill told me in her last letter that guys do that kind of thing in the basement bathroom of the WVU Library..."

Travis paused. Frowning, he cleared his throat. "Ready for that jam cake?"

"No. No, I'm not. You look sad now, Cubbie. Not angry like you were before. What's going on?"

"I got a letter from Brenda the other day. She and Bill are having troubles. Bill's got this new friend, another butch, and Brenda's jealous."

"I get that. I'd be damn jealous if you started looking at other guys."

"And why would I do that when I'm here with a muscled little stud who looks so fine in that tight thermal undershirt and those snug Levi's? I want you so bad that I can't even imagine wanting anyone else. Ever."

"I thought that way when I was in love with Randy. But then he freaked out, and then he beat me up, and now I can't fucking stand him, and now here I am with you, and happier than I've ever been. Things can change, Travis. I don't mean to scare you. My feelings run deep and they're slow to shift. But some people are different. Maybe Bill's that way."

"I hope not. I always thought she and Brenda were the perfect couple. A great love story. After all they'd been through together here in Summers County, they were so close. The thought of them maybe breaking up makes me feel sick inside."

"They didn't have a lot to choose from here. Maybe they got there and met lots of new people, and...I wonder what will happen when you get to college, who you'll meet."

"I could meet a million men, and I'd still want only you." Bending, Travis kissed Mike on the mouth, then kneaded his boyfriend's crotch.

"You say that now." Mike sat up. "Pass me that 'shine, Cubbie."

"More?"

"Yeah. I ain't sufficiently buzzed yet."

Mike took a long swallow and cleared his throat. "Look, maybe I am like Buck. Maybe I drink too much. But liquor helps me face stuff, say stuff... Look, Travis, I'm afraid. I don't like to admit it, but...I'm afraid."

Travis, unnerved by his friend's admission, tried to make a joke of it "You? Big tough Mike Woodson? I can't see you afraid of anything."

"Don't make fun of me. I'm serious. Yeah, I'm tough, but you have me built up in your mind like some superhuman hero. I'm stronger'n some, but I'm still just a seventeen year old worried about...the future. I feel real close to you, Travis...so I figured we could talk. Be honest about some stuff. As long as you won't make fun of me."

"I won't, Mike. I promise. What—what are you afraid of?"

"Hell, all sorts of crap. That's one of the reasons I act so tough, to hide how scared I am. I think lots of guys do that."

"Yeah," said Travis quietly. "I think you're right. I know I do."

"Yeah? So what are *you* afraid of? You're better at words'n me. Maybe listening to you will help me talk about my own stuff. Would you go first? Please?"

"Sure, Mike." Travis took his boyfriend's hand. "I'm afraid of...so much. So much. You promise *you* won't make fun of *me*?"

"I swear it, Cubbie."

"Hand here that jar."

Mike passed Travis the 'shine. Travis took a gulp, sat back, and sighed. "I'm afraid of losing you. I'm afraid when I go to college, we'll lose what we have and never get it back."

"I'm afraid of that too," Mike muttered. "Real, real bad."

"Yeah? It helps to know that. That we're in that fear together."

"Oh, yeah. *Oh*, yeah. We are. And it does help."

"I'm afraid you'll stop wanting me. That you'll get together with Randy again. Or take the easy way out and marry some girl."

"I've told you—"

"Yep. You have. Be quiet, please. You asked, so I'm telling you, okay?"

"Okay. I won't interrupt again. Go on."

Travis stood up and strode over to the fireplace. For a few seconds, he stared into the flames.

"I'm afraid there's no way either you or I can stay in this county, with assholes like Brent around, eager to make our lives a living hell. I want to be honest about who I am, and I can't be honest here. But I love my family. I love the farm. I love the mountains. I'm afraid if I leave, I'll be miserable. Nanny always told me that homesickness is the worst pain there is. I'm afraid I'll get to the city, to college, and I won't be happy. I'm afraid I'll finally get to experience gay life but won't be able to fit in. I'm afraid I'll be too fat, too country, that people will make fun of me. I'm afraid if you stop wanting me, I'll be alone forever."

"Travis—"

"You said you wouldn't interrupt."

"Yeah, I did. Sorry. Please go on."

Kneeling, Travis broke up embers with a poker. "I'm afraid that my family will be horrified if I come out. Nanny's so religious. It'd probably kill Mommy. And Daddy might believe that my manhood's...false. A sham. Hell, they might disown me. I don't think they would, but anything's possible. And if I don't lose them like that...there's disease. Or old age. Nanny's getting old."

Travis stood, replaced the poker, and began to pace. "Shit, shit, shit. Have you had enough? There's more if you want it."

"Yeah. If you want. Go on." Mike rubbed his forehead, then propped his elbows on his knees and his chin in his hands.

"I'm afraid I'll never be the man I want to be. I'm afraid I'll never be as strong as you. Most of all... Dammit!" Travis grabbed a stick of kindling, broke it in half over his knee, and lobbed the pieces against the wall. "I hate it. I hate it!"

Mike stood. "Travis, calm down. What do you hate?"

Teeth gritted, Travis stared at Mike's bruised face. "Those fuckers. Goddamn it. Goddamn them!" Turning, Travis swung his fist at the wall.

"Stop it!" Mike shouted, seizing Travis before he could punch the wood. "You'll break your hand! Calm down, buddy. You're acting like a crazy man."

"Yeah, I am." Travis wrenched free from Mike's grasp and sat heavily on the couch. Again he stared into the fire. "What I hate most...what I'm the most afraid of..."

"Yeah?" Mike sat by Travis, squeezing his knee.

"Look, I know you think I talk about books too much...but...in *The Iliad*, there's this great warrior, Hector, and he fights for ten years to protect his people, the Trojans, but finally he's killed in battle, 'cause his foe Achilles is too powerful, and then the Greeks get into the citadel, and his city falls...'cause Hector wasn't strong enough to survive and save them."

Travis shook his head. "What a fucking nightmare. That story makes me want to fucking puke."

"So what are you...what does that have to do—?"

"Helplessness, Mike. The thing I fear most is my own helplessness. I couldn't protect you today. I can't protect anyone. I'm only seventeen. What can I do? I have no power. I have no money. I have no fucking influence. The thing that terrifies me the most is the thought that...I'll fail the folks I love. Especially you. That I won't be strong enough to save you. From danger. From assholes like Vass and Holt. And how will I be able to live my life after that? Knowing I failed you and you suffered because I wasn't man enough?"

"God, Travis. God." Mike wrapped an arm around Travis and hugged him. "No one's that strong. No one can be everywhere at once, and no one can win every fight. We're all just human beings. We all fail sooner or later. You think I've won all my fights?"

"Probably."

"Think again. For a guy who's so smart about some stuff...well, you're just not being realistic about these things. You can't protect everybody all the time."

"I hate being human." Travis cupped his face in his hands. "Being weak and fallible. I think that's why I'm so fascinated by power. Witchcraft and magic. And superheroes. And...bondage. I want to be powerful. I want to be in control."

"All that makes sense, buddy. Look, here in a little bit, I'm going to give you...power over me. Okay? Will that make you feel better?"

Travis lifted his head and gave Mike a weak smile. "Yep. I'm pretty sure it will."

"Good. So...my turn." Mike sighed. "You ready?"

"Yep."

Mike leaned against Travis. "Well, this is gonna be shorter...'cause you've already said a lot of what I was gonna say. You leaving me behind...you meeting really cool guys, smart guys you can relate to, guys you can talk to about things like poetry and books...that's about at the top of my list. Me staying here, losing you, having to hide how miserable I'll feel without you...ending up like Buck, drinking too much, smoking too much, a bitter old bastard always snarling about something."

Mike took another sip of 'shine. "Yeah, I do like this stuff too much." Rather than putting the jar down, he took yet another sip. "Like you, I'm afraid one of these days—some lonely, drunken night at some redneck roadhouse—I'll get together with some chick—most girls really like me, so it'd be easy to use 'em the way I did Brent's sister. I'd just be fucking her 'cause I'm horny, but I'd knock her up like I did Rachel, and I'd end up stuck in a trailer with her and a bunch of brats and all of us learning to hate each other... And working in the garage the rest of my life—no money to speak of, cutting corners. Or working construction, breaking my body down a little bit more year after year like so many ole guys in this town. Ending up a goddamn hopeless wreck, drinking rotgut at three in the morning some winter night and staring at the gun rack and wishing I had the guts to just end it."

"Damn, Mike. Really?"

"Travis, buddy, you may be a farm boy, but your family has some money, some property, some education. Most of the rest of us in this county...there's not much to choose from. There's just about no way out." Mike shook his head and stood. "Okay, no more 'shine and no more depressing talk. Let's get to that cake. Might help me sober up some."

I'm glad we talked," Travis said, stroking Mike's cheek. "And I'm sorry I got so angry."

"You got a fiery temper, all right." Mike chuckled. "Glad you didn't break anything more than some kindling. For a bookworm, you can get pretty fierce. I'm glad we talked too. It makes me feel closer to you."

Dessert was done, the liquor put away. The boys sat on the fire-lit couch, sunk in the luxury of being together. Both drained by their earlier confessions, they snuggled and kissed. Soon enough libido shifted the atmosphere from fear of the future to pleasure in the present, and the boys were making out in earnest.

"Am I hurting your mouth?" Travis asked, sitting back to take a breath.

"A little. No worries. You're such a great kisser that it's worth the hurt," Mike said, unbuttoning Travis's flannel shirt. "Wish you'd brought your guitar. I love it when you fingerpick that thing and sing for me."

"I'm just your redneck troubadour," Travis said, slipping a hand under Mike's sweatshirt and teasing a nipple. "Could have played you 'Auld Lang Syne.' But I'd rather use my fingers in other ways tonight."

"Fine with me. That feels good. A little harder. Uh." Reaching down, Mike unzipped Travis's jeans before kissing him again.

A few more minutes of heavy petting, and Travis pulled away. "Lord, you have me het up. I'm about to drag you into the bedroom."

"And tie me up? And rape me?"

"Ohhh, yeah. I've been dreaming for years about doing that. I sure hope you like it. The kinky stuff."

"I 'spect I will. Though I may not like it as much as you. Can't imagine anyone liking it as much as you." Mike squeezed Travis's hard-on through his underwear. "You're stiff as a board, horse dick. I could drive nails with this thing."

"Y-yeah." Travis stammered, blushing. "I'm, uh, pretty excited."

"Eager beaver. I'm up for most anything. All that stuff you mentioned in that scene you wrote are fine with me. Just take it easy at first. Don't get too rough. And promise to let me loose if I freak out. Though I probably won't."

"I promise. You can trust me. I'd never hurt you, Mike."

"Unless I wanted you to, right?" Mike winked, kneading Travis's crotch harder. "Mr. *Drummer*."

"Uh..."

"I'm teasing you again. I know I can trust you. And you can trust me, in case you wanna bottom sometime. I think it'd be hot to ride you. You'd be my first that way."

"Maybe. I want to try everything with you, Mike. I love 'how easy it is to be with you,' as that Carly Simon song says. You know, before we got to know one another," Travis said, nibbling Mike's earlobe, "I had this silent monologue going on in my head all the time."

"I think lots of folks have that going. I sure do."

"Guess you're right. Has something to do with the contrast between the way we really are and the way we try to appear. But with you, I don't have to be someone else. That's such a gift."

"I'll give you a gift, lover," Mike said. He dropped to his knees in front of Travis and pulled out his friend's cock. "Time to have me a little appetizer."

Travis lay back and closed his eyes. He stroked Mike's hair, savoring the sensations for long, sweet minutes. Finally, he pushed Mike away.

"Wuhhff. You got me close."

"Don't take long with you. 'Rocket man,' as Elton John sings it." Mike wiped saliva from his beard.

"My jaw's numb. Is this what drunk is?" Grinning dazedly, Travis rubbed his temples and chin, then pulled his ponytail free. "I'm all turned on, but I'm tired at the same time. Kind of dizzy."

"That's drunk, all right. I've corrupted you, Cubbie. We both had a little too much. How about a shower? I didn't get to clean up when I left off at the garage."

"I can tell," said Travis. "I love how you smell."

"Well, I don't. And I still got grease under my fingernails. Come on."

Unsteady Mike helped unsteady Travis to his feet. Travis closed up the fire before following Mike into the bathroom. When Mike peeled off his T-shirt, Travis gasped.

"Oh, no. You're so bruised up." Travis ran a hand over Mike's black-and-blue side. "Oh, those bastards."

"I'm all right, Cubbie. Stop fussing over me, and don't start up again. Come on now," Mike said, tugging at Travis's shirt. "Get naked for me. Let's shower off and get me cleaned out. We got some leather lovin' to try."

Mike sat on the edge of the bed, still and silent, while Travis, his fingers trembling faintly, first tied his friend's hands behind his back, then bound his ankles together. On a bedside table, a couple of candles flickered.

"There," said Travis, finishing the last knot. "How's that feel?"

"Fine. Just fine."

"Not too tight?"

Mike shook his head.

"Can you get loose?"

Mike twisted his wrists and flexed his arms. "Don't think so."

"Good." Heart pounding, Travis sat beside Mike. He wrapped an arm around him. "You like this?"

Mike nodded toward Travis's crotch. "Sure do. I like it 'cause you like it."

"Oh, man, do I like it," Travis sighed, running a hand over Mike's densely furred torso. "You're so beautiful like this. You're like some kidnapped cowboy. Some captive forest god. Some dream come true. You're not frightened, are you?"

In answer, Mike leaned against Travis and nuzzled his beard. "No. I'm happy. I'm safe. 'Cause I'm with you, big guy. Go on now. Go for it. Do whatever you want."

"O-o-okay. Just, just stretch out now so I can taste you."

For a good fifteen minutes, Travis made love to Mike with his mouth and hands while Mike sighed and smiled, bucked and whimpered. Pausing, Travis pulled out the bandana he'd hidden beneath a pillow. He gazed into Mike's eyes, asking a silent question.

"Sure," Mike said. "Not too tight. My mouth still hurts."

Travis loosely tied the bandana between Mike's teeth. "Okay?"

Mike bit down on the cloth and nodded.

"Oh, God, you're so hot," Travis panted before recommencing his adorations with added fervor. Soon Mike was gasping, his tensed thighs shaking.

"Close?" Travis slid off Mike.

"Uh huh. Uh huh."

"I need inside you so, so bad," Travis whispered, stroking Mike's lean hip. "You ready for that? Want to get fucked? Please? Please?"

Nodding, Mike rolled onto his side. He stared up at Travis, his brown eyes wild with need, his white teeth champing the cloth. "Hell, yes. Hell, yes," he moaned, cocking his butt and bowing his head.

Travis, throat tight with gratitude, with shaking hands reached for the lube.

The lovers, both of them drowsy and spent, lay together beneath the covers, still panting, heartbeats slowing after their ecstatic exertions. Travis spooned Mike from behind. Mike, still bound and gagged, cuddled contentedly against Travis, his sweaty back nestled against Travis's sweaty chest.

"I love you." It was out of Travis's mouth before he knew it. "I love you, Mike."

Mike lifted his head and mumbled four muffled words. Despite the bandana, they were intelligible.

Travis couldn't believe his ears. "What?" He fumbled with the bandana's knot, loosened it, and pulled the moist fabric from Mike's wounded mouth.

Mike licked his lips and smiled. "I love you too."

"I...uh. Really?" Travis's voice cracked. "You do?"

"I do, farm boy, I do. You gonna let me loose?"

"Uh, sure." More rapid fumbling with knots, and Mike was free.

"Thanks," Mike said, massaging his wrists. "Was getting a little stiff there." He rolled over, pressing his face into Travis's chest hair and resting an arm on Travis's flank. "Love you a lot," Mike mumbled. "Thought you knew."

Travis was too stunned to speak. Instead he swallowed hard and stroked Mike's hair. Mike stretched and sighed. Soon he began to snore.

Travis lay there for a long time, feeling the greatest bliss he'd ever known. Finally, he rose, used the restroom, blew out the candles, climbed back into bed, wrapped his beloved in his arms, and fell into a deep sleep.

CHAPTER THIRTEEN

Furious after sixth-period Social Studies, Travis stalked down the hall to his locker. When he opened it, his brow furrowed. Someone had slipped a small red envelope inside. *Travis* was written across the envelope in familiar handwriting. He tore it open, smiling. On the cover of the card was a red bear sporting curved horns and bearing a pitchfork. Inside were printed the words *For My Little Devil. Happy Valentine's Day!* Beneath that was Mike's sloppy scrawl.

> *Working at the garage this afternoon.*
> *Get on down here. Got something for you.*
> *Love you,*
>
> Mike

"*Damn*, I'm crazy about you," Travis muttered, slipping the card back into its envelope, his mood much improved.

"What you got there?"

Travis jumped, startled. Anita was at his elbow, squinting at the envelope. Hastily, he stuffed it into his jeans pocket.

"Secret admirer, huh? Lucky boy."

"Just a joke card," Travis said, slipping a textbook into his backpack.

"At least you got one. I never get any. So why'd you leave Mr. Bennett's class in such a huff?"

Was I that obvious? Shit. "Huff? No huff. Just a lot on my mind. I better scoot. I'm walking down to the West End to lift with Mike again."

"Why do you get to spend so much time with one of the best-looking boys in Hinton High, and I don't?"

"Because you don't lift weights?"

Anita made a snarly face. "Smartass. Tell Mike I said hi. See you later. I've got to catch my bus."

Mike was dressed in mechanic's coveralls and bent over a car engine when Travis entered the warm, smelly space.

"Hey," said Travis, scanning the garage. To his relief, they appeared to be alone.

Mike looked up, his solemn face brightening when he saw Travis. Oil smudged his right cheek and the front of his garment. "Hey. You're here."

"I got your note."

"Good. Buck's not around, so I can take a short break. Gotta get back to it soon, though. Lemme wash my hands first."

Travis watched through the open door of the bathroom while Mike scrubbed his hands and tried to get the oil off his face, with only partial success. "You're sure we're alone?" Travis asked.

"Yep."

"You got any clothes on underneath those coveralls?"

"Yeah. Sorry to fall short of fantasy. It's February."

"Too bad." Travis gave Mike a bawdy grin. "I want to kiss you so bad. If I had my way, I'd lock us in the bathroom and have my way with you right now. It *is* Valentine's Day."

"Da-yum. You've become one bold bastard." Mike shook his head with mock amazement. "No way, Redneck Rapist. Buck'll be back soon. He's been especially obnoxious lately, ranting and raving, cursing the towel-heads, as he calls 'em. Patriotic zeal, I guess." Mike rubbed at his cheek a final time, then toweled his hands dry. "Can't say I blame him. That Saddam's a real son of a bitch. Can you believe all that shit that's going down in Iraq?"

"It's sounding pretty dire. I don't like to think about it. Yesterday, our bombers killed four hundred and eight civilians. We were talking about it in Social Studies. Oh, and speaking of Social Studies, Mr. Bennett said something before class that really pissed me off."

"Mr. Bennett? Dumbest assistant coach in West Virginia history? What did he say?"

"Ella had her Elton John T-shirt on, and Mr. Bennett asked her why she had a faggot on her shirt. He makes me sick. He's the kind of person who makes it impossible to come out in this town."

Mike's lips curled. He made a fist with his right hand and tapped his left palm. "Prick. Consider the source. He's dumb as a pile of horse biscuits and useless as tits on a boar-hog. Plus the man looks like a chipmunk in heat. Forget him. It's Valentine's Day, Cubbie, and I'm really glad to see you. I didn't know if you'd be able to come by, since you had your bus to catch."

"The timing was perfect. Nanny's at the beauty parlor down the street. I'm riding home with her. So, your note said you had something for me?"

"Yeah. And I better give 'em to you quick, before ole Bucky gets back." Mike fetched his gym bag from a corner and pulled out a prettily wrapped box. "Unlike you, farm boy, I *can* wrap a gift nice. Happy Valentine's Day."

"Hooray!" Travis tore off the wrapping and opened the box. "Good lord, *The Leatherman's Handbook*? Where'd you find this?"

"Where do you think? When I wrote Eddie that I was dating a cub who loved *Drummer* and *BEAR*, not only did he send the latest issues, he sent that book too. He found it in a used bookshop in Frisco. I skimmed through it. You're gonna love it."

"And what's this?" Travis held up a short piece of black leather a couple of inches wide. It had a snap at one end.

"It's a wristband," Mike said, snapping it around Travis's right wrist. "Thought when you wore it, it'd make you think of me."

"I think about you all the time anyway, but thanks. And I have a few little things for you," Travis said, pulling off his backpack and opening it. "I wanted to bring you a dozen roses, but they're super expensive and—"

"And what would people say? What would I tell Buck? That some Third Avenue whore was wooing me? Considering my reputation as a pussyhound, he'd probably believe it. No roses. Good call."

"Instead I got you this," said Travis, handing Mike a small box of Whitman chocolates. "And this," he added, dangling a black jockstrap. "I asked Brenda to find one for me in Morgantown. You're going to look mighty sexy in it, especially tied belly down to a bed with your scrumptious butt up in the air. I can't wait till we can arrange another night together."

"Cute," Mike said, taking the jock. "How about I wear this for a few days in a row, get it all smelly, and then you peel it off me and stuff it in my mouth before you fuck me?" Giving Travis one of his maddening trademark winks, he hid the jock and the chocolates in his gym bag. "That sound good to you?"

"Hell, yes. *Hell*, yes." Travis made a show of licking his lips.

"Figured you'd like that. I know you pretty well, farm boy."

"Yes, you do. Oh, God, you're just so damn hot." Travis looked over his shoulder. "You're *sure* we're alone?"

"Yeah, but..."

Travis grabbed Mike's hand and pulled him toward the bathroom. "Come on. Please? I just want to kiss on you some. Feel your nipples. Get a finger up inside you."

Mike resisted. "Travis, no."

"Please, Mike. I want you so bad. I've been aching every night to touch you. It's been so long. Weeks and weeks."

"Travis..."

Travis dragged Mike into the dark bathroom and shut the door behind them. He shoved Mike against the wall and kissed him hard, kneading his pecs and buttocks through his clothes.

"Travis, dammit," Mike muttered against his boyfriend's probing tongue.

Travis unzipped Mike's coveralls. "You're so beautiful. You're so beautiful," he panted, his hand ranging over Mike's T-shirt, pinching his nipples. "I just wanna bend you over the sink and give it to you *so* hard."

"Travis, stop," Mike pleaded. When he tried to pull away, Travis seized his wrists and forced them behind him.

"Yeah, yeah. Fight me," Travis growled, rubbing his erection against Mike's thigh. "You know how much I like that."

"Travis, I don't think—"

"Mike!" a distant voice yelled. "Where are you? Get in here. This lady needs an oil change pronto."

"Oh, no," Travis gasped. "It's your father."

"Fuck," Mike muttered beneath his breath. "I *told* you. Dammit, Travis. *Dammit.* You *got* to learn to control yourself. Your dick makes you so damn *dumb* sometimes."

Mike zipped up his coveralls. "You hide in here for a few minutes. Then use the side door and get outta here fast. I'll keep Buck distracted till you're gone."

"Mike!" Buck's voice resounded again, somewhere closer.

Travis cringed. *He'll kill us if he catches us.*

Mike slipped out the bathroom door and shut it behind him. "I was in the bathroom," Mike yelled. "Be right there."

Cursing himself, heart pounding, hands trembling, Travis did as he was told, waiting in the dark as voices receded toward the office. When silence in the garage told him that the coast was clear, he slipped out of the bathroom, snatched up his new book, and slid it into his backpack. Hunkered down, he sped for the exit as fast as he could.

CHAPTER FOURTEEN

Travis, wearing olive-drab pants and a pale green sweater for St. Patrick's Day, stood under the porch-roof of the gym, looking out into misty rain. Mike was washing up inside, he knew, and he took pleasure in picturing that sight, even if he couldn't join Mike in the shower the way he ached to. When Travis's belly growled, his thoughts shifted from Mike's wet nakedness to the meal awaiting them that Sunday evening: corned beef cooked for hours with cabbage, turnips, carrots, and potatoes, plus a cast-iron skillet of Nanny's yellow cornbread on the side, hot from the oven and ready to be slathered with butter and sorghum.

Tonight we get to sleep together, Travis thought with anticipation and relief. *It's been far too long.* Mike's old truck had been giving him fits for weeks, breaking down regularly, so Mike hadn't been able to spend any nights at Forest Hill, and that irked Travis considerably. Other than that frightening time in the garage bathroom—when Buck almost caught them together—and a few hurried and nervous gropings in Mike's bedroom after school—both of them craning for the dreaded sound of Buck's arrival—they hadn't been able to steal much time together since that cherished night at Bluestone. But that day, at least, the truck was running, so Mike was going to drive Travis home, stay over, and get them both to school the next morning.

Once the weather warms up, by God, I'm going to hike Mike's ass up to the barn, and I'm going to have him right there in the loft...dusty hay, prickly straw, and mud daubers be damned. Travis grinned, imagining Mike buck naked and bent over a bale. *Well, at least we'll be able to be together to-night, even if it's only cuddling. I'll settle for holding him in my arms. Wonder what kind of pie Nanny's making for dessert?*

A flashy Jeep was heading up Temple Street, its bass thumping. The racket annoyed Travis. He was more than annoyed when he recognized the driver. It was Brent Vass, with some companion Travis didn't recognize. As Vass drove past, Travis looked him straight in the eye and gave him the finger.

Vass's Jeep screeched to a halt. He backed up and pulled over in front of the gym. He got out.

Oh, hell, thought Travis, trying to look unafraid. *Here we go. Guess I asked for that.*

"Ferrell, you faggot. Did you just give me the finger?"

For a second, Travis felt a deep fright, but then he remembered the bruises he'd seen on Mike's face and ribs, and then he thought of those months lifting weights and working the punching bag and what that discipline had done to his body and mind.

Travis clenched his fists and stepped down onto the sidewalk. "You're damn right I did."

"I'm going to kick your ass," Brent snarled, moving closer. "Just like I did last fall."

"You think so? I kind of doubt it." Travis cleared his throat and lowered his voice. "I'm a little bigger now. And Mike's been teaching me how to fight. So you'd better think twice."

Making a show of flexing his arms, Travis moved into the boxing position that Mike had taught him. To his relief, his fear was fading, replaced by a hot surge of anger.

"I heard what you and Jack Holt did to Mike," Travis growled. "Two on one? Cowards. Damn jackals. You get any nearer, and I'll take you down, I swear to God."

Brent hesitated. "Hey, Shorty. Get over here," he yelled to the boy in the Jeep.

The guy got out. He was squat, thickly built, and ugly looking, with a Thundering Herd sweatshirt on. He ambled over, stood beside Brent, and gave Travis a threatening smile.

"This is my cousin from Huntington. Travis, Shorty. Shorty, Travis. Travis is poor white trash from the country. Plus he's a faggot."

Shorty's mouth twisted. He spat on the street. "Hate those. I got your back, cuz. What're you waiting for?"

Brent looked up and down the street. "Good question."

Moving closer still, Brent swung. Travis dodged. Brent jabbed again, and Travis parried with his left forearm.

"Goddamn you, keep still," Brent cursed, swinging a third time. Travis parried again, and then, to his own amazement, he punched Brent in the jaw.

"Holy hell!" Brent staggered back, holding his face.

"He's a faggot?" Shorty snarled. "You can't beat a faggot? Jesus. Let me do it." He lunged forward. His first blow, aimed low, Travis was able to parry, but the second caught Travis in the mouth. Pain shot through his head, and he stumbled backward. Brent grabbed him from behind, and Shorty punched him in the belly.

"Goddamn you," Travis gasped, fighting to get free.

Shorty grinned. "We're gonna tear you up, fairy boy." He balled up his fist, preparing to punch Travis in the face a second time.

"Hey!" Mike shouted from the porch. He was on Shorty in an instant, tackling him and knocking him to the sidewalk. The two boys rolled about, cursing. Shorty elbowed Mike in the mouth, and Mike punched Shorty in the side. Travis slipped out of Brent's grasp, spun around, and hit him in the right eye.

"What the fuck's going on here?" Buck, clad in coveralls, burst from the garage. In his hands he brandished a baseball bat. "Get out of here, you little fuckers!"

"Oh, shit," Brent said, bolting for his Jeep.

"Oh, damn," Shorty said, scrambling up from the sidewalk.

In less than thirty seconds, Brent's red Jeep, still blaring music, had disappeared down Temple Street. Buck lowered the baseball bat and spat out a wad of tobacco. "Who were those guys?"

"Assholes. Thanks, Buck," Mike said, rubbing another split lip.

"Thanks, Mr. Woodson," Travis said, rubbing another split lip.

"Why'd they go after you? Who started it?"

"I, uh—." Mike stepped forward. "I did."

Travis shook his head. "No, he didn't. I did, sir." He tried to meet Buck's gaze but couldn't.

"You?" Buck looked Travis up and down. "You?"

"Yes, sir. I gave one of them the finger."

"*Really?*" Buck emitted a hoarse laugh. He spat onto the pavement. "Well, I'll be damned. I thought you were a bookworm, not a brawler."

"I am, sir. But I guess your son's taught me a few things." Travis tried to smile, but it hurt too much.

"Guess so." Buck laughed again. "Well, good for you. Both your mouths are bleeding. There's some paper towels in the bathroom. Get in there and clean yourselves up. I got better things to do than deal with this kinda crap." Shaking his head, Buck headed back into the garage.

66 **A**nother fight?" Nanny gasped as soon as Mike and Travis entered the fragrant kitchen.

"Yes, ma'am." Travis hung his head.

"Oh, honey. Let me see."

For several minutes, Nanny fussed over the boys, applying peroxide and anxiety. "Why do you keep getting into brawls, son? It's that Irish blood. Courting and fighting, that's what the Ferrell men do. Next thing I know you'll be drinking. Your grandfather loved that nasty Irish whiskey."

Mike and Travis exchanged an amused look. "I guess we were just celebrating St. Patrick's Day," Travis joked.

"I can think of better ways to do that."

"Green beer?" Travis snickered, rubbing his sore abdomen.

"No. Corned beef and cabbage. How'd you get so wild?" Nanny adjusted her hairdo and reached for a cigarette. "Now go on out and check the mailbox. I forgot to yesterday. And take the trash out. Then y'all can go on in and watch TV while I start the cornbread."

"Yes, ma'am. But first..." Travis lifted the lid of the pot on the stove. He and Mike both peeked at the steaming contents and licked their lips.

"Yum. Looks good," Travis enthused. "It's gonna hurt to eat, but I don't care. What's for dessert?"

"Pie," Nanny replied, removing buttermilk from the fridge.

Mike rubbed his hands together. "What kind, ma'am?"

"You teenage boys and your appetites. Butterscotch cream."

"Praise the Lord. One of my favorites," Travis said.

"Don't take the Lord's name in vain, son. Now get on. We'll have dinner after the news. I'm so glad that awful war is done."

Letter from Brenda," Travis said, shaking out his ponytail before tearing the envelope open.

The boys, stuffed after another big meal, sprawled together in sweatpants and T-shirts on Travis's bed. On the radio, Dolly Parton quavered through "I Will Always Love You."

"Love that song. When you gonna read me some of your poems?" Mike stretched out, hands behind his head.

"Never, if you don't stop asking," Travis said, unfolding the letter and skimming it. "Sounds like Brenda and Bill are still having problems."

Frowning, Travis read the letter more carefully, then put it on his desk. "I worry about them. Well, nothing I can do about it tonight. Ready for bed, Studly?"

Mike nodded. They stripped to their underwear.

"The black briefs I got you," Travis exclaimed.

"Yep," said Mike, hands on his lean hips. "I wear 'em all the time. Reminds me of a certain tall, handsome Cubbie and how sweet he treats me."

"And so I shall," said Travis, turning off the radio and bedside lamp before pulling back the blankets and climbing into bed. "Git in here, fur-face. I want to hold you hard."

"Roll over, sad eyes," demanded Mike. "This time *I* spoon *you*."

"I'd like that," Travis sighed, acquiescing.

For a long time, the two boys cuddled without words, Travis clutching Mike's hand and Mike stroking Travis's thick hair.

"What if they break up? If they can't make it, who can?" Travis muttered. "They're so much in love. Like I'm in love with you." Lifting Mike's hand, Travis kissed the back of it. "They're the ideal love, like you're the ideal man."

"Ideal? Oh, Lord. Things happen, Travis. We've talked about this before. Those ideals of yours...you gotta learn to focus on the real, not the ideal. Relationships ain't always what they look like from the outside. I know that from watching my parents. Before Mom got sick, she almost left ole Bucky twice. He was mad about her, but he didn't treat her real well half the time. He was crazy-jealous of other guys. Used to accuse her of having an affair with a neighbor of ours, then a mechanic in the garage, then even the postman. He even hit her once. I saw him do it. I also saw her take a skillet to his head right after, so I don't think he ever hit her again." Mike sniggered. "Got more'n he bargained for that time. Anyway, love's complicated, big guy. Life's complicated. And not always fair. And a helluva lot harder than it ought to be half the time."

"It shouldn't be complicated. It should be simple. I know one thing that's simple and true."

"Yeah? And what's that?"

"The way I feel about you. Like Dolly said, I will always love you."

"I hope you will, Travis. But you gotta remember that other song you sing me sometimes, that Joni Mitchell tune. Something about blazes burning down to ash."

"We won't be like that."

"Maybe not. I hope not. Who knows? Maybe it's the intensity of the heat that matters, not the duration of the fire." Mike ran his fingers through Travis's chest hair. "God knows we got the heat. I bet some folks never find this. Poor bastards."

"We're lucky, that's for sure. Mike?"

"Yep?"

"I really wish I could make love to you tonight. I've been fantasizing about...I'd like to tie you down and tape your mouth and lick you all over."

"Tape? Sounds hot. Sounds like one of those stories in *Drummer*. But I can hear a 'but' coming."

"But I'm kinda sad 'cause of Brenda's letter, and Nanny..."

"I know, big guy. I know. Shhhh. Just snuggling is wonderful."

"Yeah, it is. Thanks for saving my butt today. They would have clobbered me."

"Glad to be there. You were great. You've come a long way since last fall. How many times did you punch Brent?"

"Twice. I can't believe I did it. It felt good. Real good."

"I'll bet it did. My big butch warrior." Mike squeezed Travis's meaty chest.

"Rraawwrrr!" Travis giggled. "I'm your berserker."

"Huh?"

"That was a kind of Norseman who went crazy in battle and acted like a wild animal, a wolf or bear."

"My were-bear. Love it. How's your mouth and belly?"

"Sore. You?"

"Sore," Mike admitted.

"Think we'll get into any trouble? Last I heard, Brent's father was on the town council."

"Maybe. Probably not. If I know Brent, he wouldn't want folks to know that he'd gotten whipped by a faggot."

"I didn't exactly whip him."

"You did well enough." Mike rubbed Travis's belly, then probed his navel.

"No tickling." Travis tensed. "Hey, do you have any idea when you might get your truck fixed?"

"Hell, I don't know. Why?"

"I think...some weekend...could we go to Morgantown? I want to see Bill and Brenda, find out what's going on. I'd love for you to meet them. And I could check out the school while we're there. I still have some extra money from all that farm work I did last summer for the Pences and the Springstons, so I could pay for the gas."

"Sure, Cubbie. Maybe in a few weeks. Once I get the old girl running good again. Now get some sleep. We got to get up early tomorrow. I got Shop first period. Ungodly early. God, I can't wait to graduate."

"Me too. Except..."

"Right. Except a few months after that, you leave for college."

"Yeah." Travis kissed the back of Mike's hand again. "I don't think I can live without you."

"You're such a romantic, Travis. Of course you can."

"Well, I don't want to. Come with me. Why stay here?"

"I'm not the college type. But we'll see. We got nearly six months to think on it." Mike gave Travis's butt a soft slap. "Now shut up, berserker, and get some sleep."

CHAPTER FIFTEEN

"Damn chilly for mid-April," Mike groused, rolling up his window as they approached Morgantown on I-79. He was wearing the outfit Travis most loved to see him in: jeans, cowboy boots, tight black T-shirt, and faded Levi's jacket. Travis had on jeans and cowboy boots too, with his black leather vest over a tan button-down shirt, the leather band Mike gave him for Valentine's Day around his right wrist.

"Chilly means good cuddle-weather," said Travis, patting Mike's thigh. "Sorry we had to get up at the crack of dawn."

"Your grandmother's biscuits and gravy made the early hour worth it. And those pimiento cheese sandwiches she packed were pretty damn good too." Mike checked his wristwatch. "Nearly one. We woulda got here a lot sooner if the damn engine hadn't heated up and we hadn't had to pull over so many times. I don't know what's wrong with the stupid thing. I thought I had it fixed."

"Doesn't matter. We're here now." Travis's right leg bounced excitedly. "Wonder what the campus will look like?"

"What's that thing? It looks like a giant clam." Mike pointed to the top of a distant hill to the right of the interstate. "Or a UFO."

"The Coliseum. That's the basketball arena. That's where Bill took her karate classes."

A few miles later, Mike took the Star City exit. They drove over the Monongahela River, up the hill, and turned left near the Coliseum into the Evansdale Campus. "That's the Creative Arts Center," said Travis, scanning the map in his lap and nodding to his right.

"Looks like a big toilet to me. How much farther?"

"Not far," said Travis, after consulting the directions Bill sent him. "You turn right up there, near those towers, and that'll take us into the Downtown Campus and to Bill's dorm."

One thirty on a Saturday afternoon, and the Arnold Hall cafeteria was nearly empty. Bill, a solidly built young woman with short ash-blonde hair, was dressed in an apron and clearing a table at the room's far end when Travis and Mike walked in.

"Hey! We're here." Travis shouted, loping toward her.

"My God, you've gotten so big." Bill grabbed him and they hugged each other hard.

Travis stepped back, poked his belly, and made a face. "I haven't gained that much weight."

"Not that kind of big. Muscle-big. You're looking tough in that vest. I'm so glad you could come." Bill turned to Mike and extended a hand. "And you must be his weight-trainer."

They shook. "Yep," said Mike. "He's come quite a long way."

"I can tell. Glad to meet you, Mike. Travis has told me lots about you. I hope y'all enjoyed that book."

It was the first time Travis had ever seen Mike blush. "Yeah, we did. Uh, thanks." He grinned and shuffled. "Kind of you to send it."

"You bet. So I'm about done here," Bill said, removing her apron. "If you two can wait out in the lobby for a few minutes, I'll be right out. There are some things I need to tell you."

Something in the tone of Bill's voice made Travis worry. "Uh, okay."

The boys found a lounge area down the hall. It was empty of students, except for a girl at the far end who was bent over a book. Long diaphanous curtains billowed and waved in the breeze pouring in through window screens. The boys sat side by side on a couch.

"Something's up," Travis said, his brow furrowed up. "I've known Bill for years. I can tell."

"You worry too much, bud. What would you do without something to worry about?" Mike grinned. "Always wanting the weight of the world on your shoulders."

"Atlas."

"Huh?"

"Forget it. So maybe we'll go to the gay bar tonight. It'll be our first. I wonder if...oh, here she comes."

Bill strode toward them. Studying her serious expression, Travis's heart sank. *Oh, no. I think I know what she wants to tell me.*

Bill sat beside Travis. "Little brother, I'm really glad you all came. It's so good to see you. But you need to know something important." She placed a hand on his shoulder. "I hate to tell you this, because I know how upset you'll be, but...Brenda and I broke up."

"Oh, no," Travis whispered. "Oh, no."

"We both think it's for the best. We've both been unhappy for a while now. Brenda's moved in with a friend off campus, Farron, a gay guy we know. I'm staying in our dorm room here in Arnold Hall."

Travis wiped the wet from his eyes. He didn't want either Mike or Bill to see him cry. "But I thought, I mean, you two loved each other so much. I saw it. What happened?"

Bill gave Travis a grim smile. "I *really* hate to tell you this."

"Let me guess," Travis said, trying to suppress the sarcastic tone he yearned to use. "Brenda said you had a butch buddy you were spending a lot of time with."

"Yes. Cin. I'm with Cin now."

Travis wanted to shout "Oh, shit. How could you?" and lob something breakable against the wall, but all of his background in good country manners prevented such a scene.

"I don't know what to say," he muttered. Resting his face in his hands, he rubbed his temples and wiped away the seep of tears. "I think I have a headache. Shit."

"Cin's upstairs in my room. I'd really like you to meet her. Would you, Travis?"

Again, manners and passion clashed inside Travis's head. *Hell, no. The bitch! She broke you up.* "Oh, man. Really?"

"It would mean a lot to me," Bill said, rising. "Please? Then we can take your stuff up to Brenda's. Y'all will be spending the night there.

Since most of us are underage and can't drink at the bar—at least not legally—she and Farron decided to throw a party at their place tonight so you guys can meet everybody."

A thin girl in a green T-shirt and blue jeans was lying on one of the two beds when Bill led Travis and Mike into her dorm room. The stranger's features were sharp, her wavy brown hair cut short. She rose as they entered.

"Hi," she said. Stepping forward, she kissed Bill on the cheek.

"This is Cin. This is my little brother, Travis, and his honey, Mike."

"H-hi," said Travis, shaking her hand but unable to meet her eyes for fear she might see the anger there. Mike, shooting Travis a concerned look, shook Cin's hand as well. "Nice to meet you," Mike murmured.

"So, uh, Cin, are you living here?" Travis moved to the window. He wanted to glare at her but his deep sense of what was polite wouldn't allow that. Instead he stared down into the street.

"Sort of. My room's just down the hall, but my roommate's a ditz, so I spend most of my time here. Bill, I'd better get on to the track. Good to meet you guys. I'll see you later tonight." Grabbing a Levi's jacket that matched Mike's, she gave Bill another quick kiss and left the room.

"Cin's on the track team, but she majors in forestry. I thought you could talk to her at the party, Travis. I know that's one of the majors you're planning on."

"Forestry, yeah."

"There's a state forest not far from here where Cin and I have done some hiking. It's called Coopers Rock. Tomorrow, how about the four of us drive up there? It's really pretty. Really popular with forestry students. There's a beautiful cliffside overlook. You can see for miles. "

"Maybe. Don't know if we'll have time," said Travis, far from eager to expend any more energy being polite to Cin. "We need to get home tomorrow night, since we have classes Monday morning. So, how long have you two..." Travis trailed off.

"We've been dating for about three weeks."

"I can't believe you left Brenda," Travis blurted. "So you don't love her anymore?" He sat heavily in a chair. Mike rested a comforting hand on his shoulder.

"Of course I love her. But not that way. Not anymore."

"But Cin's butch. I thought you liked femmes."

"Things are complicated, little brother." Bill shrugged and sighed. "I'm sorry to see you so sad. Brenda and I will both be fine. Now let's get you all up the hill. Brenda's got lunch waiting for you. You know what a good cook she is."

Brenda was more animated than Travis had ever seen her. A slender girl with curly brown hair and stylish glasses, she moved around the kitchen in her flowered sundress serving borscht and chicken-salad croissants and talking nonstop: about her absent roommate Farron, about her classes, about the men and women she was seeing, including one of her male professors. Travis ate and stared, not knowing what to think. Beneath the table, Mike rubbed Travis's thigh, as if to say, "I know you're hurting and confused. Relax. I'm here. I got you."

The old house on Willey Street was only a couple of blocks from Arnold Hall, and it had been, according to Brenda, "in the family" for years, which was to say populated by queers. Jerry and Leroy lived upstairs, and Franny had the attic apartment.

"Tonight will be fun," Brenda exclaimed. "I'm going to make spaghetti and garlic bread and salad. Franny's ordering pizza and bringing wine. Laura's bringing vegetarian chili. Farron's making a coconut cake. Leroy and Jerry already brought down the grain punch. They might even come in drag."

"Really?" Travis didn't know whether to be horrified or anticipatory. He'd never seen a drag queen before. There used to be rumors that poor Martin, whom Brent and his pack had tormented so unmercifully, had become a drag queen after he'd left Summers County, but Travis had no idea whether those stories were true. "How in God's name did you meet drag queens?"

"Well, they live upstairs, but I first met them at the bar, the Firefox," said Brenda, refilling Travis's glass of sweet tea. "They have shows there every now and then. Jerry prides himself on his resemblance to Suzanne Somers, and Leroy does a great Reba McEntire. Trust me, you'll love them."

"But...why do they want to be stereotypes and dress in women's clothes?"

"Travis, not all gay guys are like you and Mike or even want to be. Some folks *are* stereotypes. It's just the way they are. Look at Bill. She's butch. Or Jean. They're 'ferocious bull-daggers,' as my father used to call them."

"Yeah, but...I like them. I like butch." Travis patted Mike's knee.

"I'm not butch," Brenda said. "You like me."

"True. So how do I treat them? Drag queens?"

"Like ladies. You're a Southern boy. You know how to treat a woman like a lady, don't you?" Brenda took the boys' emptied plates to the sink and then started doling out lime sherbet.

"He does. Believe me, he does," said Mike. "He got 'Most Polite' in our senior class. All sorts of girls have crushes on him."

"You're crazy, Mike. When's the party?"

"It starts at seven."

"So where will we sleep?"

"We have a futon in the living room that folds out, so you boys can sleep on that tonight. Right now, let's have some sherbet, and then, if you'd help me fetch some groceries, I can show you around the town and campus afterwards."

Travis sat in the corner sipping pink punch, feeling mildly drunk and completely overwhelmed. The room was full of young people, laughing, drinking, and dancing. He couldn't believe there were so many gays and lesbians in Morgantown. He couldn't believe that Morgantown was so big and the WVU campus so sprawling and complex. Scanning the room, he tried to remember the names of all the folks to whom he'd been introduced.

Bill and Cin—much to Travis's smoldering but silent disapproval—gyrated in the middle of the room, dancing together to Stevie Nicks' "I Can't Wait." Near the door to the kitchen, Brenda, ignoring her former lover, spoke in her roommate Farron's ear. Farron was taller than Travis, with an angular, good-looking face, light brown hair, glasses, a thin frame, and very large hands. Beside them, Laura, looking somehow both elegant and athletic with her bobbed hair, fedora, and tight black dress, sipped white wine and watched the dancers. On the far side of the room, Mike leaned against the wall, holding a bottle of beer and talking to a buxom blonde girl named Martha who showed off her curves in a sexy dress. *Just my luck,* Travis thought, biting into a liquor-soaked strawberry. *He's talking to the only straight woman at the party, and a pretty one at that.*

"Way different from Hinton, huh?" Jean, with beer in hand, sat beside Travis. She had curly dark hair that framed her round face. She would have had a linebacker's build were it not for her large breasts.

"Lord, yes. I can't believe all these folks are gay."

"Believe it, darlin'. You're looking mighty cute in that vest and wristband. You're becoming a little leather stud. Where'd you get them?"

"Mike," Travis sighed. His grin was dreamy and drunken. "He's mighty good to me."

"Didn't he used to play on the Bobcats football team?"

"Yeah. He was a guard. He was real good."

"Wish I could have played. And speaking of football, how about them 'eers?" Jean said with a grimace, pointing to her blue-and-gold WVU Mountaineers jersey.

Travis grunted. "Four wins, seven losses? I watched the Syracuse game on TV. That was awful. And a female mascot? Heresy."

"Hey!" Jean nudged him in the side. "First one ever. I thought she was pretty cute."

"I much prefer the male version, thank you."

"Right up your alley, huh? A bearded guy dressed in buckskins and a coonskin cap and carrying a musket? Your new sweetie there could pull that off."

"Don't I know it." Travis took another swig of punch. "Damn, this is only my second glass, and I'm already half-drunk."

"Grain's strong. Watch yourself. Me, I'll stick to beer. Or Crown Royal when I can afford it. So you really love that guy, huh? He's pretty good-looking."

Travis took a deep breath. "God, yes. I've never been in love before, and now I'm so eaten up with it, it scares me."

Jean nodded. "I felt that way about Cathy. We were great together. Until..."

Travis scowled. "Yeah, I know. Till that slimy guidance counselor found out and told her parents. Where are they now?"

"Alaska." Jean finished her beer and rose. "Fucking Alaska."

"Pizza's here," yelled Franny from the kitchen. She was a smaller version of Jean, a short, solid girl with medium-length brown hair, ruddy cheeks, and a cheerful expression.

"Want some pizza?" Jean asked.

"Not now. That spaghetti was so good I had to have two plates of it. Had three pieces of garlic bread too. Brenda cooks as well as my grandmother does."

"Always has. I never miss an opportunity to eat here. Be sure to get a piece of Farron's cake. He can cook just as well as Brenda can. Here he comes now. I think he's been wanting to talk to you." Jean tugged on Travis's ponytail. "Hey, I know you're bummed about Bill and Brenda. I am too. You hang in there, okay? Things'll turn out all right."

"Okay. Thanks."

"I need another beer. I'm going to get some pizza, and they'd better have some with pepperoni on it. Not all us lesbians are vegetarians, damn it."

"Hey, Travis." Smiling, Farron took Laurie's seat. "You having a good time?"

"Oh, yeah, thanks." Nodding, Travis took a nervous slurp of punch. Farron's stylish clothes and classy ease thoroughly intimidated and impressed him. Travis felt like a sloppy country hick in contrast. "I really appreciate you letting Mike and me stay over tonight."

"No problem. Brenda's going to make one of her famous breakfast glops in the morning. Want to dance? I like this song."

"Don't know how to dance. Sorry," Travis admitted, sucking down another mouthful of punch. "So, Bill told me you were a painter. And Brenda said some of the paintings in here were yours. They're really cool. Sort of dark and gothic. You an art major?"

"Sculpture, actually, though I paint too. I'm going to Rome this summer as part of a Study Abroad program to study the sculpture and architecture there."

"Oh, man." Travis's eyes lit up. "I've got a Latin class right now. I'm dying to go to Rome."

"You'd love this trip then. We're going to see the Vatican, the Pantheon, many of the churches, Castel Sant'Angelo, the Baths of Caracalla, and the Colosseum, of course."

He knows more about Rome than I do. "You're so lucky. I'd love to hear about your trip sometime."

"Well, you'll be attending WVU this fall, right? Come up for dinner sometime and I'll tell you all about it. I hope to have some photos to show you."

"That'd be great. I hear you're a good cook. Like Brenda. I love to eat. You can probably tell." Travis rubbed guiltily at his midriff.

"Then you need to try my coconut cake. Want me to get you a piece?"

"Aw, naw." Travis clambered to his feet. "I'll get it, thanks. And I need more of that punch."

Music's too loud, Travis thought. He wove toward the kitchen, eyes ranging the room for Mike, who was nowhere to be seen. Bill, dancing now with both Cin and Laura, gave Travis's shoulder a friendly slap as he crossed the room. *I can't believe you left Brenda for Cin,* Travis thought. *She isn't half as pretty.*

In the kitchen, Travis replenished his drink. At Franny's urging, he gobbled two slices of pizza, then sampled a cup of Laura's vegetarian chili. He was halfway through a thick slice of Farron's delicious coconut cake and, inspired by the concept of *Carpe diem,* was contemplating a second piece when Brenda touched him on the arm.

"Hey, Travis. I'd like you to meet Bob."

Travis turned to find a guy in his mid-twenties smiling up at him. Bob was swarthy and very handsome, about Mike's height, with a black beard and moussed hair. His tight black T-shirt and black jeans showed off a compact build.

"Howdy." Travis put down his plate, and the two shook hands. *Wow, you look like Mike,* Travis thought. *You're hot.*

"Bob's a truck driver from Clarksburg. He's been wanting to meet you," Brenda said, before moving to the stove to stir the spaghetti sauce.

"I've heard loads about you, Travis. Bill and Brenda talk about you all the time."

"Yeah? Bill mentioned you in her letters. So you're Italian? I don't think I've ever met someone Italian before."

"Italian-American. My grandfather came over to work in the mines. Lots of Italian folks in Clarksburg. We even have an Italian festival every Labor Day weekend. Best pepperoni rolls you'll ever have. And Oliverio's canned peppers. Good music too. And wine."

"Pepperoni rolls? I've never had them."

"It's dough, and sometimes cheese, wrapped around pepperoni and baked. It was an easy lunch for guys to carry into the mines."

"That sounds wonderful. We don't have a lot of, uh, difference, diversity, where I'm from, down in Summers County."

"There used to be lots of Italians in southern West Virginia. We had cousins in McDowell County and Mingo. So, tell me," said Bob, plucking at Travis's vest, "you into leather?"

"Um. I-I guess so. Don't know much about it, really."

"If you're into leather, you need to go to the Eagle," Bob said, tapping his own well-defined left pec. "It's in DC."

Travis peered. On Bob's T-shirt was the small image of a big-built, bare-chested man in black leather chaps and black cap, holding a whip. Behind him, a huge eagle spread its wings.

"It's a leather bar?" Travis said.

"*Oh*, yeah. It's great. Lots of hot studs and daddies. Porn videos. Even some action in the right corners."

"Really? Like, sex in public?"

"Not exactly public. You should go if you get a chance. You'd really like it. And while you're in DC, you should hit the Leather Rack. You can buy all kinds of toys there. Dildos, handcuffs, harnesses, porn."

"Really?" Travis, feeling dizzy, pulled his ponytail free and massaged his jaw. *Farron knows more about Rome than I do, and Bob knows more about leather. I am definitely out of my league.*

"What you two talking about?" Mike appeared at Travis's elbow, smiling thinly, a plastic cup of brown liquor in his hand. His dark eyes were glassy with drink.

"Uh." Travis took a swig of punch. "Bob, this is my boyfriend, Mike. Mike, this is Bob. He was telling me about a leather bar and a leather store in DC."

"Cool," said Mike, wrapping an arm around Travis's waist. "So, Travis, wanna dance?"

"I don't know how to—"

"Yeah, yeah," said Mike impatiently, nudging Travis in the small of the back. "But I do. C'mon. Nice to meet you, Bob."

"Same to you. Travis, if you end up at WVU this fall, maybe we can check out the Italian festival in September," said Bob, reaching for a plastic plate. "Or the Buckwheat Festival. That's fun too."

In the living room, a slow song, Cyndi Lauper's "Time After Time," had come on. Bill and Cin were swaying to it. Jean, Farron, and Franny sat on the couch, sipping their drinks and chatting.

"So what you drinking?" Travis nodded at Mike's cup.

"Switched to Wild Turkey. That pink punch crap's too sweet for me."

"Where'd you go?" Travis asked. "I couldn't find you earlier."

"Back porch. Martha and I were having a smoke. Shit, I'm drunk." Mike said, pausing in the doorway. He knocked back his cup of bourbon.

"Meeee too." Travis finished his drink as well. "I love these strawberries."

"Think we've both had enough. So, Bob, he was pretty good-looking, huh?"

"Yeah, he was. He reminded me of you. Kind of a Heathcliff. Dark and brooding. How do you know how to dance?" asked Travis, as Mike grabbed his hand and led him into the middle of the room.

"Randy taught me," Mike said, wrapping his arms around Travis's waist. "Just do as I do. Arms around my waist. Good. Now, just shuffle in a circle. Good. Not too complicated, right?"

"Randy taught you? You're shitting me."

"True. Not Randy. He wasn't exactly a romantic. Though he sure could fuck. I took Rhonda Cantrell to a dance at the Armory once. She showed me."

For a few minutes, the boys swayed unsteadily together. *God, how I cherish you,* Travis thought, pulling Mike closer. In response, Mike rested his cheek against Travis's shoulder.

"This feels so good. You smell so good," Travis murmured, inhaling Mike's scent. He could detect tobacco, liquor, and fruit, and beneath that, the rich body-musk Travis so adored. "I can't believe we're doing this in front of other people."

"Does feel kind of incredible," Mike said, hooking his thumbs in Travis's belt loops. "I'm glad you're leaving Hinton and coming up here. I'm glad you'll have all these folks to look after you."

"I want you to come too. There have got to be garages up here looking for help." Travis stepped on Mike's foot and stumbled. Mike righted him.

"We'll see. I don't turn eighteen till November, remember? Don't worry, Travis. We'll work something out." Mike nuzzled Travis's beard. "Stop planning out the future and focus on tonight."

"Okay, yeah. But can you imagine? We could share an apartment like this. We could spend every night together. We could dance together all the time."

"You like this, huh? Dancing with me?"

"Lord, yes. We need to do this again. And I think we can soon. Real soon. In my room," Travis said, kissing Mike's black bangs. "Nanny's planning to visit her brother in Lewisburg in a few weeks. You want to stay over? We can celebrate Beltane together."

"What's Beltane?"

"It's the big Wiccan spring festival. It's all about love and fertility. People used to burn fires on hilltops and dance in standing stones. They used to drink and feast. They used to fuck in the greenwood. *We* should do that."

"The way you're swaying, I think you've had enough drink tonight. So, a hot date for Beltane? A fuck in the greenwood? Here I've gone and started dating a high priest of the witch cult. Damn. You gonna sacrifice me to the dark gods?"

"Yep. Tie you down to the altar and ravish you in unholy ways." Travis slapped Mike's butt once, then twice.

"Wow. How drunk are you?"

"Give it to him, baby brother," Bill yelled over the music.

"Yeah," shouted Jean. "Show that boy who's boss."

Travis looked around the room. "Oh, Lord. Everybody's watching us."

"Who cares? Do that again, sir," Mike said, cocking his rear. "Spank your bad boy, sir."

Travis obliged with a duo of hard swats. "Cock tease. You know just what to say, don't you? God, I love it when you call me 'sir.' God, I love your ass. So hard and round. And tight."

"And I love the way you use my ass. You're not a pussyhound, you're an asshound. An asshound berserker."

The Lauper song ended. Madonna's "Vogue" started thumping. Roughly, Travis pushed Mike backward into a corner.

"Easy, sir. Don't hurt me, sir," Mike said, squirming provocatively.

"You're driving me crazy, you little bastard," Travis growled, digging his fingers into Mike's denimed ass-cheeks. "One of these days, I'm going to tie you up and stuff your briefs in your mouth and take a belt to your butt, the way Daddy used to spank me. I'm going to get that furry white rump of yours all red."

"Oh, you are, are you?" Mike kissed Travis's chin and groped his crotch. "Fine by me. And then what, Mr. *Drummer*, sir?"

"Then I'm going to—"

The boys' inebriated erotic moment was shattered, when, three feet from Travis's elbow, the front door burst open with a bang. "Here we are, girls!" shrilled a large woman of Travis's height. She appeared to be in her thirties, with heavy makeup and blonde hair that puffed over her forehead and curled about her shoulders. She wore a frilly blue dress, long pink gloves, and white high heels.

"Let the royal festivities begin," she announced, striding into the room.

"Miss Jerry!" Bill hooted.

"And Miss Leroy!" Jean added, as a second woman entered. This one was younger and shorter, with voluminous dark brown hair beneath a broad-brimmed purple hat and a purple gown of darker hue. "Where's my fruit punch, bitches?" Shimmying to the music, she crossed the room toward the kitchen. "Mamma's parched. My throat's dry as my grandaunt's pussy. I pity that punch bowl tonight."

"Fetch me a glass, honey," the tall blonde shouted after her companion. Mike and Travis leaned against the wall, staring at Miss Jerry as she made her way around the room greeting each partygoer with effervescent gestures.

"She's dressed mighty elegant," Travis muttered. "Like one of those well-off Bellepoint society ladies back home."

"He. He's mighty elegant. Those are the drag queens," Mike said. "God, that one's big. Wouldn't want to cross him for love or money."

"Those are men?" Travis rubbed his eyes, feeling profound unease. "I can't believe it."

"Miss Jerry, you're a vision," Brenda said, kissing the tall blonde's hand. "Come on over here. I want you to meet Travis and Mike. They're in town for the weekend."

Miss Jerry regarded them. *Oh, Lord,* Travis thought, struggling to meet the big blond's eyes and trying not to cringe.

"Why, ain't y'all cute? What a pair of little studs. Why, I'd climb all over either one of you. You look like James Dean with a beard," she said, squeezing Mike's hand. "All muscle and smolder."

"Well, thanks, ma'am. That's sweet of you to say." Mike summoned one of his cocky catfish grins. To Travis's amazement, he looked as unruffled as ever. "And you look like Marilyn Monroe."

"That's the idea, honey. I love a pretty man with a pretty mouth." She took Travis's hand and patted it. "And you, sugar, with those whiskers and all that hair, you're like a baby Kris Kristofferson. Huskier, though. I like a man with some meat on his bones." She pinched Travis's love handles with both hands.

"Thank you, ma'am," Travis said, flinching and flushing. "That's quite a compliment."

"Am I your first drag queen, honey?"

"Yes, ma'am. How did you know?"

"Because you look like you don't know whether to run, shit, or go blind. Now don't you be afraid of me. Just think of me as a glamorous aunt. You remind me of a little bear I used to date up in Pittsburgh. Y'all ever been to Pittsburgh?"

"No, ma'am," said Mike.

"Oh! We must go!" Miss Jerry said, grabbing both Mike's and Travis's hands. "It's not far. We could dance at Pegasus. Those rough biker daddies would eat you alive at the leather bar. And I could give you my Suckee Suckee Tour."

"What's that?" Travis asked, wide-eyed.

"I could show y'all all the places where I've sucked cock. Down on Liberty Avenue and up in Shadyside. Over in Mount Lebanon. Beside the Incline. In the shadow of the Cathedral of Learning."

Travis had absolutely no idea how to respond to that, but fortunately Brenda appeared, holding a cup of punch. "Miss Jerry, Leroy sent you this drink. And I have a lot of food in the kitchen."

"*Food?* This dress is tight enough. Where is that whore Leroy anyway? Probably on her knees in the bushes out back. So nice to meet you boys," she said, chucking Travis under the chin. "I know we'll be great friends." With that, she turned and swept off between the dancers.

"Wow," muttered Travis.

"I figured you needed a break," Brenda said. "He can be pretty outrageous, but he's got a good heart, Travis. I'll bet you like him once you get to know him. God knows he's been kind to me. The night that Bill and I broke up... Well, that's a story for another day. You both look exhausted. And shitfaced, as they say around here. Why don't you all go lie down on my bed? I need to stay up till the party's over, so I can take the futon tonight."

Both boys, still clothed, took off their cowboy boots and plopped down on Brenda's blue coverlet. The lamp-lit room spun about Travis. He propped himself on an elbow and shook his head. "Ugh. Agh."

"The dreaded whirlies, huh? Are you gonna puke?"

"Don't think so. Thank God I didn't drink any more of that stuff." Travis sat on the edge of the bed. "Just going to sit up for a while. What time is it?"

"Two. Sounds like the party's winding down." Mike rolled onto his side and regarded Travis. "So what were you and Farron talking about?"

"Rome. He's a sculpture major. He's going there this summer. He promised to have me up for dinner this fall to tell me about it and show me his photos."

"Sculpture major? What kind of job can you get with that?"

"Sculptor? I don't know. He paints too. Those were some of his paintings in the living room."

"That black and gray stuff with the bones? Pretty weird, if you ask me. Are you attracted to him?"

Travis raised his head. "What? No. I mean, he's handsome, but he's not my type."

"But Bob is, isn't he? You said he was good-looking."

"*You* said he was good-looking."

Mike rolled onto his back and stared at the ceiling. "You think he's hot."

"I think he's hot because he looks like you."

"Man, you were busy tonight. Two invitations for this fall. First, dinner with cosmopolitan Farron, and then some Italian festival with another bear into leather. I'll bet you won't be missing me at all."

Travis turned toward Mike, brow furrowed. "You're jealous?"

"Damn right I'm jealous. You were flirting with those guys."

Travis rolled his eyes. "Please. I don't even know *how* to flirt. You were the one out on the back porch with Martha."

"She smokes. I smoke."

"You thought she was pretty."

"She *is* pretty. Lots of girls at the party were pretty. Brenda. Laura."

"But Martha's straight. And you're bi. You haven't been with a girl for a long time. Did you want her?"

"I'm not interested in Martha. Don't be childish."

"I'm not being childish. You started it."

"Yeah. Yeah, I did," Mike sighed, scooting to the far side of the bed and turning his back on Travis. "Let's get some sleep. We got a long drive tomorrow, especially with that goddamn engine acting up."

Stomach churning with both emotion and alcohol, Travis moved to an armchair. For a long time, the room kept spinning. He dozed off in the chair, only to wake with a start. Mike lay snoring, his back still turned. Travis joined Mike on the bed. He stared at his lover's broad shoulders, then rolled away from Mike, hugged his pillow, and passed out.

The next morning, Travis woke to find Mike cuddling him from behind.

"You awake?" Mike asked.

"Yeah," dry-mouthed Travis croaked.

"Look, Cubbie," Mike said, taking his hand and nuzzling his hair. "I'm sorry about last night. Woke up this morning and realized I was acting like Buck, all jealous and possessive. I don't wanna be that way, I swear."

"I'm sorry too. I was so drunk I didn't know half of what I was saying. I don't want to be with anyone but you."

"I need to hear that. I don't know why I get so insecure sometimes. I just love you so much, and the thought of you with another guy makes me sick. That Bob, he was sexy, and Farron, he's smart like you. You can talk to him about things I can't. Cultural stuff. You fit in here. I don't."

"Bob's sexy, but you're sexier. And I enjoyed talking to Farron, but I don't want to sleep with him. I'm in love with you, Mike, not them. I don't want to sleep with someone I don't love."

"I love you too, Travis. I guess I'm just afraid of ending up like Buck did when Mom died. All bitter and lost. I don't know what I'd do if you ever stopped wanting me."

Travis snorted. "*That's* not going to happen. What time is it?"

"Nine. I think Brenda's up. I can smell sausage cooking, and coffee brewing too."

Travis rolled over and groaned. "Oh, man," he said, clutching his head.

"First hangover, huh? I know all about doctoring that."

Mike slipped off the bed and left the room. He returned with two big glasses of water and a bottle of Tylenol.

"This'll help," he said. "Brenda's cooking her glop. Looks like a tasty combination of fried potatoes, peppers, and eggs. Plus she has a fruit salad. Should all be ready in about fifteen minutes, she said. Plus she made ham salad sandwiches for us to take on the road."

"Okay. Thanks." Sitting up, Travis gulped a couple of pills down. "If we start to feeling better, let's check out that state forest before we head home."

"With Bill and Cin?"

Travis made a face. "What do you think?"

"Yeah, I know. Just the two of us is fine by me. Long as we start back to Hinton by two P.M., we should be home by dark...long as the damn truck doesn't break down."

Mike pulled off his T-shirt and smiled. "Wanna take a quick shower together? I don't care if my head hurts. I wanna blow you bad. *Carpe diem*, right?"

Coopers Rock State Forest was thickly wooded, set along the top of Chestnut Ridge, a high mountain just east of Morgantown. Mike parked the truck in the big gravel lot at the end of the road. Under spring-green trees, families and groups of college students grilled food beneath long wooden picnic shelters.

"Ack. As far away from breeders and brats as we can," Travis said, leading Mike past a crew of parents with shrilling children.

"Not planning on having an adorable passel of kids, huh?" Mike said.

"God, no. Do *you* want kids?"

"Not especially. After having Buck as a father, I doubt that I'd make much of a parent."

That's a relief, Travis thought. *A desire for kids would be just one more reason for you to drop me for a girl.* "Come on, there's a sign for the overlook."

The pair made their way down a dirt path between rhododendron bushes and chestnut oaks, then over a stone-and-wood bridge and onto a fenced-in expanse on top of a huge flattish boulder. All about them, sheer cliffs dropped. Far, far below, the Cheat River glistened green. The boys could make out in the far distance the urban structures of Morgantown. To Travis's delight, the two had the overlook to themselves.

"We're above the birds," he said, looking down into the clear air of the gorge. "I think that there's a red-tail hawk. And those are turkey buzzards."

"You know so damn much. Wow. We're high up. I'm a little afraid of heights."

"Me, too, actually. But, man, the air smells so clean." Travis looked around before taking Mike's hand. For a few minutes, they simply stood there, alternating between taking in the view and looking over their shoulders for fear of hostile witnesses. When Travis heard voices approach, he dropped Mike's hand.

"I get so goddamn tired of worrying about what people might do if they saw us touch," Travis growled. A few loud college boys in Greek-letter T-shirts sauntered over the bridge and onto the overlook.

"Might be not so bad in a university town," Mike said. "Might be better than back home. C'mon, let's walk in the woods a little bit, and then we'd better head on down the road."

They strolled back over the bridge and into the shade of the forest. Travis reached up every now and then, stroking leaves. "Sourwood," he said. "Funny little flowers in the summer. The bees love 'em. Sourwood honey..."

"Guess you might be studying all that tree stuff this fall, huh?" Mike kicked a chunk of fallen bark out of the way.

"Yeah." *Without you. Nearly four hours' drive away. Damn.*

"While I'll be pissing with carburetors and dealing with Buck's bad moods."

Travis scuffed dead leaves. "You ought to come with me. I've told you that before."

"Hell, Travis. I figured before we ever got up here that I wouldn't belong here and you would. And now I know. All that educated talk last night. None of 'em asked me what I did. Most of 'em didn't even talk to me. Probably because they could tell I was lowbrow."

"You're *not* lowbrow. Martha talked to you. She was probably wanting to climb all over you."

"Don't start that. Most of 'em ignored me."

"That's not true. I saw all kinds of folks talking to you."

"A few, I guess. But they could probably smell the car oil on me. They were probably wondering why a guy like you is with a blue-collar dude like me. Lowbrow. Lowlife. Yep, I'm your blue-collar dude, through and through."

"You're always bringing that up. Nobody is looking down on you 'cause you're a mechanic."

"Nobody's looking down on me? You've got a lot to learn. How many degrees do you plan to get anyway? Going to grad school, I bet."

"I don't know. Maybe."

"You'll probably end up with a PhD. What the hell does a PhD have to say to a mechanic?"

Travis stopped in his tracks. "So what are you saying? You can't imagine a future with me if I get more educated? Do you want to break up with me like Bill did Brenda? Is that what you're trying to say?"

"Maybe we *should* break up. That might be better than me lying in bed this fall, wondering what you're doing and who you're with, waiting for a phone call or letter, trying to hide how much I miss you. You'll be improving yourself, and I'll be the same ole Mike, 'another year older and deeper in debt,' as the country song goes."

Travis stopped in his tracks. He turned toward Mike, face flushed. "Damn you. You really want to dump me?"

"No. Not really, but—"

"Maybe it's for the best? That's the phrase Bill used." Travis clenched his fists.

"Maybe it is. If I'm going to lose you, maybe it would be easier sooner than later. What? Are you going to hit me?"

"I want to."

"*Do* you? Last fall, you came to me and asked me to make you strong," Mike said in a low, even voice. "And so I did. Now you have strength *and* a bad temper *and* not much self-control. Bad combo. I think you like to break things just to feel powerful. Now that you're strong, you want to break me?"

Mike shoved Travis in the chest. "Huh, big man? Huh?"

Travis staggered back, then regained his footing. "Don't."

"Why not? Here's your excuse. I'd rather you break my face now than break my heart later."

Mike shoved Travis again. "C'mon. Show your blue-collar boy-toy who's boss."

"Don't, Mike," Travis said, glaring.

"Third time's the charm." Mike shoved Travis again.

"Damn you!" Travis roared.

Leaping forward, he tackled Mike to the ground. The two thrashed back and forth in the leaves and mud, cussing and snarling, fighting for an advantage, before Mike finally maneuvered himself on top of Travis and pinned him down. Travis strained against Mike's grip, then suddenly stopped struggling. Panting, they stared at one another for a long moment.

"Fuck this," Mike said. Sliding off Travis, he slumped back into the leaves.

"Fuck this," Mike said again, rolling away from Travis, his back to him.

"Oh, damn. Oh, damn. Mike. Mike?" Travis edged toward his boyfriend. "I'm sorry. I'm sorry. You're right. I need to learn to control myself. My own anger scares the shit out of me sometimes. Mike?"

He laid a hand on Mike's shoulder, but Mike jolted away.

"Mike? Did I hurt you? Come here."

Travis rolled his boyfriend over. Mike's dirt-streaked face was expressionless, but his cheeks were moist with tears.

"Oh, God, you're crying?"

"Hell, yes, I'm crying." Mike stared up into the canopy of leaves, his lips curled in a faint smile. "You think a rough old redneck boy like me is too proud to cry? I guess I usually am. But my pride... I don't know how to hold onto you and my pride too. I don't, Travis. I don't."

Mike got to his knees, then his feet. He extended a hand to Travis, who took it and righted himself. For a few seconds, the boys wiped mud from their clothes and pulled twigs and leaves from their hair and beards.

"You're a crazy boy," Mike said. Wetting a finger, he rubbed at dirt on Travis's cheek. "You may end up with ten college degrees, but you'll still be one crazy hillbilly. I'll love you till the day I die, though you may never bring yourself to believe it, and that fact's part of our problem. You're probably the most passionate guy I'll ever meet. Whether that makes you or breaks you—and the people around you—I guess the future will find out, whether I'm around to see it or not."

Mike lifted Travis's hand to his mouth and kissed it, then dropped it as if he were suddenly weary and it had become a great weight. "Come on, berserker. Let's go home."

Not much was said on the long drive south. The truck overheated near Flatwoods, so they pulled over till the radiator cooled. At the overlook between Birch River and Summersville, they gave the truck another break while wolfing down Brenda's sandwiches. The truck overheated a third time near Beckley.

Every now and then the boys held hands above the gearshift, but Mike's touch seemed different. *What have I done?* Travis thought, stealing glances at Mike's face, then gazing out over the mountainous landscape. *What kind of guy damages what he finds most precious? A fool. A fool. A fool. A fool. A fool.*

CHAPTER SIXTEEN

"I'm so glad you could come up for Beltane," Travis said. "I've really missed you."

The first of May was warm and sunny. The two boys strolled the Ferrell property in hiking boots, jeans, and T-shirts. It was the first time they'd been together since the trip to Morgantown.

"Like I said, we've been slammed at the garage. Plus you kept telling me how busy you were with school work, so I figured you needed some space."

Convenient excuse. You're still sore over our fight at Coopers Rock, and I guess I don't blame you. "Yeah, I've been swamped, all right. Physics is driving me crazy."

"Physics. Uck." Mike grimaced. "I'll stick to Shop."

"I would too. I hate numbers. They're slippery. They're not like words." Travis took Mike's elbow. "Hold on." He plucked a tiny, many-legged form from Mike's back.

"Damn ticks. Going to have to check you for 'em when we get back to the house. It's prime tick season around here," Travis said. "If I were a Christian, I'd say they were pure proof of Satan."

The two boys followed the line of a breezy ridge. In the deep dell to their left, red cedars composed a dense thicket that descended to the banks of the pond. To their right, the pasture sloped down toward the barn and the Ferrell family farmhouse. Beyond that stood the white church and the few houses that composed Forest Hill, a crossroads hamlet surrounded by low wooded hills leafing out with the green-gold of May.

"So your parents are coming home next month?" Mike asked.

Travis nodded, chewing contemplatively on a stalk of sweet grass. "In time for graduation."

"Right. Congrats, Mr. Valediction. So remind me again: why are you slumming around with an uneducated guy like me?"

"That question again." Travis patted Mike's rear. "There's your answer."

"You horny Ferrells just gotta get you some strange, huh?" Mike heaved a mock sigh. "I'm just a piece of ass."

"A piece of ass I heartily adore. You got on that black jock I bought you?"

"As you ordered. Sir."

"Yum." Travis gave Mike's rump another appreciative pat. "Good boy. So, why were you so quiet when you first got here? Seemed like something was on your mind. Are you...are you still pissed about what happened at Coopers Rock?"

"Naw." Mike shook his head emphatically. "I goaded you. I asked for it."

"Naw. I was an asshole. It was my fault."

"You can't forgive yourself for anything, can you?"

Travis's smile was doleful. "I guess not. I was reading Sylvia Plath's journals the other day, and she said, 'Not being perfect hurts.' I think I want a T-shirt that says that."

"Plan to spend your life hurting, huh? Not planning to put your head in an oven any time soon, I hope."

"Don't make fun of Sylvia. She's my favorite poet."

"Sorry. I'm just in another grim mood." Mike made a face. "Ole Buck and I got into it again."

"Oh, Lord. Now what?"

"Remember me telling you about how Buck pitched a fit when I brought my black buddy Eugene home once? Eugene was a teammate of mine. Well, this morning Buck got a call from his sister, my Aunt Drema up in Nimitz, and she was all hysterical about how her daughter Darlene was dating 'a nigger.' Turned out said 'nigger' was Eugene. So Buck was yelling about how he was going to kick Eugene's ass, and I was telling him he'd damn well better not."

The boys paused at the gate, looking out over the tiny community below. To the west, the sun was slipping beneath the hilly horizon. "Buck scares me, I've got to admit," said Travis. "If he feels that way about blacks and whites seeing one another, how would he feel about gays? If he found out we were lovers, I'm afraid of what he'd do."

Mike scowled. "Well, he'd beat me to death first. He might or might not come after you."

"That's not exactly comforting, Mike. Why are people so damned concerned with other people's love lives?"

"I don't know. Mind your own goddamn business, that's what I say."

"Me too. I got to know Eugene and his sister Wilma about the time I realized I was gay, and I think one of the reasons I like them, and a lot of other black folks, is they're a minority and we're a minority, so I can't help but feel a kinship, you know?"

"Yeah, I do. But the minister of that black Baptist church down in Hinton might not feel the same." Mike chewed his lip, then pulled out a cigarette and lit it. "I hear he's always preaching about the sin of Sodom. Speaking of race, you know the John Henry statue?"

"Sure. The one at that roadside park on Tunnel Hill, down near Talcott."

"Been meaning to tell you this. I'm pretty sure that Buck was one of the guys who vandalized it last time. He came home drunk that night making some vague boasts about 'putting the jigaboos in their place.'"

"Vandalized? Really?"

Mike inhaled, then released a smoke ring. "Really. Whoever it was shot at it, and somebody painted 'Nigger' with white paint across the big guy's chest. Hell, a good while back, some dickheads even chained it to the back of their truck and dragged it down the hill."

Travis groaned. "Daddy told me about that. Backwards bastards. Reminds me of something Wilma told me in Physics last week. It turns out the Moose Club won't let black folks in. Neither will that roadhouse up on the Greenbrier. Can you believe it? How do they get away with stuff like that?"

Mike shook his head and spat into the grass. "They all need a good ass-whupping, I know that much. Okay, enougha that. This shit's depressing me. It's supposed to be your big holiday, witchy boy. Let's head us down the hill and have that May wine you promised me. Whatever the hell that is."

"Shower first," Travis said, heading toward the bathroom. "Time for that tick-check. Plus I want to see you in that jockstrap."

Mike stripped to the jock and posed. Mike strutted in a slow circle. Mike turned his back to Travis, bent, grabbed his knees, and waggled his rump. "Like what you see?"

"Work of art," Travis sighed. "God, the curves of your chest and your ass. All that fur. Michelangelo would have loved you. You're a poem, Mike. You're my poem."

"All right, all right," Mike said, shucking down the jock. "Blarney Stone again."

"Damn, your butt is a national treasure. Reminds me of that old joke about what you get when you cross a donkey with an onion."

Mike sniggered. "I know that one. A piece of ass so beautiful it brings tears to your eyes. Enough flattery, farm boy. See if I got any damn bugs on me."

Nodding, Travis undid his ponytail and stripped. Laughing, the boys fingered and fondled each other's bodies, doing their best to make an unpleasant task enjoyable and succeeding gloriously in that attempt. Travis found a tick crawling on Mike's calf; Mike found one nesting in Travis's hair and another preparing to burrow into the nape of his neck.

"Foul fuckers," said Mike, facing twisting with disgust.

"Hate 'em," Travis said, corralling the bloodthirsty bugs in his palm.

"As much as you do homophobes?"

"Not quite," replied Travis, flushing the ticks down the toilet before carefully combing out his shaggy hair. "They're all the same kind of nasty in my book."

The friends wedged into the shower stall together. They spent a happy interval giggling and groping, shampooing one another's beards and soaping up one another's furry bodies.

"Leave your shirt off, Studly," ordered Travis as they toweled dry. "I want your chest bare. And no deodorant. I like your natural smell."

Mike pulled on his jock. "Bossy. You're taking this leather Top thing to wild new extremes, Mr. *Drummer*, sir. As I said before, I've created a monster." Mike tautened his towel and slapped Travis on the ass.

"Ouch! Dammit." Travis tried to return the favor, but his towel fell short.

"Hell, I never could do that towel thing. You do everything better than me."

"Guess so," Mike replied, snapping the towel again. This time he caught Travis on the thigh.

"Stop it! That hurts. You're bucking for a punishment, aren't you?"

"Maybe so, sir. You did promise to take a belt to me sometimes. I'm still waiting for that."

Travis lifted an eyebrow, dubious. "Sure you're up for it?"

"Sure. If it turns you on. Can't be half as bad as how Buck used to whale on me. I'm a tough dude, right?"

"That's for damn sure. One of a slew of things I savor about you."

"Then bring it on." Winking, Mike dropped the towel and slipped on his jeans. "I'm starved. What's for dinner? More of your grandmother's yummy leftovers?"

"Nope," said Travis, pulling on gym shorts and an A-shirt. "Tonight I'm doing the cooking. Always dreamed of having some hairy little stud to cook for, and here you are, so here I go."

In the kitchen, Travis found a country music station on the radio before pouring them glasses of the May wine he'd started steeping in the fridge as soon as Nanny had left for Lewisburg. It was pale yellow and perfumed with an herby scent. "It's a German recipe I found in one of my witch books," Travis explained. "Even grew the woodruff myself. I have a little herb garden going out near the rhubarb patch."

The barefoot boys sipped wine and complained about classes while Travis cooked and night fell. Soon they were tucking into oven-baked barbeque chicken with macaroni and cheese on the side. After slices of pound cake topped with ice cream, they took to the couch, Mike's head resting in Travis's lap, and watched TV, first *The Young Riders*, admiring the good looks of the actors in their Western wear, then *Golden Girls*, hooting at Rose's wide-eyed stupidity, Sophia's outrageous comments, Dorothy's acerbic wit, and Blanche's bawdy enthusiasms. After that, Travis cut off the television and sat back in the dark, running his fingers through Mike's soft hair.

"I've always loved cowboys," Travis said. "You remind me of one, strutting around in your tight jeans and boots."

"Too bad I can't ride."

"Me neither," Travis admitted.

"You can ride, all right. You can ride me all night."

"I fully intend to. Not much sleep for you tonight." Travis flicked one of Mike's nipples, then the other.

"Ummmm. Oh, yeah. The more you do that, the more I want ridden."

"Another of the million things I love about you. Your sweet, hairy tits. Your scrumptious butt. That black beard of yours. Damn, Mike," Travis sighed. "This is the kind of evening I want, the kind of life I want. A little house in the country with you, evenings drinking and cooking, watching TV, and making love."

"No bar hopping in big cities? No cruising the DC Eagle with Eyetalian Bob?"

"Forget about Bob. No bar hopping, no."

"I want that future too, Travis. And today I did something that might help us get it."

"What? Really?" Travis grabbed Mike's hand. "What did you do?"

Mike sat up. "I don't know how you'll feel about this."

"What? What did you do?"

"I drove up to Beckley and talked to an army recruiter."

Travis's face fell. "What? Why? Why would you do that?"

"Travis, there's a thing called the GI Bill. If I serve in the army for four years, I can come back here and the government will pay for me to go to college. Who knows, with my grades, if I could get in, but it's worth a try. And I could make real money in the army, better than helping Buck in the garage."

"But we'd be apart for four years." Travis's face paled. "And you'd be in danger. You might even have to kill people."

"Maybe. Maybe those crazy bastards in the Middle East who pulled all that shit in Kuwait a few months ago, maybe they ought to be killed. That shithead Saddam sure does. Who knows what he'll do next? Look, Travis, you've known ever since we met that I'm interested in the military. I'd be defending my country and making money and working towards a future with you, all at the same time. I might even become an officer one of these days."

"But the *army*?"

"Look now. Buck was in the army. It did him good. It helped him get started. Ain't nothing wrong with the army."

"Aren't you too young to sign up?"

"Naw. I asked about that. Seventeen year olds can join up with a parent's permission. Buck might let me go if he can find someone else to work in the garage."

Travis rubbed his forehead and shook his head. "You might be hurt or killed, Mike. You might not come back. And what would I do then?"

"Of course I'm coming back. The war's over. Besides, ain't no A-rab going to end Mike Woodson."

"You can't know that, you cocky bastard. Another war might start up. Why can't you move to Morgantown with me and find a job as a mechanic?"

"I could. But eventually you'd have a degree and then a career and then a real paycheck, and I'd still be coming home in greasy coveralls with oil under my nails. You'd have smart, slick friends who'd be wondering why you were wasting your time with a loser like me. And you'd be paying more than your share of the bills. That's not the life I want with you. I got some pride. I gotta pull my weight."

"I don't care about who pays the bills. We can live in a trailer out in the woods, for all I care. As long as we're there together."

"Well, that's another option. Look, big guy, don't be upset." Scooting closer, Mike took Travis's face in his hands. "This army thing was just an idea. I ain't committed to anything. I just wanted you to know that I've been thinking hard about...well, last fall, at Kirk's on my birthday, I said something about wanting to stay here and maybe take the easy route and settle down with some girl...but I don't feel that way any more. I've fallen in love with you, farm boy. I want to be with you. And with your smarts, you *gotta* go to college. I'm just trying to figure out ways for us to be together once you leave here."

"Okay, I get that, and I'm very glad to hear it. And I must admit I love seeing you in camo," Travis said, grinning bashfully. "But the military? Killing? Hell, the only things I can bring myself to kill are houseflies, ticks, and potato beetles. When we find wasps or spiders in the house, I catch them under a glass and take them outside. I've always had a soft heart that way. That's why I didn't want to go deer-hunting with you."

"I know, Travis. And I love that tender heart of yours. But sometimes killing's necessary. Think about Hitler. I know some of your heroes are military men. You admire Jackson and Lee, don't you?"

"Sure. Like I told you, one of my ancestors was a Rebel soldier, and I'm damned proud of that."

"And you ought to be. Let me put this another way. What would you do if you saw someone try to hurt me? Or your grandmother? Or your parents?"

Travis's face darkened. "I'd kill them. I'd slaughter them."

"Right. See? The military ain't all about killing. It's about protection and defense. Ain't that what you've been doing since September, with the barbell and the punching bag?" Mike gently thumped Travis's chest. "Trying to get strong so you can defend yourself if necessary? Or protect the folks you care about?"

"Yeah. Yeah, you're right there."

"The army's about strength, big guy. You love strength. I know it. You love my strength. You've said so. And when you have me tied up, don't that make you feel powerful? And don't that feel good?"

"*Hell*, yes, it feels good. As good as it can get. But the army? It's one thing to read all those war books of yours, but... Look, Mike, I'm sure you'd be a damned fine soldier. You already have the physique, the confidence, the determination, and the bearing. But you'd have to hide who you are. The military doesn't want gays, lesbians, or even bisexual folks, from what I've heard."

"Hell, I'm used to hiding. I grew up in Hinton, right? Look, Cubbie, I don't wanna talk anymore." Mike kissed Travis on the lips. "Let's not waste the little bit of time we have together arguing. Take me to bed, farm boy. Please."

"You promise we can talk about this more? You promise you won't sign up without telling me?"

"I promise. I swear. I swear on your horse dick. And my hairy ass. And the hot times they find together."

Travis laughed. "Okay, okay, Private Woodson. That's a holy oath indeed. That's a manly trinity." He rose, then pulled Mike to his feet. "Time to get you out of those clothes. Let's brush our teeth, clean out your, uhm, nether regions, and head to bed."

Travis drew the bedroom drapes and lit candles around the room. Mike stripped off his jeans, then, at Travis's request, stood in the middle of the room wearing nothing but his jockstrap.

"I love it when you're nearly naked and I've still got clothes on." Travis switched on the radio and tuned to a soft rock channel. "The contrast turns me on."

"You like a man vulnerable, huh?"

"Damn straight I do. All nekkid and needy and at my mercy. Want to dance?"

"You bet," Mike said, hooking a finger under the waistband of Travis's shorts and pulling him close. "Who needs the goddamn Prom anyway?"

"Ummm, the Prom. We should go," Travis said, wrapping his arms around Mike's shoulders. "I can see it now. The two of us in tuxedos slow-dancing...the shocked looks on everyone's faces. Wouldn't that be a night to remember?"

Mike snickered. "True enough. Brent and Rhodetta and that whole crew of ass-wipes would probably faint."

The boys fell silent. They slow-danced for a long time, first to John Waite's "Missing You," then Cyndi Lauper's "True Colors," then Berlin's "Take My Breath Away," kissing and beard-nuzzling softly.

"I forgot. I got you a Beltane gift." Mike pulled away long enough to fetch something from his duffel bag. It was a black leather strap with silver studs and a buckle.

"It's a dog collar," Mike said. Beaming, he handed it to Travis. "Eddie bought it for me. He got it in one of those Frisco leather shops. I thought you'd like it. Do you?"

"Do I?" said Travis. "What do you think? I love it." Eagerly he buckled it around Mike's neck. "Lord God, you look so hot in it. You should wear it all the time."

"The fine folks of Hinton would love that."

"It'd look great with your mechanic's coveralls. While we're at it," said Travis, opening the drawer of his bedside stand, "I know how to make you look even hotter." He held up two green and black mottled bandanas. "Here's a little camo for you, soldier boy."

"Uh, oh. Looks like I'm going to be abducted again."

"Yep. You're going to be my prisoner of war. Now keep still and behave." Grabbing Mike's wrists, Travis bound them together behind him with one bandana. With the other, he blindfolded him.

"Whoa," muttered Mike. "Now I really am at your mercy."

"Ohhh, man," Travis moaned, stepping back to study his boyfriend. "You look superb."

"I'll have to take your word for it. Never been blindfolded before."

"You all right like this?" Travis fondled Mike's bound hands.

"Damn, yes," Mike sighed, tickling Travis's palm with a crooked finger. "I really need to be...your captive tonight. Make me helpless. Take care of me, Travis. I need...I need you to take care of me."

"You bet I will. Going to treat you right. But first, one more tune," said Travis, wrapping his arms around Mike again. "I love this old song. Dan Hill's 'Sometimes When We Touch.'"

Again they circled to music, while Travis massaged Mike's rear and Mike ground his jock pouch against Travis's thigh.

"Travis?" Mike whispered.

"Yeah?"

"I am a little scared about joining the army, gotta admit."

"Then don't. There's got to be another way for us to be together."

"Maybe I won't. Travis?"

"Yeah?"

"Give it to me good and hard tonight," Mike said, his voice hoarse and deep. "I want you to...I want to...give myself to you...I want to... put my...my life in your hands. Keep me tied good and tight. Don't let me go. Use me hard. Please? Please? Get rough, as rough as you like."

"God, Mike," Travis croaked, his throat dry and his cock achingly stiff. "I will. I will. Oh, man, you are turning me on."

The song faded away. Travis whispered, "All right. Time I had me some poontang, soldier."

"Do it," blinded Mike muttered, licking his lips. "Enough romance. Take me, dammit. Get to it."

"We'll get to it, all right." Fetching rope, Travis added several feet to Mike's wrist-bonds. Mike leaned against him, rubbing his hard-on against Travis's thigh and murmuring, "Yeah, good and tight. Good and tight. Own me, man. Make me yours. Make me your prisoner. Don't let me loose. Don't let me go."

Done with his knot-work, Travis grabbed Mike by the arm, led him to the bed, and shoved him belly down across it.

"I got a couple more surprises for you, Private Woodson. Here comes the first one."

Mike flinched as a ripping sound filled the room. "What's that?" he said, rolling onto his back.

"Duct tape. I need to keep you extra quiet for what I got planned next." Travis straddled Mike's waist. "Don't want you shouting for help or bothering the neighbors. Those Hutchinsons across the road are good Christian people."

"Do it. Fucking shut me up. Gag me good and tight and then hurt me, man. Beat me. Ride me till I fucking sob."

"Don't have to tell me twice." Roughly, Travis plastered tape over Mike's mouth. "Now you look even hotter. Can you breathe all right?"

"Mmm hmmm." Mike nodded.

"Good boy. Here we go," Travis said, lying on top of his captive.

For a long while, Travis teased and tormented Mike's nipples with his fingers and teeth while his lover whimpered and writhed. Then he climbed off, helped Mike up, then pushed him to a kneeling position on the floor and bent his torso over the edge of the bed.

"Want me inside you?" said Travis, stripping off his clothes.

Mike nodded and grunted. "Uh *huh*."

Another sharp sound filled the room, this time a loud crack. Mike jumped.

"Got something else in mind first. So I hope you were serious earlier? About the belt? About wanting a little hurt?"

Mike took a deep breath and nodded.

"Good. If you want me to stop, just shake your head hard and wiggle your fingers around." Travis took a deep breath and began.

"Ouch! Damn. Pulls my beard," Mike groused as Travis peeled the strip of tape off Mike's mouth.

"Sorry," Travis said. He crumpled up the tape and tossed both it and the tube of lube on the floor. Leaving Mike's hands still bound and his eyes still blindfolded, he pulled up the sheet and light blanket, then slipped into their customary spoon, snuggling against Mike from behind.

"I'll let you loose in a little while, okay?" Travis said, kissing Mike's white shoulder. "Right now, I just want to hold you like this."

"Fine. Feels great. Snuggling with you is always great."

"Your hands all right?"

"Oh, sure, Cubbie. Snug but not too tight."

"Was that...good?" Travis stroked Mike's butt-curves, feeling the flushed heat the belting left behind. "D-did you enjoy that?"

"Hell, yes. I needed that bad, to...just give up control for a while. To struggle and shout and just let loose and get wild and know I couldn't hurt anyone or break anything. It was like some scene outta one of those *Drummer* stories. You liked it, right?"

"Liked it?" Travis laughed softly. "I loved it. It was amazing. A dream come true. Thank you so much for letting me...indulging my..."

"Kinks? No problem. The leather stuff's real hot, actually. Like every time we touch, it's an adventure. Bondage is probably not something I ever would have tried on my own, but since you like it, I do too, and now I'm really getting into it. Mainly 'cause I love you and I trust you. And tonight...man, I was really in the mood for it tonight. I've just been so stressed out about so much shit, I needed it real intense."

"Rope therapy?"

"Kinda."

"Catharsis?"

"Huh?"

"More Greek stuff. Sorry. Your butt sore?"

"Yeah. Both hole and cheeks. But good-sore. Like love left me a souvenir."

"Was I too rough?"

"Naw, not at all. You actually could have laid it on harder."

"I was just so afraid of really hurting you, or doing something that would turn you off."

"You need to relax about that, big guy," Mike said, nudging Travis's groin with his rump. "Believe me, if I don't like something, I'll let you know big time."

"I don't know why the leather stuff turns me on. It has something to do with my power...and your trust in me...and how you surrender even though you're strong too." Travis sighed, fondling the fingers of Mike's bound hands. "Sometimes I wish I were vanilla. Sometimes I feel like a freak. Like a monster. Like I'll grow up to become someone dangerous."

"Bullshit. That'll never happen. You have such a sweet soul, Travis. And we're all freaks. At least the interesting kind of people are. As for why you like to tie me up, well, why do I like your hairy little belly and the shape of your shoulders? And your smile when you're feeling shy? Why does that retard Brent Vass always go out with blonde girls with snub noses? Why does Buck favor slutty redheads? Why does my cousin Darlene fall in love with black guys? It's all a mystery. Don't look a gift horse in the mouth, that's what I say."

"Yeah, I guess. Why *do* people find beauty where they do? Why do they love the people they do? Why are some folks gay, and some straight, and some bi? I read a book once—"

"Of course you did. No wonder you got 'Biggest Bookworm' in our class as well as 'Most Polite.' Go on, Brainiac. What book?"

"Well, Brenda turned me on to some historical novels by Mary Renault, including that one I showed you about Alexander the Great, and those led me to read a bunch of Greek literature. Classics in translation. Plays by Sophocles and Aeschylus and Euripides and poetry by Sappho, who wrote about her passion for girls."

"I sense a lecture coming." Mike rolled over to face Travis. "Hold on, professor. Please take the blindfold off. I want to see your eyes. I want to see your face."

Travis loosened the knot behind Mike's head and removed the bandana, revealing his lover's fond brown eyes. Mike leaned forward and kissed him. "There's my sweet bear cub. There's my ruthless bondage Top. You're so damn handsome."

"You really think I'm handsome?"

"Christ. Leos. How many times do I have to say it? Yes. Thank you, handsome Travis, for treating me to such a brutal fucking. Now go on."

"You sure? I'm not boring you, am I?"

"Naw. Go on. I like it when we learn from each other."

"Okay." Travis flushed and grinned. "So anyway, the Greek philosopher Plato wrote a little book called *The Symposium*. It's a bunch of Athenians drinking and talking about love. They talk about beauty, and they talk about the love of men for men, and how love for physical beauty leads to spiritual maturity and the love of ideal beauty."

Reaching over, Travis stroked Mike's black beard. "There's also a story that tries to explain sexual orientation, about how human beings were double-sided once, and the gods got angry at their presumption and decided to punish them by splitting them in half. The guys split from other guys were gay, the women spit from women were lesbians, and the creatures that were part man and part woman, well, after they were split, they were straight. So now we're all seeking our lost halves and aching for them. I think about that sometimes when we're apart. When I'm lying here in bed alone and wishing you were with me."

"Yeah. I know that feeling. I felt that for Randy, but he didn't deserve it. Now I feel that for you."

"Someone else in the book says that if you were to compose an army of male lovers, you could lick the world, because the guys would all be super-brave and determined not to appear like cowards in their lovers' eyes."

"Sounds like St. Patrick's Day, the two of us fighting those assholes in front of the gym."

"Yeah. Plato says that lovers would sacrifice their lives for one another."

"Makes sense to me. What kind of man are you if you ain't willing to sacrifice yourself for someone you love? Or for your country? A pussy, I'd say."

Travis fell silent and bowed his head. When he raised his face to Mike's, his eyes were moist with tears. "You're my ideal, Mike. You're what's most beautiful to me. *Please* don't go into the army. I don't want to lose you. I'll never find anyone like you again."

"Untie my hands, Cubbie."

When Travis did, Mike grabbed him and held him. "I may not go. But if I do, I'll come back, buddy. I swear. I'll come back."

"You damn well better. I don't want to end up like Heathcliff pining by your grave."

"Heathcliff? Another book?"

"Yeah. *Wuthering Heights*. This sexy guy, all dark and brooding—I picture him kind of looking like you—he loses the love of his life, Cathy—she marries someone else and then she gets sick and dies—and he roams the moors, miserable and bitter for the rest of his life, and he starts being haunted by her, and eventually, they end up in the same graveyard, their bodies mingling."

"Pretty gothic, huh?"

"Yeah. Mike?"

"Yep?"

"We talked about our fears, that night at Bluestone. Aren't you afraid of dying? Now that you're talking about joining the army, now I'm afraid...you'll be killed in action. I'm afraid of your death more than mine."

"Yeah, sure I'm afraid of death. Though, when I look at Buck, the way he went all to hell when Mom died, I guess I'm like you: the death of someone I love seems worse than dying myself."

Travis nodded. "That must have been awful, losing your mother when you were so young."

Mike slid down in the bed so he could press his face against Travis's torso. "Your chest hair tickles my nose," he said, his sad tone belying the words. He rested an arm athwart Travis's hip.

"I remember too damn well...she'd been losing weight for months and kept putting off going to the doctor...we'd never had much money or much in the way of health insurance...Buck considered insurance a waste...and by the time she finally got a check-up...by the time the test results came back..."

Mike kissed Travis's right nipple. He continued, his voice flat. "I only got to visit her in the hospital a couple of times. It was liver cancer, and it moved fast. She'd always boasted that cigarettes never did her any harm, and she was dead by the time the doctors figured out that the cancer had started in her lungs, then spread to her liver."

"I'm so sorry, Mike."

"Me too." Mike wiped at his eyes. "Shit. Here I go again. Why am I always crying around you?"

"Shhhh. I got you. I got you. Just get some sleep."

Travis stroked Mike's thick hair till his boyfriend slipped into slumber. He gazed into the darkness and rocked Mike gently, but inside he ached with unwelcome realizations. *Love, it's not just touching. It's not just kissing and fondling and romantic walks and sex. It's becoming attached to a body as mortal as your own, a body as susceptible as your own to danger, disease, and death. It's having more and more to lose. It's facing new depths of fear.*

"**D**amn. Nice spread," said Mike enviously. "You Ferrells got some fine land. You're like rural royalty."

"That's the Old Homeplace," Travis explained, as the boys—sated after a big breakfast of bacon and buckwheat cakes—pulled into the grassy drive beside a sprawling white house with columns. Behind it, pasture stretched in a slow slope up to a small cemetery and thick pinewoods beyond.

"Biggest chimney I've ever seen," said Mike, turning off the engine. "Is this what you wanted to show me?"

"Not exactly. It's locked up now. A distant cousin owns it, an old woman in Roanoke. Pisses me off. I wish Daddy could buy it. Anyway, it's where Nanny grew up, and her grandfather, the Confederate soldier. When I was a kid, and had more kin left, we all used to have Christmas parties here. Now it's mainly only opened for funerals. That's the family graveyard up there. That's what I want to show you."

"Y'all have your own graveyard? Exclusive. We Woodsons end up in Hilltop Cemetery above Hinton. Mom's buried there. Maybe I could take you there sometime."

"I'd like that. I wish I'd met her."

"Me too."

Travis and Mike, carrying coffee in travel cups, climbed out of the truck and strode into the May morning. It was chilly but sunny, everything green with spring. Travis opened the white pasture gate, in the process smearing his fingers with old paint dust.

"That outbuilding there, beneath the maple, that's where my older cousin Ann and I used to hide and drink cups of liquored-up Presbyterian punch we'd sneak at the Christmas parties. I guess I got my taste in seventies music from her."

"And where is she now?"

"Down in Kentucky. She's a Mary Kay gal. Her mother, my daddy's sister, Aunt Doris, used to live just down the road, in that red farmhouse." Travis turned and pointed. "But she moved to Kentucky too, just last year. I miss her. She was a serious farmer. Raised ducks and chickens and lots of spaghetti squash. Made the best pecan rolls you'll ever taste. And her homemade bread, well, it—"

Mike interrupted. "Can we hold hands here?"

Travis looked around. "Uhh, I…"

"Please?"

When Travis saw the beseeching look in Mike's eyes, his uncertainty dissolved.

"Sure." He seized Mike's hand. "Almost no traffic on the road, plus not likely anyone would see us up here."

The lovers made their way up the hill to the top. The Ferrell family graveyard was small, scattered with trees, and protected from pasture-grazing cattle by a chain link fence. Travis opened the metal gate and they entered. Sipping coffee and holding hands, they strolled from grave to grave.

"These are my great-grandparents, Erastus and Arminta. See, that's their names in their own handwriting. And Aunt Gus. And Earl Senior, my grandfather. And here's my Rebel ancestor, Isaac Ferrell." Releasing Mike's hand, Travis pulled up weeds surrounding the grave plaque.

"Did he survive the war?" Mike peered. "Died 1932. I guess he did."

"Sure did. His two brothers did too. They were all in Lowry's Battery together. Didn't you say you had an ancestor in that battery?"

"Yep. A great-great-granddaddy, I think. That's pretty cool, isn't it, that they fought together against the Yankees, and now you and I are together?"

"Fighting the world," said Travis. "Or at least the gay-haters." He looked out over the property, to the Old Homeplace and the wooded hills beyond. "I wonder what it felt like, coming back here after that war, knowing you'd put your all into it, and lots of your friends had died for the cause, and you'd lost anyway? I've seen pictures of him when he was young. He looked a lot like me."

"All burly, bearded, and handsome?" said Mike, taking Travis's hand again. "Maybe, once you're done with college—"

"And you're done with the army?"

"Maybe. I still think it's a good deal. And God knows you've trained me how to say, 'sir,' right, sir? Anyway, maybe some day we can buy this place and live here."

"God, that would be super. But how would we make a living?"

"Uhhhh...you'd be a professor at Virginia Tech, and I'd own my own garage...and have some amazing career based on stuff I learned in the army?"

"Who knows? And then we'd grow old together. I bet your beard would look pretty nice with streaks of gray in it. And then we'd be buried side by side in this very graveyard. Or better still, in the same grave. Like Achilles and Patroclus, or Heathcliff and Cathy."

"More literary references. You already have us buried, buddy. Let's live our lives first." Mike kissed Travis's hand, then kissed his lips.

"Sorry about that. I guess I got some gloomy goth in me, huh? So, I need to do some Physics and History homework today, but I have a few hours yet. You want to drive around? Or hike the farm? Or check out that Wakerobin Gallery? I want to find some little arts-n'-craftsy thing for my mother's birthday."

"When's your grandmother due back today?"

"Around dinnertime."

"How about we go back to your room, get naked, cuddle in bed, and watch junk TV? Or sports? Whatever. Seize the carp, I say."

"You just failed your Latin quiz. It's *Carpe diem*, silly boy."

"I know, I know. I'm joshing you. You think because I'm so damn handsome I'm stupid?"

"No. You're smarter than most folks I've met."

"Bullshit. I'm a C student. C+ at best."

"There are lots of ways of being smart. I'm learning that from you."

"Smart enough to love you," said Mike, leading Travis toward the cemetery gate. "Getting on toward lunch, isn't it? Any of that pound cake left?"

CHAPTER SEVENTEEN

Travis's parents got home at dusk, just in time for a late supper. Travis sauntered out to meet them. Beneath the great oak, fireflies were rising from the grass and blinking in the warm June air.

"Howdy!" he shouted, hugging his mother Frances hard. She was a slender, pretty woman in her early fifties with brown eyes, curly dark hair, and, Travis thought, a vague resemblance to the Queen of England.

"Mercy, you didn't used to hug like that."

Travis stepped back, grinning. "Guess I've grown up some."

"I guess you have. Look at your arms. Earl, look at this boy."

Travis flexed proudly. "I've been lifting weights with a friend."

"You've been working out, huh?" said Earl, shaking Travis's hand. Earl was built like Travis, tall and burly, with a clean-shaven face, blue eyes, and short graying hair. "Transformed yourself from an endomorph to a mesomorph, looks like. Good for you. Why don't you use those new muscles to give me a hand with these bags?"

"Yes, sir," Travis said, hauling two suitcase from the back of the Honda station wagon.

"How are your grades?" Earl took a bite of wilted lettuce salad while Nanny doled out bowls of buttered peas and new potatoes.

"Good. A's in everything but Math, and that's an A-."

"I never much liked Math either," Earl admitted.

"Valedictorian," Frances enthused, passing Travis a cut-glass dish of pickled beets. "And the Honor Society and the Latin Award. I'm so glad we could get home in time for your graduation."

"Garden's looking a little ragged," said Earl. "Tomorrow I want you to help me weed."

"So you got to go to Morgantown?" Frances spooned up cheese-topped stuffed peppers for the men, then served herself.

"Yep, with a new buddy of mine."

"Did you like the campus?" Frances asked.

"I did. It's really big. So big it's scary. But I met a whole bunch of people, friends of Brenda's and Bill's, who said they'd show me around, help me get used to it all." *If you only knew what kind of people,* Travis thought, slicing his pepper in half.

"Bill?" said Frances. "You mean that mannish girl from Indian Mills?"

"Uh, yeah. Her real name's Diana, but everybody calls her Bill."

"She's up there?" Frances pursed her lips.

"Yes, ma'am. She and Brenda both are."

"Are you all still friends?"

"Yes, ma'am. We've been exchanging letters. They've both been real nice to me. Why shouldn't we be friends?"

Nanny took her seat and tasted her peas and potatoes. "Needs salt," she declared. "They were talking about that Bill Walker the other day in Mizz McNeer's beauty shop. Her mother, that busty, chubby redhead, had just been in. Hair like a wildfire, I swear. Anyway, Mrs. Fitzsimmons said that Bill Walker was a morphodite."

Travis had never heard his grandmother—or anyone else for that matter—use that word. "I beg your pardon? Hellgrammite?"

"No, son, that's fish bait," said Earl. "Your grandmother means a hermaphrodite. Or a homosexual."

Oh, shit. "A homosexual?"

"Travis, please. You're already a pretty well educated boy. You know what a homosexual is. When I was a boy, I had a guitar teacher who was one. When he made a pass at me, I stopped taking lessons. Pass the beet pickles, please."

"Who's this new friend who drove you up to Morgantown?" Frances said.

"Mike Woodson. He's the one I lift weights with. There's a new gym down in the West End."

"Buck Woodson's child?" said Frances.

"Yes, ma'am."

"Aren't they a mite trashy? That Buck Woodson is a womanizer and a drunk, from what I hear," said Frances, pushing back her plate and wiping her lips.

Travis frowned. "Mr. Woodson is a little rough, but Mike's been great."

"Travis is right, Frances," Nanny said. "That Mike's been up here for dinner a few times, and he's mannerly as all get out. Very handsome boy. He helped Travis around the farm. He even backed up Travis in a fight on St. Patrick's Day. Both of those boys showed up to dinner with busted lips."

Oh, hell, thought Travis. "May I have a second stuffed pepper, please?"

"A fight?" Frances gasped. "When did you start fighting?"

"Christ, Frances. Boys fight. You two shelter Travis too much. He was nearly ten when he learned the word 'piss,' and *I* had to teach him."

"Earl!" Nanny said. "Not at the table."

"Fighting?" said Frances. "I leave you here a mannerly, scholarly boy, and I come back to find you've been fighting? Hardly what a gentleman would do. I think that Mike Woodson is a bad influence. I don't want you spending time with him."

"What? He's my only friend," Travis sputtered. "No way I'll stop hanging out with him."

"Don't backtalk your mother, Travis," Earl ordered. "Frances, for God's sake, at least meet this kid before you ban him."

"Frances, Mike really is a nice boy," said Nanny. "I think you'd like him once you got to know him."

"We'll see. I just worry about what people would say." Frances gathered up the few plates already emptied, then stalked into the living room and lit up a cigarette.

"What people say? Who cares what people say?" Earl muttered. "Great meal. The German food was good, but I missed good old-fashioned West Virginia home cooking. What's for dessert, Mother?"

"Lemon meringue pie," said Nanny, rising. "Your favorite. Travis, you saved room for some, didn't you?"

"Hell, yes," Travis said.

"Travis!" Nanny gasped.

"Are you cussing in there?" Frances piped from the living room. "Bad influence, I tell you."

Earl chuckled. "Mother, just cut the boy his pie."

The graduation ceremony was finally over, and the stuffy hallways of Hinton High School milled with robed graduates and family members in dress clothes. Travis, mortarboard in hand, left Earl, Frances, and Nanny chatting with other adults from their end of the county while he searched for Mike. He found his friend enjoying the evening breezes near the propped-open front door. Wiping sweat from his brow, Mike stared into the illuminated glass awards case.

"Hey, Mike. Where's your father? Didn't he come?"

"Yeah, but he's already left. Said it was hot as hell and he needed a beer bad. I second that. Frigging ceremony took forever." Mike jabbed a thumb at the inscribed plaques and gleaming awards. "Never did win anything. Maybe I should have stayed on the team. A football scholarship might have gotten me to Morgantown. Ain't your name gonna be on that one?" He pointed to the plaque inscribed with the winners of the Latin Award.

"Yeah," Travis replied with shy pride.

"You're a winner, man. Me..."

"*Don't.* Look, I want you to meet my parents, okay?"

"Oh, Lord." Mike brushed bangs off his brow and straightened his tie. "Yeah. Okay. Glad that Buck left already. Otherwise he might embarrass me. I think he had a damned flask in his back pocket and already had a buzz on. My luck, he'd cuss your father for no good reason and then make a pass at your mother."

"That wouldn't exactly be the way to win them over. Follow me. They're down this way. Remember, be real polite. Mommy thinks you're...well, try to impress her, okay? Good manners go a long way with her."

"Argh. No pressure or anything. Want to lend me some of that blarney of yours?"

Travis led Mike down the hall. The two boys waited until Earl and Frances had finished their conversation with a neighboring farmer whose pretty daughter had just graduated as well, then they stepped forward.

"Folks, this is my buddy, Mike Woodson. Mike, this is my mother and my father."

Earl shook Mike's hand. "Nice to meet you. I hear you've been teaching Travis to lift weights."

"Yes, sir. He's come a long way."

"We can tell. My mother says you've been helping Travis in the garden too. Good for you. So you work in your father's garage?"

"Yes, sir."

"Good honest work. Maybe you could teach Travis a few things about cars. He's not as practical as he should be."

"Thanks a lot," Travis muttered. *One of these days soon, I'll be leaving, and I won't be around for you to criticize or order around anymore.*

"Are you planning on going to college, Mike?" Frances asked. Travis could see the dubious look on her face.

"No, ma'am. I don't have the grades or the money. But I wish I could." Mike bowed his head and polished his right dress shoe against his trouser-covered left calf. "Your son here has really taught me a lot...about literature and history and the importance of, uh, education. He's the smartest guy I know. And the most mannerly. He's a real...gentleman. He's, uh, like a brother to me."

Mike stuck his hands into his pockets and smiled at Travis. "Y'all have really brought him up right. He's awful lucky to have parents like you. And a grandmother like Mrs. Ferrell here," he added, nodding at Nanny. "While y'all have been overseas, she and Travis have been real, real kind to me. I haven't had much of a home life since my mom died—I'm sure you've heard I'm kind of from a rough background, and I guess that's true—so it's been a real privilege, a real luxury to spend some time at your all's farm. It's so pretty and peaceful there. And I think I've gained five pounds in the last few months enjoying all those pies."

To Travis's relief, Frances gave his friend a bright, genuine smile. "Well, that's really sweet of you to say, Mike. You come up and help Travis around the farm whenever you'd like."

"Thank you, ma'am. I'd like that."

Good job, Mike! Let's get out of here before something goes wrong. "Hey, would it be all right if Mike and I went to a party in Bellepoint? Just for a few hours?"

"A party? Would there be drinking?" The dubious look returned to Frances's face.

"It's Bellepoint, Frances. Where the sophisticates live. It couldn't be too bad," Earl said. "Go ahead, son. You two ought to celebrate some."

"Don't stay out too late," said Nanny.

"And no alcohol," ordered Frances.

"**G**raduates. At last," sighed Mike, patting Travis's thigh.

"God, yes," Travis replied, sipping his vodka and lemonade.

The boys sat in Mike's truck, in a tree-lined turnout above Brooks Falls, staring out over the moonlit whitewater of the New River as it rushed by over jagged rocks. Both had torn off their hot graduation robes at Mike's house and changed into tank tops and shorts before hopping into his truck, eager to be alone together.

"So what'd your parents get you for graduation?" asked Mike, topping off his drink from a Thermos he'd wedged beneath the driver's seat.

"I asked them for another night at Bluestone so you and I could have another, uh, cabin experience, but I got luggage instead. *Luggage.* You'd think they were eager for me to leave. What did Buck get you?"

"You know the answer to that. Jack shit. Well, okay, this vodka we're drinking," said Mike, jiggling his cup.

"Tastes pretty good. Did you notice how efficiently Brent Vass avoided us as we left? I think he's afraid of us."

"Believe so. Here's to us. Here's to intimidating assholes," said Mike, lifting his drink, "and graduating and, with luck, never seeing the motherfuckers ever again."

"Hear, hear," said Travis, bumping Mike's cup with his.

"You gave a great speech tonight, Travis. I was so proud of you. I liked the Emerson and Thoreau quotes. Didn't much like reading that stuff in English a few years back, but I liked hearing you say it. Made sense. 'Fuck conformity' seemed to be the main message."

"Yep. Speech would have been a lot shorter if I'd said it that way. And you were the best looking man in that auditorium," Travis said.

"Thanks, Cubbie. Me, I'd say you were. But thanks. Man, it'll be nice to get away from all those people and their petty rumors, and all those teachers who thought I was dumb."

Travis frowned. "You know you're not dumb. I've told you that a million times."

"Yeah, you have. And, thanks to you, I'm inclined to agree with you. But the teachers... Look, bud, you don't have any sense of this 'cause you're so good with the book-learning and all, but those teachers all just assumed I was stupid 'cause I was a mechanic's son. And pretty soon, if people think you're stupid and don't expect you to do well, well then, you don't do well. You stop caring. Does that make sense?"

"I guess. They all assumed I was smart because Daddy used to teach there before he started consulting."

"Plus your parents pushed you to study. Buck, he didn't care about my schooling, he just wanted me to help him in the garage. So I didn't study, which meant my grades ended up being just what the teachers expected. Mediocre. You end up with a 4.0, and I end up with a 2.9. Now I'm regretting all of it, 'cause I can't come to college with you. At least now I'll be working in Buck's garage pretty much full-time, and I can start making some money."

Travis took a big swig of his drink. "You got some Certs on you?"

"Yeah. But that's why we're drinking vodka, Cubbie. Can't smell it on a guy's breath."

"Are you still thinking about the military?"

"Yep. Though Buck said he wanted me to stay and work the garage at least a few more years. 'Cuse me. Gotta piss."

"Me too. Like a racehorse."

Both boys climbed out of the truck and relieved themselves over the ledge of the rocky riverbank. Both zipped up. Mike turned to Travis. "When you moving to Morgantown?"

"Late August. I've been assigned a dorm room already. Boreman Hall. It's just down the hill from Arnold Hall, where Bill still lives.

I hope my roommate isn't some kind of troglodyte. Ack. I hate the idea of sharing a space with someone I don't know."

"So you want me to drive you up there when the time comes? If Buck'll give me time off? And if it's all right with your mother? All that stuff I said to your parents tonight was true, but I was also doing my level best to impress her."

"You did a fine job. You looked like a real gentleman in your suit and tie. Sure, you can drive me." Travis hugged Mike hard. "Oh, God. I don't want to leave you."

"Me neither, Cubbie," said Mike, hugging Travis back and kissing his fuzzy cheek. "I can't imagine life without you."

"I said something like that once," Travis murmured, "and you said I was being a romantic."

"Guess it's contagious then. C'mon, let's get you home. Don't want to get you back too late and lose that ground I made with your mother."

CHAPTER EIGHTEEN

Travis's and Mike's bodies ran with sweat. They took turns gulping eagerly from the jar of cold well water Frances brought them.

"You're a good worker, Mike," Frances said. "We'll have y'all a nice dinner once you boys are done," she added before heading back to the house.

Late June, and the sky was cloudless, the sun bright and hot. All morning and much of the afternoon Travis, in overalls and T-shirt, and Mike, in camouflage pants and tank top, had ridden around the pasture in the bouncing bed of the old farm truck. When Earl came to a halt by a group of rectangular bales, the boys leaped off, heaved the bales onto the truck, then clambered back on, clutching the rails as Earl steered the truck over the sloping pasture toward the next pile of bales. Now, to their exhausted relief, the work was done, except for arranging a few more bales in the loft.

Earl waved as he bumped by in the old blue Chevy. "Nice use of those muscles, boys. Good work. See y'all at dinner."

Once the friends had finished the jar of water, they climbed up to the loft and began stacking the last batch of bales. "Yeah. Good. Crisscross, like this," Travis instructed Mike. "Helps keep out the mold. Helps the hay air out."

Finished, the two stripped off their sweat-sodden shirts and sat panting on the hay. Thanks to summer sun beating down on the tin roof, the loft was very hot, making the cross-breeze wafting through the high doors especially welcome.

"Thanks so much for helping us," Travis said, taking a swig of water from the canteen Mike had brought. "Supposed to rain tomorrow. If that hay had gotten wet, it would have been a mess. Mold. Even spontaneous combustion. A cousin of ours lost a barn like that."

"Hard work. But it was worth it. I think I might have really won your mother over."

"I think your, uh, 'graduation speech' already did that. You sure as hell won over Daddy. Anybody who can put in a hard day's work is just fine in his book. Man, you look so sexy with all that sweat on your shoulders and chest. And, ummmm, do you smell good." Travis swiped a forefinger through the feathery hair in Mike's armpit and licked it off. "Taste good too."

Mike fondled Travis's navel and moist belly hair, then lapped Travis's sweat from his fingers. "You too. Yum. We gonna be alone for a few minutes?"

Travis peered out the loft window. "Ummm. I think so. Daddy's got the truck parked down at the house. Looks like he's digging another batch of new potatoes."

"How about I suck you off?"

Desire decapitated caution. "Hell, yes. Been too long, between my parents being home and you working so much for Buck. Better still," said Travis, grabbing Mike's wrists and pulling him to his feet, "how about I tie you to this post, stuff a rag in your mouth, and jack you off? Got lots of baling twine around here."

"Damn, yeah. A quickie in a barn? Sounds hot as hell. Do it."

Grinning with delight, Travis pushed Mike back against the post, unbuttoned the fly of Mike's camos, and pulled them down around his ankles. He forced Mike's wrists behind him and licked sweat off his pecs. He was burrowing his tongue between his fragrant friend's lips when they heard Frances calling outside.

"Travis? Travis, honey?"

"*Damn* it," Travis hissed. "Get your pants on."

Being gay sure makes you an adept actor, thought Travis, leaning from the loft window and regarding his mother in the barnyard below. "Hey, Mommy, what's up?" he said, as calmly as he could. "Dinner ready already?"

Frances looked solemn. "Travis, honey, there's someone on the phone for Mike. His father's had some kind of attack. He's down at Summers County Hospital."

"Oh, nephew! Praise the Lord! I'm so glad you came." Mike's Aunt Drema rose from her seat in the hospital waiting room. A short, fat woman in a paisley dress, she had wavy bottle-blonde hair and pink cat glasses, and she carried an enormous purse.

Mike gave her a quick hug, then introduced her to Travis. "So how's Buck?"

"He's all right. Thank the good Lord he survived."

"Damn, that's good to hear," said Mike, brushing bangs off his brow. "What happened?"

"Those A-rab doctors said he had a heart attack."

"Can I see him?"

"He's sleeping, honey. He's in ICU, they say. It was a pretty bad attack. He's going to need lots of help, I think. You're going to have to run the garage for a while."

"I can do that. I've been working there full-time since I graduated."

"I think I may move in with y'all for a while. The Lord knows you two need a woman around the house. Last time I came by, the house was a pigsty. Beer cans and fast-food wrappers and cigarette butts and empty bottles of Mad Dog and malt liquor... It looked like a nest of sinners. If y'all came to the Lord, you'd know better than to live like that," Drema said breathlessly, shaking a finger.

"I'm sure you're right. How's Darlene?" asked Mike, his expression mischievous. "I heard she has a new beau."

"Don't you even mention that. Darlene and I have been fighting like cats and dogs since she started seeing that...that Eugene, so it'll be nice to get out of the house for a few weeks."

Drema paused to rummage in her purse. "Cherry Life Saver?" she said, holding up a roll of candy.

"No, ma'am," said Mike, smirking. "Now, if y'got a cigarette in that big ole bag, or a flask, or a joint, that's another matter. I'll bet you got a joint. Ole Buck always said he couldn't pry you away from that marijuana."

"Nasty. You're always teasing me," said Drema, popping a red Life Saver in her mouth. "It's sins like that that led to Buck's heart attack. That, and lust. I said that floozies would be the death of him, and he nearabout proved me right."

"Floozies? Do you mean his girlfriend Janet? What did she have to do with it?"

"Well, now." Drema looked around the room, then ushered Mike and Travis into a corner as far from other people as possible. "Those paramedics are terrible gossips, so people'll be talking about this. I guess it's best that you know," Drema whispered.

"Know what?"

"The, uh, scandalous circumstances of your father's heart attack. You see, Buck didn't have his attack at home. He had it at the Coast to Coast Motel!"

"What? What was he doing there?"

"Well!" said Drema, eyes gleaming. "Turns out that he was going out behind Janet's back. He was shacked up at the motel with Wanda Grimmett, that trash from up Wolf Creek, the one that waitresses at Pack's, that bar on Third Avenue? But the receptionist at the Coast to Coast—Marsha Ellison, she's a sweet little thing who goes to my church—well, Marsha is the cousin of a friend of Janet's sister Lois, so Marsha called Janet, and pretty soon Janet was pounding on the door of that motel room and making all kinds of ruckus, and when Buck finally opened the door in his underwear, Janet just barged in, and that strumpet Wanda was a'hiding in the bathroom, naked as a Jezebel and wrapped in a sheet, and Janet grabbed her by the hair and tried to scratch her eyes out, but Wanda got loose and ran out the door, that sheet just a'flapping in the wind and her breasts bouncing up and down like basketballs—that girl was nigh about buxom at birth, which is clearly the root of all her problems—and Janet started to chase her down—Lord, if she'd caught her, she might have drowned her in the river—but about that time Buck came roaring and tearing after Janet, and she turned and kicked him in the balls! And then he grabbed his crotch, and then he grabbed his chest, and then he just crumpled, he just crumpled up, he just crumpled up into a *heap*!"

"Well, damn." Mike rubbed his jaw. "Reminds me of when ole Buck and I used to catch night crawlers for bait, in the yard after a rain.

When he grabbed up two worms that were so busy fucking they were easy to catch, he'd say, 'Damn fool. Lost your ass over a piece of ass.'"

Travis suppressed a chuckle and tried to look sad. Drema, on the other hand, gasped.

"Michael Wayne Woodson! You're as vulgar as your daddy."

"Sorry, ma'am. You know what they say about the apple and the tree."

"I hate to say this about my own brother, but the wages of sin is death. Only thing that saved him this time was my prayers, I suspect."

"I'm sure that's true," said Mike. "So is there a doctor around I can talk to?"

"One of those camel-jockey doctors was in here earlier. Y'ought to ask at the desk over there. I'd better head home. Got church tonight. I'll see you in a few days. Nice to meet you, Travis." Hefting her great bag, she waddled off.

"Great," muttered Mike, heading for the reception desk. "My dad's a slut-collector, and my born-again aunt is moving in."

Once the boys got back to Forest Hill, Travis's mother, much to his surprise, insisted that Mike spend the night. "There's no reason for you to go home to an empty house," Frances said. "You shouldn't be alone. Travis has a spare bed. You can visit your father in the morning."

"Thanks, ma'am." Mike looked equally surprised. "That's real kind of you."

"A crisis calls for kindness, that's what my father used to say. Y'all wash up and I'll heat some leftovers for you. We have green beans, mashed potatoes, and meatloaf. Apple crisp for dessert."

The two famished boys kicked off their shoes, washed their hands, grabbed the plates Frances had prepared, and ate heartily. After watching *Murphy Brown* and *Designing Women* with Travis's family, they said their goodnights and retired to Travis's bedroom. Travis locked the door, but Mike stretched out on the spare bed nonetheless.

"Maybe I should sleep over here."

"Why?" said Travis, turning on the window fan. "No one's coming in. I locked the door, and they always knock. I don't plan to get frisky. I just want to cuddle. You've been through a lot today, and I want to hold on you some."

"It just feels funny to... I mean, I know your mother didn't think much of me at first, and now she's being real nice to me. But if she knew that you and I... I just get tired of deceiving people, you know what I mean? What would they do, your family, if they knew?"

Travis sat on the spare bed beside Mike. "I don't know. Freak out. Nanny would pray and talk about the Bible. Daddy'd grouse about grandkids, then probably tell me that he didn't much care as long as I could still do farm work and didn't move to some big city. Mommy'd drop down dead of a heart attack."

"Are you serious?"

"Naw. But I'm sure she'd wring her hands and worry about what people would say. Probably try to send me to a psychiatrist."

Travis untied his ponytail and sighed. "I get tired of lying too. They've all brought me up to be honest and tell the truth, but this is a truth I'm pretty sure they wouldn't want to hear."

"It sure would be sweet to live some place where we wouldn't have to constantly lie. Only reason I'd ever move to a city." Mike closed his eyes and rested the back of a hand on his forehead. "Damn," he said huskily. "Damn. I can't believe my dad almost died. I mean, he's an asshole half the time, but still. Oh, shit. I, what would I do if—?" His voice rose and broke. "Half the time, when he's being a shit, I wish he was dead. But now, damn."

Buck's mean to you. You might be better off if the guy died. Maybe you could move in here, help my family keep the farm up while I'm at college. When I graduated, I could come back here and we could buy some property nearby, maybe the Old Homeplace, and move in together. Shit. Okay, Travis, you're being real selfish. If Buck died, Mike would be in pain, and you don't want that.

Travis took Mike's hand. "What would happen if..."

"If Buck kicked the bucket? Shit, I don't know. God knows he doesn't have any savings to speak of. Spends it all on booze and cigarettes. Guess I do that too. The house ain't paid off. The damn bank'd take the house and the garage. Hell, I guess I'd have to live with Aunt Drema till I turned eighteen. Ugh. She'd be whining at me to read the

Bible and go to church with her. I think I'd rather camp out on the riverbank. Or go right into the army. The Middle East would be way better than that. Damn, Travis. What *would* I do?"

"Come on, Mike. You're sleeping with me. No two ways about it." Rising, Travis took Mike's hand and hauled him to his feet. Travis pulled off Mike's tank top and helped him off with his pants, then unhooked his own overalls and stripped down to his briefs. After switching off the light, Travis led Mike to the big bed. There, the boys curled up together in the fan's artificial breeze.

Mike's body trembled against Travis. Travis caressed his face and hair till his shaking ceased. Outside, distant lightning flashed, and, after a long moment, thunder rolled.

"Storm's coming," murmured Mike.

"Yep. Just as predicted. Glad we got in that hay today."

"You need to learn Dylan's 'Shelter from the Storm,' Cubbie."

"Sure. I should be able to figure it out."

"Shelter. You're my shelter." Mike twined his fingers in Travis's, heaved a raspy sob, cuddled closer, and fell asleep.

Travis held him, silently thanking whatever powers brought them together and praying that they might never part. The storm moved closer. Travis listened to Mike's soft snores. Heart welling, he kissed Mike's broad back. He cupped one of Mike's furry pecs in his hand and felt his lover's heart beating against his palm. He thought of the great passions he'd read about in literature—Alexander and Bagoas, Cathy and Heathcliff, Achilles and Patroclus, the heroes of the gay novels Brenda had given him—sorting through the ways in which they were at last separated, the ways in which their love ended. He thought of the future, swamped alternately with hope and with fear. Only after the rain had begun its soothing rush did Travis finally bury his face in Mike's thick hair and join him in sleep.

CHAPTER NINETEEN

The New River in its grand gorge was low with July, but Sandstone Falls thundered on, a great torrent of green and white. Cicadas buzzed and pulsed in the mountains' summer-thick foliage. It was early evening, the sun riding the ridge, most of the riverbank fishermen already gone home. Travis and Mike walked to the end of the boardwalk to take in the view of the main falls, a cascade of water twenty-five feet high, then returned to the lower, smaller set of falls for a swim.

"This is gonna feel fine," said Mike, as both boys took off their baseball caps and tank tops. Clad in nothing but ratty shorts and tattered tennis shoes, they waded into the chest-deep jade-green pool at the foot of the falls. As young men will, they wrestled, dunked one another, and splashed around. Mike's black beard glittered with water droplets, and Travis's auburn hair hung wet about his shoulders. They clambered up the ledge into the dim and mossy grotto behind the cascades. There, concealed by the rushing wall of water, they hugged and kissed.

"Think I need a massage," said Mike, leaning forward into the torrent.

"Feels like a Sumo wrestler's fists pounding my shoulders," he shouted, laughing and gasping.

My lover. My lover. My river god, thought Travis, watching water rill down the smooth, muscled skin of Mike's back.

The sun had set over the mountain by the time they slid down the slippery ledge and back into the wide pool. They floated on their backs for a bit, watching the sky's pale blue grade into indigo. "I think we're alone," said Travis, after scanning the river's sycamore-green banks.

"Good. I have something to show you." Mike climbed up onto the ledge between twin torrents of white, unbuttoned his shorts and dropped them to his knees. He bent forward and wiggled his pale, hairy butt. Travis was about to make a salacious comment when he noticed a small dark splotch on Mike's right ass-cheek.

"What's that?" asked Travis, wading closer. He reached out and fingered the smooth spot. It lay in the center of a square of white skin from which the fine dark hair of Mike's butt had been shaved away.

"A little surprise for my hunky boyfriend. I drove over to Blacksburg and—"

Mike was cut short by the sound of approaching voices. Over the rushing of the falls, a man shouted, "Norma! Bring the cooler," and a child shrieked, "Daddy! I want to swim!"

"Yikes," said Mike, pulling his shorts up fast. "More damn people. I'll show you when we get to the campsite. It's only a few miles downriver. C'mon, Cubbie. I'm starving."

Twilight was falling as the boys reached their destination. Travis hopped out of the truck long enough to unlock the aluminum gate and, once Mike had pulled onto the property, to lock it behind them. Mike steered his pickup a quarter of a mile down a narrow dirt road lined with woodland. He parked in a grassy clearing edged with trees on three sides, the steep riverbank on the other. The boys got out and surveyed the area.

"Nice," said Travis. "All you can hear's the river and the night bugs."

"Buck's employee Russ Gunnoe bought this piece of land the first of the month. He's gonna set him up a camper here for fishing weekends. His wife drives him crazy, he told me, so this'll be the place to get away from her. He said I could use it anytime."

"Nice of him to let us camp here," said Travis, taking Mike's callused hand. "Why'd you wait till now to invite me? If he bought it weeks ago? I've been missing you awful bad."

"A couple reasons. I've been so damn busy in the garage that I just got around to buying the air mattress last week. Plus I thought it'd be fun to hit the falls first, but I couldn't swim till yesterday."

"Couldn't swim?"

"'Cause of this." Mike turned his back to Travis and tugged down his shorts again. "My first tattoo. Y'aint supposed to swim for two weeks after you get one."

Fondly cupping Mike's butt cheeks in his hands, Travis bent and peered. "Too dark to see it well. Wow, I can't believe you got a tattoo."

"You'll like it, I think," said Mike, pulling up his shorts. "Let's get a fire going in that pit there. I brought some wood, and there's gotta be some kindling around here."

Another summer thunderstorm was rumbling in the distance by the time they'd gotten a good fire burning. "Hope it doesn't rain before we get this stuff cooked," Mike worried, wrapping ears of corn in aluminum foil. "This corn'll take a little bit. How about you get out that CLC and pop, and we'll have a few drinks before I start grilling the steaks and mushrooms? I brought a bottle of Gallo to go with dinner."

"You bet," said Travis, hauling out the cooler.

Soon the boys were sitting by the fire in lawn chairs they'd brought and sipping quietly. About them, mountains loomed, black against black. Above them, summer stars glinted. Somewhere, tree frogs started up their rhythmic song.

"Muggy," said Mike, pulling his tank top off and scratching the thatch of black hair on his bare chest. "You gonna play that new dulcimer for me?"

"You bet. After we eat. I learned a few songs just for tonight. But first, Mr. Woodson, the viewing of the tattoo."

"Oh, right." Again Mike pulled down his shorts, turned his back on Travis, and wiggled his rump in the firelight. "Whaddya think?"

"Oh, my God," whispered Travis, lightly fingering the ink. It was a small Celtic knot with the initials TF and MW intertwined. "I can't believe you did this."

"Travis Ferrell and Mike Woodson. Your name in my skin. Forever."

"Mike! Oh, man." Travis leaned over and kissed the tattoo. "Amazing. I love it."

"Guess you own a little part of me now," Mike said, tugging up his shorts. "I know there ain't much summer left, and you'll be leaving for college in a few weeks, so I...I just wanted to show you how much I care. I—"

Mike turned away. He cleared his throat. Bending, he picked up a small flat stone, rubbed it, then lobbed it into the river. "Guess I'd better grill those steaks."

"**G**lad the rain's held off," said Mike, tipping back the bottle of Gallo. "But it's clouding up there to the west."

"That was all really tasty, thanks," said Travis, collecting the scraped-clean plastic plates. "I brought some store-bought fruit pies we can have in a little bit. Apple for you, coconut for me. And I brought some peaches and blueberries for breakfast. And Suisse Mocha."

"Sounds great," said Mike, gazing blankly into the fire. "How about that music, farm boy?"

"Sure. Need a seat without arms, though. The truck tailgate will work."

Travis opened the back of the truck and fetched a long green corduroy bag from atop the air mattress Mike had already inflated for their night together. "Pretty, isn't it?" he said, pulling the dulcimer out and placing it on his lap. "Black walnut. Nanny got it for me up at the Pipestem State Park gift shop. Early birthday present."

"Whatcha gonna play me?"

"Well, I just learned 'Amazing Grace.' Nanny plays it all the time on her piano."

"I thought you were a pagan," said Mike, smiling faintly. He stood, took another swig of wine, and poked at the fire.

"I am. I just like the tune." Travis strummed a few bars absently, then hummed the melody. Throat tightening with wonder, he watched the firelight flicker over Mike's naked torso.

Thunder sounded again. A breeze picked up. "'I once was lost, but now am found,' murmured Travis. "Talk about amazing grace. You're so beautiful, Mike."

Mike turned. The gleam of firelight made his brown eyes seem wet.

Travis smiled. "I love your body. I love the ease you have in your body. Always stripping to the waist and knowing you're doing the world a favor. All those muscles, all that body hair. Those sweet little nipples, like fur-roses. I love your confidence, your macho swagger."

"Aw, Cubbie." Mike waved away the compliment and added a stick of wood to the embers. "I ain't swaggering. I'm just feeding the fire."

Travis plucked a chord. "In Wicca, we believe that divinity is embodied, that the god or goddess is in each of us. The Christians talk about 'theophany,' when God manifests. You're my theophany, Mike. You're my Horned God in human form."

"Travis. Lord, lord." Mike shook his head, gave Travis a sideways grin, and returned his gaze to the flames. "Play me another one before I get a swelled head."

"Okay. This one's 'Loch Lomond.'"

Travis fingerpicked the melody, then sang the song in his quiet baritone.

> *You take the high road and I'll take the low road,*
> *And I'll get to Scotland afore you.*
> *For me and my true love will never meet again*
> *On the bonny, bonny banks of Loch Lomond.*

"How'd you like that?" Travis said, as the last note faded.

For a long moment, Mike didn't answer. He kicked at a charred stick and took another slug of wine. "Really pretty," he said finally, rubbing at his right cheek. "And really sad. You have such a sweet, deep voice. I—I'm so glad we could come here. I really needed to be with you tonight."

"Me too," said Travis, returning his dulcimer to its bag. "Man, I miss our times at the gym. I never get to see you enough, between your job and all the work I'm doing on the farm. I wish—"

Lightning flashed, and thunder sounded again. A few drops of rain fell.

"Here comes the rain," said Travis, putting the dulcimer back beneath the covered truck bed. "Better gather stuff up. You want to grab the cooler?"

Mike didn't respond. The rain began in earnest, but still Mike stood staring into the hissing fire, as if mesmerized by its embers, while Travis folded up the lawn chairs and stowed them in the cab.

"Mike?" Travis said. "You'll get drenched." Striding over to his lover, he took his hand. "Mike, buddy, what's wrong?"

Mike turned. Rain trickled down his shoulders. Fire-lit rain beaded on his mustache and in his chest hair. His jaw trembled. His long-lashed eyes were moist.

"Are you crying?"

Mike wiped his face and smiled weakly. "Y-yeah. So much for macho swagger, huh? I'm gonna douse this fire just in case and then let's get inside. We ain't done with that bottle of CLC yet."

Within minutes, the boys had stashed everything away and were lying on the soft mattress in the sheltered dark of the truck bed. The rain, coming hard now, beat on the roof, and thunder boomed.

"Let's get naked," said Mike. The boys pulled off their moist garments and underwear, then stretched out side by side.

"Why were you crying, Mike?" Travis asked.

Mike sighed. He opened the bottle of CLC and took a swig. "Part of it was that song. Never meeting again. Some days I wake up and think we'll be together forever, somehow or some way. Other days, I'm convinced you're gonna get up to WVU and meet some other guy, some smart dude you can have educated talks with, and you'll leave me the way your friend Bill did Brenda."

"That's *not* going to happen. How many times have I told you that?"

"You can't know for sure."

Travis took the bottle and sipped. "I've also told you again and again that you should come with me."

"Yeah." Mike was silent for a moment. "Look, there's another reason I'm real sad tonight. I was real sad before you even played that song. My mom died seven years ago tonight."

"Oh, Mike," said Travis, propping the bottle against the side of the truck bed. "Oh, man. Come here."

Both boys rolled onto their sides, facing one another. Mike rested an arm on Travis's hip; Travis wrapped Mike in his arms. Mike stroked Travis's beard; Travis kissed Mike's hair.

Mike took a deep breath, then exhaled slowly. "I think about her a lot when I'm with you. 'Cause no one since she died has been as good to me as she was...till I met you. It's like God finally felt bad for taking her away and decided to send me you, Cubbie."

Travis grasped Mike's hand. "I'm so glad we met. I know you're a little younger than me, but you've taught me all kinds of things about being a man."

"Like drinking and cussing?" Mike chuckled softly and tweaked Travis's nipple.

"Among other things. You make me want to be strong. Like you."

"You *are* strong, Cubbie. I keep telling you that."

"Well, stronger then." Travis gently kneaded Mike's chest. "And I ain't just talking about bench pressing."

"Strong's good, but so's tender. Don't lose that, Travis. When you make love to me, I think the best thing about it is how rough and wild you can be one minute and how tender and gentle you can be the next."

Mike nuzzled Travis's neck and sighed. "Tomorrow, when I drive you home to Forest Hill, I want to stop by Hilltop Cemetery on the way and put some flowers on Mom's grave. That all right?"

"You bet, buddy."

Violent lightning flashed outside. The rain thickened.

"Damn, it's really coming down. So what do you think happens when you die?" said Mike, pressing his palm against Travis's chest. "When your heart finally stops? What would happen if, God forbid, some homophobic assholes caught us here together and took a shotgun to the both of us, like what happened a few years back to that lesbian couple on the Appalachian Trail? Or if I joined the army and some Iraqi whack-job blew me to pieces?"

"Don't even say that." Travis shuddered.

"Sorry. It ain't exactly a visual that appeals to me either. Do you think we'd end up together in some kinda afterlife?"

"Well, the Vikings believed that there was a special heaven for warriors who died in battle. Valkyries—those were sort of like butt-kicking female angels—carried their souls to a great hall called Valhalla where they feasted for eternity. Wiccans believe in reincarnation. Each soul is kind of a spark off the great bonfire that is God, or the gods. And after death the soul rests in the Summerlands, a kind of Elysium, before being reborn in another human body, in another time and place."

"Huh. So you do believe we have souls? You believe in God?"

"Oh, yeah. There has to be a benevolent deity in the universe for something as splendid as you to have come to pass." Travis lightly brushed Mike's chest hair and kissed him on the nose.

"I'm serious."

"So am I. When I look at beauty—your face, your body, the mountains all around us—I have no doubt there's a God. My faith in that is as strong as Nanny's belief in Jesus. And if I need salvation...I don't really believe in that concept, but if I did...I'll be redeemed by how much I love beauty, the beauty that the gods brought into being. Beauties like you."

"I want to believe in God. I really do. When the Christians say 'God is love,' I can buy that, when I think about how my Mom loved me and how you love me and how lucky I am to be loved like that. Of course, the same Christians, most of 'em at least, would want to run us outta town on a rail if they knew *how* we loved."

"If they caught me tying you up and giving it to you hard up the butt, as, here in a bit, I fully intend to?" Travis snickered. "Yum. Yeah. If they only knew."

"So if we're reborn in some future life, then we had past lives too? Think we were Rebel soldiers together? Or members of Alexander the Great's army?"

"Undoubtedly." Travis squeezed Mike's butt, then traced a fingertip over the shaved skin bearing the tattoo. "This means so much to me, Mike."

"Together forever in ink, big guy. Thanks for the talk, but..." Mike rubbed his rear against Travis's hand. "I think it's time for some action, don't you? I'm feeling a lot better. Time to seize the carp. Where'd you put the rope and lube?"

The rain had stopped by dawn. Careful not to wake his lover, Travis clambered out of the back of the truck. The humid clearing glistened with wet. He urinated over the riverbank, then stood there for a moment watching the green waters swirl by on their way to the Ohio, the Mississippi, and the far-off Gulf of Mexico.

When Travis returned to the truck, he found Mike on his side, snoring softly. He'd thrown off the light blanket and was curled into a ball, like a large, hairy-thighed infant, his hands folded together as if in prayer. As Travis gazed at Mike, his beloved's nakedness illuminated by the slanting light of the rising sun, words began to fill his head. Fetching a notebook and pen from his backpack, he sat on the open tailgate and began to write.

CHAPTER TWENTY

"Thanks again for the gift certificate. Now I can lift weights with Bill when I get to Morgantown," said Travis as he and Mike, in shorts and tanks, made their way past high rows of corn toward the barn. "She says Prairie Street Gym is a great little place."

It was the morning after Travis's eighteenth birthday. The day before, Mike had been invited to the Forest Hill farm for an overnight. He and the Ferrell clan enjoyed a celebratory spread of crookneck squash, half-runners, corn on the cob, pulled-pork barbeque, cole slaw, and sour-cream cucumber salad, followed by a coconut birthday cake and the opening of presents. After a few hours of television, Travis spent a happy night behind his locked bedroom door sweatily snuggling with his lover despite the early August heat.

"Glad you liked the gift. Gotta keep those Cubbie muscles up, right?"

"You bet," said Travis, flexing as they entered the barn. "Got to stay strong so I can keep wrestling you down and ravishing you."

The boys climbed up to the breezy loft, opened the door there, sat on the edge, their feet hanging over, and took in the view of the farm and the hills beyond.

"I'm so glad you could spend the night," said Travis, kissing Mike's cheek. "I figured you'd have to be working in the garage today. So what did you want to talk to me about? You've decided to move to Morgantown with me, I hope."

Mike shook his head. "This is probably the worst timing ever, but... I'm so sorry to have to tell you this right after your birthday. I would have told you yesterday, but I didn't want to ruin things."

Travis's face fell and his belly tightened. "Oh, no. What?"

"I'm living in Russ Gunnoe's shed. Buck kicked me out. Fired me too."

"*What?* Why?"

"Aunt Drema is why, the pious *cow*. Turns out she's been making some extra money cleaning house for Brent Vass's mom, and Mrs. Vass told her about the fight we got into with Brent and that ape of a cousin in front of the gym on St. Patrick's Day...and then she told Aunt Drema about..."

"Oh, hell. That bitch! About how Brent—"

"Yep. About how Brent thought we were fags. So guess what holier-than-thou Aunt Drema did next?"

"Oh, no. What? She told Buck?"

"Not quite. Better'n that. She searched my room for evidence."

"And?"

Mike rolled his eyes and spat over the side of the loft. "And she found that book you lent me months ago. *The Fancy Dancer*, about that affair between the motorcycle stud and the priest. Worse, some of those *BEAR* and *Drummer* magazines Eddie sent us. And, of course, *The Joy of Gay Sex*. And my dog collar. Though, knowing her, the fat-assed retard, she'd think that just meant I was planning to adopt a pit bull."

"Oh, no," Travis moaned, shaking his head. "Oh, no. It's all my fault. I should never have— You should have told them all that stuff was mine. That way—"

"Don't you even *start* that." Mike slapped Travis's thigh. "Or, next time we're getting it on, it'll be your butt beneath the belt, not mine. So, of course, Aunt Drema showed all that stuff to ole Bucky and we had a 'family conference,' as he put it, with him screaming at me and Drema waving around the leather porn and tsk-tsking like a nesting hen. And Buck responded pretty much as I feared. Well, actually, he didn't try to kill me, which was the worst scenario. Probably didn't get violent since Aunt Drema was there. I would've hated to have had to break my own father's face. But he threw me out and he fired me, though he let me keep the truck, thank God, I guess since he knew I'd drive outta there as fast as I could. And he told me I was welcome to join the army 'cause he thought that might be the only hope of straightening me out. They'd 'beat the faggot outta me,' is how he put it."

Mike bent his head, kneaded his brow, and cleared his throat. "So I did two things. I asked Russ Gunnoe if I could camp out on his land in my truck, but he told me I could crash in his shed. If Buck talks to Russ, he may throw me out too, but my guess is that Buck doesn't want anyone to know he has a perverted cocksucker for a son. On the other hand, with Aunt Drema, she's such a sanctimonious gossip...the news might be all over town soon. I can just see her presenting those *Drummer* mags to her church congregation as evidence of satanic abomination and sin. Pitchforks and torches and an angry mob coming after me... That's one of the reasons why..."

"What else did you do? Did you... Oh, no. Did you..." Travis trailed off, his voice quavering.

"I signed up for the army. I'm heading out for basic training right after you leave for college. I know you don't want this, but—"

"You're *damn right* I don't want it. You told me you'd consult with me before you signed up. How could you do this?" Travis scrambled up and leaned against the loft wall, eyes moist and face distorted.

Mike stood too. "I'm sorry! I should have told you. But I panicked, I guess. There I was, stuffing all my shit into the back of the truck, with no place to live and no job and hardly any savings...and thinking that the whole town would be talking about what a sick queer I was—"

"Mike, damn it! Come to Morgantown with me!"

"I can't, Travis. With no money and so little work experience? Like Buck would write me a recommendation? Where would I live? Not in the dorm with you. What would I do? I hardly have the cash to eat or gas up the truck. I don't have access to money like you and your family do."

"We'll get money somewhere. My parents."

"I ain't borrowing money from your parents. Fuck that. In the army, I'll learn skills, and I'll have a salary. Maybe I can visit you at WVU if I can get furloughs. I'll come back in a few years, and I'll have saved money and I'll be employable, maybe, in a range of ways. I'll be more than a grease monkey. People will respect me. Maybe I can do that G.I. Bill thing and get a degree and have a career like you're planning to. And then we can be together. As equals. You sure as shit ain't gonna keep me. I got too much pride for that."

"You're too damn proud. And too damn reckless. Running off to join the goddamn army and leaving me behind." Travis pounded the side of his fist against the slatted loft wall. "Damn you! Who knows what'll happen to you or where they'll send you? Maybe that fucking crazy Middle East. And one of these days I'll get the news that you've been killed."

"Please don't be this way. We only have two weeks left before I drive you to Morgantown."

"I don't know if I want you to drive me to Morgantown," said Travis, teeth gritted and eyes glaring. "Maybe my parents can take me."

"What? Are you serious?"

"Damn right I am." Travis kicked a bale, starting up a cloud of dust. "Damn, I'd like to punch you in the jaw right now. You've ruined everything. I can't believe you're leaving me."

"You're the one going off to college. You're the one who's doing the leaving. You're choosing that. Now that Buck's thrown me out, I don't have much of a choice."

"Go home, Mike," Travis said, turning away. "Go home."

"*Please* don't be like this, buddy. *Please.*" Mike's voice cracked. "I love you. I swear I do. I'm just trying to work for a future with you. Me being in the army for four years'll be like you being in college for four years. After we're both done, we could—"

"Git! And don't let the barn door smack you in the ass on the way out."

"You don't have to tell me again," muttered Mike. He wiped his cheek, lowered his head, and climbed down the loft's ladder. In another minute, Travis could hear Mike's old truck roar into life and tear out of the driveway.

Travis stomped around the loft for a good five minutes, cussing, punching and kicking things, and spitting into the hay. Finally, exhausted, he sat on a bale, put his head in his hands, thought of a future without Mike, and sobbed.

Travis stood in the hall of his home, the phone to his ear. He had a few minutes of privacy, since his grandmother was washing the dinner dishes and his parents were watching TV.

"Hello, Mr. Gunnoe? This is Travis Ferrell. I heard Mike was staying a while with you. Could I talk to him?"

"Sure, Travis. He's back in the shed. Hold on a minute."

Travis waited. In the background a TV was chattering, and a dog barked. A door slammed, and a shrill woman's voice started up. *Must be that gorgon of a wife,* thought Travis, grimacing. *I'd want a fishing camp too.*

"Hello." Mike's voice was sullen and deep.

"Mike, it's Travis. I...I'm so sorry I acted like such an asshole this morning."

"Can't really talk here," mumbled Mike.

"Then just listen. I'm really, really sorry. The thought of losing you just maddens me. Look, I still hate the idea of you in the army, but... I'm going to think of it as your version of college, okay? And I'll be as supportive as I can. I—I promise."

"Okay," said Mike. "Okay."

"So can I see you soon? Apologize in person?"

Mike paused. "Uh, wanna hit Kirk's tomorrow for lunch? I could do with a couple of their hot dogs. I got a few bucks left."

"Yeah. I'd like that a lot. I can pay."

"Naw. It's my turn."

In the background, the shrill female voice rose and fell. "Christ, she's a banshee," Mike groaned. "How can anyone talk so much? I gotta get back to the shed before my eardrums burst. Look, you still want me to drive you to Morgantown? Or are your parents taking you?"

"I'd like you to take me. Please. If your truck's running right."

"It is. Miraculously. Okay, I'll take you. But you gotta pay for the gas, 'cause I don't have jack shit in funds. I tried to get some part-time work at that garage in Avis, but they'd heard the rumors... Thanks to Aunt Drema and her Church of the Holy Loudmouths."

"I can pay for gas, no problem. And I just got a letter from Brenda. Franny, the girl we met at the party? She lives in the attic apartment of Brenda's house, but she's been staying over a lot with her new girlfriend, Lisa, so she said we could spend the night there, after I drop off my stuff at the dorm."

"Good. That's good to hear," said Mike. "Look, I gotta go. Jesus! Whatta shrew. Whatta fuckin' harpy. Russ, the poor bastard... I'll pick you up tomorrow around noon, okay? And since I suddenly find myself free of, uh, job-related duties, maybe we can schedule another camping trip down Sandstone before you go?"

"That'd be great, Mike."

"Okay. Uh. Thanks for calling, Travis. Bye."

Before Travis could respond, Mike hung up. Travis fled to his bedroom. There he stripped to his underwear and plucked at his dulcimer for a few minutes, trying to calm himself. He started to cry, then, cussing, wiped his face and choked back further tears. He blew his nose, threw himself on the bed, watched heat lighting flare in the windows, and tried to get some sleep while the melody of "Loch Lomond" looped over and over in his mind.

Travis watched university buildings blur by in late-August sunshine. The Coliseum. The Creative Arts Center. Towers. The long slope of University Avenue down into Sunnyside, then the Downtown Campus. On the Saturday before classes resumed at WVU, the town was packed with traffic. When the boys reached red-brick Boreman Hall, so many other students were moving in that they had to circle the block a few times before they found room for Mike to pull up onto the curb.

"Let's get this over with," said Travis, climbing out. "I'm starved. Bill's going to take us to lunch after we're done."

When they got to Travis's assigned room on the second floor, a shapeless lump of a boy with unkempt dirty-blond hair and a ruddy face was already there, unpacking his belongings.

"Howdy," said Travis, offering his hand. "I'm Travis. This is my buddy, Mike. You must be Rodney. You're from Lewisburg, right?"

"Yep." Rodney gave both boys rapid handshakes. "That's your bed there, by the window."

In four trips, Mike and Travis had all of Travis's boxes stacked on the floor. Travis hung up a few clothes, tucked some underwear and T-shirts into his dresser, and unboxed some books.

"We're gonna head out to lunch. Going to spend the night with some friends. See you tomorrow," said Travis, shouldering his backpack.

"Sure," Rodney replied. Pulling a poster from a folder, he affixed it to the wall above his bed. The full-color image was that of a buxom brunette, completely naked, cupping her breasts and spreading her legs.

"Miss November," Rodney grunted. "Damn. Sure would like to take a crack at that."

Travis suppressed a grimace and a satiric comment. As soon as he and Mike had reached the stairs, Travis groaned. "I specifically asked for no troglodytes. Damn, his idea of decoration is vaginas on the wall? How about a Georgia O'Keeffe calla lily painting instead?"

"Well, at least I don't have to worry about you leaving me for *him*," said Mike cheerfully, patting Travis on the arm as they clattered down the stairs.

The boys' last afternoon together passed quickly, as time always seems to do when lovers are about to part. Bill treated them to burritos and French fries with blue cheese dip at Wings Olé, on the humid deck overlooking the Monongahela River. She and Cin drove them up to the Virgin Hemlock Stand on Chestnut Ridge for a hike, then on over to Coopers Rock. Politely pretending that they'd never been there before, Travis and Mike stood once again on the rocky overlook above the Cheat River and watched buzzards riding updrafts in the gorge. All day, Travis fought back tears, and all day, whenever there were no strangers about, Mike kept taking Travis's hand.

After Bill and Cin had said their goodbyes to Mike and dropped them off at the house on Willey Street, Farron and the boys drank beer on the front porch, high above the street, and watched twilight fall and traffic go by. Inside, Brenda prepared a big meal she dubbed the "Welcome-to-Morgantown Italian Spectacular." When everything was ready, Farron opened a bottle of rosé, and the friends dug into a big Caesar salad, pasta carbonara, and focaccia, followed by a Tuscan lemon cake Farron had baked that afternoon.

Travis helped Brenda clean up the kitchen while Mike and Farron chatted in the living room over the last of the wine.

"So he's still going into the army?" Brenda asked, handing Travis a plate to dry.

"Yep. Signed up for four years. He says it's like me going to college. So we can both prepare for our future together."

"My mother and two older sisters were all in the military, Travis. A lot of poor kids from the mountains who have few other options join up. It's not a bad life. Mike could come back in a lot better position to make a living. It did my sisters a world of good financially."

"That's what he tells me. But what if there's a war? What if he's hurt? Or worse. I have nightmares about...about that beautiful body of his torn to shreds by some bastard's bomb. Or what if he meets someone else? He's bi. He might meet a woman. Or another man. He might not want to be with me anymore. That would break my heart."

"Like Bill met Cin?" Brenda brushed a curl behind her ear. "Travis, you're like a little brother to me. I won't lie to you. Anything's possible. Any one of those fears of yours might come true. But you were always writing to me about how strong and tough Mike is, and how you wanted to be that way too. So here's your chance."

"I know." Travis hung his head. "It's just that...for the gods to send such a love to me, and then to take it away?"

"Maybe they're not. You never know. What happened to me might not happen to you. 'God works in mysterious ways,' those rabid Christians down in Hinton used to say. I think most of their beliefs are vile rubbish, but I think they're right about that."

Brenda handed Travis a wet plate and patted his arm. "That's enough. It's getting late. I'll do the wineglasses. Why don't you and Mike go on up to bed? I know you must want some time together, just the two of you. Why don't you all sleep in tomorrow? Farron and I will make us all a nice brunch before Mike has to leave."

Franny's attic apartment was small and stuffy, with angled ceilings and a window with a view out over the street. Within minutes, the boys had stripped off their clothes and flopped down onto the mattress on the floor.

For a long time, Travis and Mike simply lay side by side, their fingers intertwined.

"Travis?" said Mike, bending over to kiss Travis's shoulder.

"Y-yep?" *Oh, God. Our last night together till who knows when?* Travis was doing his best not to break down and sob.

"Don't you cry on me. I can hear it in your voice. One of these days, we're gonna be two old men living together in a log cabin on a ridge, rocking on the front porch and watching the leaves changing with autumn and reminiscing about all our years together, and we'll remember tonight and how sad we were, and we'll laugh."

"Maybe so," Travis said, exhaling slowly. "Maybe so."

"Travis, I don't want to talk tonight. We can do that tomorrow before I leave. We're alone now, and we're together. And I want us to make love. Tonight...I want to be the Top. Please? I want to fuck you. Would that be all right? I won't hurt you, I swear."

"Oh, yes. Oh, sure. I really want you to be my first that way."

"I'll be real careful, real slow, real gentle. And tomorrow morning, I want you to tie me up and gag my mouth and tug my tits and pound me hard. Ride me till I'm hurting, okay? I wanna drive home with a sore butt and think of you. Kind of a parting souvenir, okay?"

"It's a deal, Mike. It all sounds wonderful. Could we snuggle first? I know it's hot up here, but I really just want to hold you for a while."

"Sure, Cubbie," said Mike. Moving closer, he kissed Travis on the lips. Travis, eyes welling with tears, pulled Mike into his arms.

The young lovers lay in a slant of sunlight, Mike's head resting on Travis's chest, Travis playing absently with the curls of black hair around Mike's navel. Both were moist with sweat and sticky with lube after a rough and lengthy bout of lovemaking. A mess of rope and bandanas scattered the floor.

"It's 'Morning Morgantown,'" whispered Travis. "That Joni song I used to sing you." His fingers ranged over Mike's ass, stroking the tattoo upon which hair was growing back. *MW and TF,* Travis thought. *Our initials intertwined together, inside your flesh forever.* "Sore?"

"Yep. Feels good. Just what I needed. Your butt sore too?"

"A little. Not bad. Thanks for going so slow. It hurt at first, but then it felt real, real good, just like you said it would. And this morning... being inside you...it was just incredible. Thank you."

"Thank *you*." Mike squeezed Travis's limp dick. "Ole Horse Cock gave me a ride to remember. Hold on. Gotta piss."

Mike rose and trotted to the tiny bathroom. By the time he'd returned, Travis had fetched his omnipresent backpack and, sitting cross-legged on the bed, was digging through it.

"I have some things for you," Travis said solemnly. "First of all..."

He handed Mike a small cloth bag of black velvet. Mike sat on the bed, loosened the drawstring, and dropped stones into his palm.

"Pebbles? What're these?"

"The pink one's rose quartz. A few weeks before I came to the gym with a busted lip and asked you to help me lift weights, Bill mailed me this. It was a love charm from Laura. I prayed to the Horned God that I would find someone to love. And I have. I don't need it anymore. I want you to have it. Not so you'll find someone else, of course, but to remind you of me."

"I don't need any reminders, Cubbie. I'm not going to forget you. I'm not going to fall in love with someone else. I'll be back for you, I swear."

"I hope so, Mike," Travis said, bowing his head. "I'm so afraid."

"Don't be. I love you. So what's this? Looks like a blue arrowhead."

"It's lapis lazuli. It's a protection charm. So you'll come back all in one piece."

"Thanks, buddy." Mike kissed Travis on the cheek. "I'll be fine."

"I have one other thing for you." Travis pulled a thin notebook from his backpack. "Remember when you asked about those poems I was writing about you? Well, I copied them all into this book. So you can take them with you and remember our times together."

Mike took the notebook and flipped through it. "There are quite a few here."

"You're quite a muse."

Smiling, he handed the book back to Travis. "Would you read a few to me?"

"Uh."

"Please?" Mike lay back on the bed, propped his head in his hands, and winked.

Travis nodded. He opened the book and, in a shaky voice, began.

By a snaky green river,
In the hard gray rain,
Broken I saw
You in the leaves of summer.
Brought down by grief,
Rain in your black hair,
Caught in your mustache like dew.
Rain trickled down your bare chest,
Dripping silently through the soft dark hair
Like your tears glistening in long-lashed eyes.
Vulnerable in the storm you stood,
Muscles wet and smooth,
Till we bolted into the truck,
Cozy womb of CLC escape.
I shall walk the woods
Alone for a while
Without you,
Your example to follow.
Mike, I'll see the storms as baptism
And be all the better for it.
Mike, you've been on my mind.

"Wow, Travis," Mike murmured. "I don't know much about poetry, but that's real pretty. Would you read some more?"

"Just a couple more. Both are real short."

Sad-eyed angel,
I'll drive away the wolves.
I have rough rope for you in return,
And guitar strings at twilight.
It's a package deal.

Mike heaved a low laugh. "Yeah, I know what that one's about. A honey-sweet deal, I'd say."

"One more," said Travis.

> *Seeing your smooth body*
> *At midnight*
> *In the blood of fire*
> *I saw God.*

"That's beautiful, buddy," Mike said, giving Travis's big toe a fond squeeze. "Thanks for giving me copies. I'll cherish 'em. Truly. It'll be like carrying a little piece of your heart with me."

"I guess. Don't know how good they are, but I'm glad you like them." Travis blushed. "At least they're better than the stuff I used to write. Before I met you, I piddled with poetry, but it always sounded childish or trite. This stuff isn't quite as bad."

"And why is that?"

"Because...I met you. I've changed. Grown up some. The poems I used to write weren't about real stuff. They were about infatuations, dreams, and fantasies. Shallow things. Unreal things. These poems are about something...deep and real."

Mike smiled sadly. "Yeah? And what is that?"

Travis gazed at Mike's nakedness, consciously trying to preserve every detail of his lover's beauty in his mind. "What I feel for you."

Mike took Travis's hand and pulled him to him. For a long moment, they silently clung to one another. Travis stared at the alarm clock on the floor beside the bed and grimaced with the sick sense of time running out.

"It's nearly eleven," he said. "Guess we'd better strip this bed, take a shower, and get downstairs."

Little was said over brunch. Farron had helped Brenda prepare another amazing spread: one of her potato/pepper/sausage/cheese/scrambled-egg glops, blueberries in cream, croissants with butter and jam, and mimosas, which Mike refused since he had the long drive back to Hinton soon to make. They talked a little about the classes Travis would start the next day; a little about Farron's latest sculpture project; a little about Brenda's interest in Dona, a handsome butch who lived across town; and a little about Mike's hopes for success in the army. Once the plates were cleared, Brenda and Farron politely disappeared into their respective bedrooms, leaving Mike and Travis alone. The two sat on the couch for a few minutes, leaning shoulder to shoulder and holding hands.

"Better scoot," said Mike, checking his wristwatch. "Got a ways to go."

They both stood.

"Well, Cubbie, this is it." Mike took Travis's hands in his. Travis, mouth trembling, looked into Mike's brown eyes.

"I guess so," said Travis. "Will you write me?"

"Of course I will. And how about you write some more poems about me and send 'em to me?" Mike tugged at Travis's wristband and managed a wet-eyed wink. "That'll be good ego food for me."

"I will. Send me your address and I will."

"Cubbie," Mike said, "four years is a long time. I hate to think of you with another man, but...you got your whole life ahead of you...and you'll meet all kinds of cool folks in college. I'm so glad you already have so many friends here, 'cause they all seem like great people, and I think they'll take care of you while I'm gone...but you might meet some other guy..."

Travis frowned. "No, Mike. Please don't say it."

Mike stopped, bowed his head, then continued. "No, now listen, Travis, buddy...you're gonna meet other guys...and one day you might meet one you're gonna...gonna want...so...it's okay with me if you... I don't want you to feel tied to me. So you're free, is what I'm saying. Free to..."

"Mike! No. I'll never want anyone else."

"You might. You might. Look, I..."

Mike seized Travis and hugged him so hard Travis gasped. Then, just as abruptly, he released Travis and stepped back. Mike's face was streaked with tears. "Bye, Cubbie. I love you," he choked out. "Always will. Now I gotta go!"

Before Travis could respond, Mike had snatched up his duffel bag from the floor, bolted through the kitchen and out the back door. Travis followed, only to see Mike rushing up the concrete steps to the parking lot behind the house. By the time Travis had reached the top of the stairs, Mike had backed his truck up with a screech of tires. He paused to wave. Travis waved back. Then Mike wiped his face with the back of his hand and drove down the alley and out of sight.

There was a sharp knock on the attic apartment door, and then it swung open.

Travis looked up from Franny's moist pillow, his eyes red, his sinuses swollen and aching from a long bout of crying. Bill, in jeans and a button-down Western shirt, stood in the door, along with a blond man in his thirties, dressed in white slacks and a lime-green polo shirt.

"Oh, honey. You poor sweet little thing. You're just a mess, aren't you?" said the man.

"Hey, Travis," said Bill. She strode over to the bed, bent down, and stroked her friend's mussed hair. "Brenda said you were up here. So Mike's gone, huh?"

Travis heaved himself up into a sitting position. He put his head in his hands and rubbed his throbbing temples. "Yep. And I just sobbed myself into one hell of a headache. Howdy, sir," he said, remembering his manners even amid his misery. "I'm Travis."

"Honey, we've met. At the party."

"This is the Fabulous Miss Jerry," said Bill. "The most glorious drag queen alive."

"Oh. Okay. Sorry. I didn't recognize you—"

"Without my finery? High heels and a ball gown wouldn't be proper attire for what we have planned, or so Bill has regretfully informed me."

"Planned?"

"We think you need some air," said Bill, handing Travis a Kleenex.

"Yes!" added Jerry breathlessly. "Come with us now, boy. Let us enter the wilderness together...where—ack!—many creepy-crawly mysteries await. This fierce butch—the Golden Lion, as Cin calls her—and I—the Unspeakably Exquisite Queen of Hearts—plan on making you feel better."

"Good luck," said Travis. He blew his nose, then rose obediently. Bill hugged him, and then she and Jerry led him down the stairs and up to the parking lot.

"They call this the Core Arboretum," Bill explained, as they pulled into a gravel lot not far from the Coliseum. "As much of a country boy as you are, we figured you could do with a walk in the woods."

Beyond the parking area was a flat space in which gravel paths wove through grassy clearings and between clumps of trees. "The plants are labeled," Bill explained as they climbed out of Jerry's sporty car. "Cin tells me a lot of forestry classes come here. There's thick woods just over the hill, and paths that lead down to the railroad tracks and over to a pond and bottomland and then the river."

"It's pretty," Travis said. "Thanks for bringing me here. It's nice to get away from the traffic and all the people in town." He bent to sniff the fragrant star-like flowers of a clambering vine that sprawled over the hedges edging the parking lot.

"What's that, honey?" asked Jerry. "I'll bet a mountain man like you knows all about these exotic botanicals."

"Virgin's bower," said Travis. He smiled, thinking of how tenderly Mike had topped him the previous night.

The three walked for a while. They read the plaques: "Kentucky Coffee Tree," "Sweet Gum," "Paper Birch." Travis rubbed the sticky buds of a balsam poplar and snuffled the resin on his fingers. *Smells like Mike's pits. Smells like Mike's crotch,* he thought. For a moment his vision blurred with sorrow, and then they continued on down the path, entering the forest proper.

They descended narrow, shady dells where Travis plucked spice-wood leaves and sniffed them. They crossed the railroad tracks, where Travis fingered the silica-rough stalks of ribbed horsetails. Around the pond, red-winged blackbirds clattered and cattails grew thick along the banks. On the far side, a Great Blue Heron stalked fish. As they got closer, it spread its wide wings and soared off through the woods.

Soon the three had reached the edge of the river, where sycamores, box elders, and silver maples grew in profusion. They stood quietly on the root-gnarled banks. Travis leaned a hand against a scaly maple trunk and watched the stream's slow flow. "The water is wide. I cannot cross o'er," he whispered, recalling a song he'd once sung to Mike.

"The Monongahela," said Bill. "It's an Indian word. It means 'River of Crumbling Banks.'"

"I'm already numb," Travis said calmly. "It's like Mike never was. Like he was just a wonderful dream, but then some cruel person shook me awake."

"Does he love you?" asked Jerry. "Was it, miracle of miracles, mutual?"

Travis plucked up a dead sycamore leaf, fiddled with it, then cast it onto the water, where it drifted leisurely downstream. "Yep. I'm pretty sure he does. A lot."

"Then, even so young, you've had something I've never had, honey. I've loved plenty of men, but none of them's loved me back. They've fucked me, and they've used me, and we've had some fun together, but..."

Jerry shrugged. "Her subjects keep deserting the queen. Poor benighted commoners." He mustered a theatric sigh, then smiled at Travis. "Off with their heads, the stupid pricks."

"Jerry's right, Travis," Bill said, wrapping an arm around her melancholy friend. "Count your blessings. I saw how Mike looked at you. He would have done anything for you."

"Anything but stay with me." Travis rubbed the black leather of his wristband. "What will I do if he doesn't come back? If he's killed overseas, or if he meets someone else like you did Cin? I'll never find a love like that again." *God, Mike. I wish you were here. Will I ever see or hold you again?*

"You can't predict what will happen to you and Mike by basing it on Brenda and me. Every love's different, Travis. My heart changed. His might not."

"And every great love affair has got to end sometime, just like Romeo and Juliet or Antony and Cleopatra. That's what makes it all so bittersweet, tragic, and romantic," said Jerry. "Who knows, honey? Maybe your soldier boy will come back and y'all will shack up together somewhere and live in married bliss. Or maybe you'll drift apart and lose touch for years and then find one another again when you're both scruffy salt-and-pepper daddies and rekindle the romance. Anything's possible, believe you me. Lord, the things I've seen in my eighty-plus years."

Jerry nudged Travis in the ribs, making him giggle despite his deso-
lation. "You've escaped that pissant fundamentalist town of yours.
Don't be sad. It's time to celebrate! Your little stud may be gone for
a while, but you got your friends. 'You got to have friends,' sings the
Divine Miss M. Why, honey, you already have a whole clan of queers
to take care of you. And you'll need 'em, as tenderhearted as you appear to be. There's big butch Bill here, and Cin, and Brenda, and Farron, and Laura, that seductive witch. And Franny and Jean. And Mizz
Leroy, that rampant whore. Watch out for that savage queen, honey,
if she ever gets you alone. She might make a quick meal out of you
if you're not careful. She's like a red-legged tarantula that way. And
then there's me, your own private Marilyn Monroe, your own private
Venus." Jerry flipped imaginary Cher-hair back and forth, making
Travis giggle again.

"Give me a hand, you ferocious dyke," Jerry said to Bill, "and let's es-
cort this inexcusably cute cub out of this dirty wilderness. The gnats
are trying to dine on my royal blood, and I'm terrified I'm going to
see a snake or a mouse at any minute. You will protect me against
the wildlife, won't you, Travis? I'll bet a big boy like you isn't afraid
of anything."

Travis wiped his wet eyes but couldn't help but grin. "Yes, ma'am, I
will. I mean, 'Yes, sir'?"

"'Ma'am' is just fine, sugar."

Jerry took Travis's left arm, and Bill took his right. They headed
back along the woodland path. Travis stared into the thick foliage,
but he wasn't seeing trees and leaves, he was seeing Mike's cocky
catfish grin, his seductive winks, the way his bare torso looked in rain
and firelight. *Horned One, Lady of the Moon, protect him from harm and
lead him back to me,* thought Travis as they crossed over the railroad
tracks and headed up the steep, wooded hill. *And if that can't be, may
his life be long and fulfilling, and may he remember me.*

"You're looking sad again, honey," said Jerry. "I think you need some
booze and a good dinner." He patted Travis's little belly. "You look
like an eater to me."

Embarrassed, Travis flushed. Then, remembering how Mike used
to rub his belly hair after they'd made love, he gave Jerry a shy smile.

"Yes, ma'am, I am. A ferocious eater. We hillbilly boys can make a serious dent in a meal."

"Can you cook too?"

"Yes, ma'am, some. Mainly just simple down-home stuff."

"Ever made pizza dough before?"

"No, ma'am. Just piecrust and biscuits. Is it hard to do?"

"It's child's play. My maternal grandmother grew up in Clarksburg, and she was a nasty hag who used to scare the piss out of me when she got wild on red wine, but she could cook. And I have her recipe book. How about the three of us go back to my royal quarters, which is to say my firetrap of an apartment, and I make us a deep-dish pizza? From scratch? Mushrooms and black olives and pepperoni and Italian sausage? We'll just get out the wine coolers and toast to your future and eat till we're big as beanbags. How's that sound? We can even pick up some of that delectable ice cream from Chico's. Would that make you feel better?"

"Sounds like a grand plan, Miss Jerry," said Bill.

"Food, drink, friends, and a Grand Queen's sparkling wit. That'll pull you through when love isn't around. Mark my words, child." Jerry dropped Travis's arm and gave his butt a sharp slap. "Now buck up! Mother doesn't want any Eeyores at her table."

"Yes, ma'am. That pizza sounds mighty tasty. That would make me feel better indeed," Travis said. Lifting his hand to his nose, he sniffed his fingers, breathing in the aroma of balsam poplar resin lingering there. He thought of musky, black-bearded Mike in bed that morning, bound and moaning, bucking passionately beneath him.

How many people over the centuries have had to part from those they cherish, have felt what I'm feeling? Untold billions, generation after generation. What bliss it is to love Mike. What suffering it is to lose him. I've got to hold onto him somehow—how brave and beautiful he was. I've got to endure this pain and remember. I've got to capture and commemorate what we had together.

"Wait just a second, folks," Travis said, stopping abruptly in the middle of the trail. Pulling out a tiny notebook and pen from his baggy shorts pocket, he wrote down the date, then began scrawling notes for a poem.

J EFF MANN grew up in Covington, Virginia, and Hinton, West Virginia, receiving degrees in English and forestry from West Virginia University. His poetry, fiction, and essays have appeared in many publications, including *Arts and Letters*, *Prairie Schooner*, *Shenandoah*, *Willow Springs*, *The Gay and Lesbian Review Worldwide*, *Crab Orchard Review*, and *Appalachian Heritage*. He has published three award-winning poetry chapbooks, *Bliss*, *Mountain Fireflies*, and *Flint Shards from Sussex*; four full-length books of poetry, *Bones Washed with Wine*, *On the Tongue*, *Ash: Poems from Norse Mythology*, and *A Romantic Mann*; two collections of personal essays, *Edge: Travels of an Appalachian Leather Bear* and *Binding the God: Ursine Essays from the Mountain South*; two novellas, *Devoured*, included in *Masters of Midnight: Erotic Tales of the Vampire*, and *Camp Allegheny*, included in *History's Passion: Stories of Sex Before Stonewall*; two novels, *Fog: A Novel of Desire and Reprisal*, which won the Pauline Réage Novel Award, and *Purgatory: A Novel of the Civil War*, which won a Rainbow Award; a book of poetry and memoir, *Loving Mountains, Loving Men*; and two volumes of short fiction, *Desire and Devour: Stories of Blood and Sweat* and *A History of Barbed Wire*, which won a Lambda Literary Award. He teaches creative writing at Virginia Tech in Blacksburg, Virginia.